C

Or, Vicki Cochr

By Victor Olliver

A novel set in late 1980s London, Brightworth and Beyond

Published by Equinox Books and printed by Amazon 2013

Copyright © 2013 by Victor Olliver

All rights reserved. No part of this publication may be reproduced, distributed, or transmitted in any form or by any means, including photocopying, recording, or other electronic or mechanical methods, without the prior written permission of the publisher, except in the case of brief quotations embodied in critical reviews and certain other noncommercial uses permitted by copyright law.

For permission requests, email the author: Volliver5@aol.com

First published as *Farce Hole* by Citron Press in 1998

Front cover: *Blue Angel* by Hilary Gialerakis, reproduced by kind permission of Antonia Gialerakis. Photograph of *Blue Angel* by Roger Smith

To my mother

Contents

MEDIA REVIEWS... 7

PART ONE: BRIGHTWORTH... 9

Chapter One... **10**
Chapter Two... **16**
Chapter Three... **33**
Chapter Four... **44**
Chapter Five... **50**

PART TWO: RAVEN'S TOWERS... 57

Chapter Six... **58**
Chapter Seven... **92**
Chapter Eight... **111**
Chapter Nine... **126**
Chapter Ten... **128**
Chapter Eleven... **137**
Chapter Twelve... **146**

PART THREE: CURTAINS... 163

Chapter Thirteen... **164**
Chapter Fourteen... **185**
Chapter Fifteen... **193**
Chapter Sixteen... **194**
Chapter Seventeen... **206**

END NOTE: HILARY GIALERAKIS... **209**

Selected reviews
(*Curtains* originally published as *Farce Hole*)

"Dealing so much with the ephemeral, journos instinctively tend to knock out facile hit-and-run novels. Olliver is an impressive exception. His metaphysical morality tale about the emotional cost of pursuing a brittly fashionable life is a sophisticated serving of the imagination, sensibility and sly humour. It's a quirkily stylish debut."
Jeremy Jehu, ITV Teletext

"Victor Olliver's funny and stylish clever satire on the world of glossy magazines and contains some sensationally catty dialogue."
Linley Boniface, *Hampstead and Highgate Gazette*

"This elegantly wicked satire of the vain world of the glossy magazine is a first novel which the author will find hard to follow. Surreal and catty, and yet at times strangely sympathetic to the characters for a satire, the novel is in fact brilliant…Victor Olliver could become Britain's answer to Tom Wolfe."
Nesta Wyn Ellis, author of *John Major* (Warner)

"A brilliant and acute book that gives a literary treatment to a very non-literary world."
Heidi Kingstone, *The Star*, South Africa

"Victor Olliver is clearly intelligent and, if he'd toned down the farcical elements just one notch, his debut could well have turned out to be a biting satire on the fashion industry, a British rival to Brett Easton Ellis' *Glamorama*. Like his characters, though, Olliver is trying too damn hard to impress."
Spike Magazine

"Mr Olliver is a talent to watch. His caustic and very funny narrative, set exotically between London and Brightworth (where Max sets up home at the end of the Pier), has a cast of bitches, temptresses, queens and roughs worthy of grand opera, and just asking for the book alone should provide mirth at the checkout. And that's before you've even opened it."
Christie Hickman, *Midweek*

"This is one of the funniest and nastiest novels I have read in a long time, highly readable and chock-a-block with sly tricks, twists and turns."
Amazon customer

PART ONE

BRIGHTWORTH

CHAPTER ONE

I could be wrong (don't take my word for it) but I, Vicki Cochrane, editor-in-chief of Glossy International *magazine, and all its foreign editions, have every reason to believe that my bodily body has just passed out of fashion and now lies crumpled between two groynes on the beach in Brightworth.*

The ignominy! Even a cast-off Chanel does not end up thrown onto a bric-a-brac stall.

My head reverberates with the roar of the blast that blew me off my feet, sent me soaring in fact, and threw me onto what I think coastal poets call the littoral - that area where the tide ebbs and flows but is in practice the final resting place of contemporary (and please excuse any lapse in taste – I am not quite myself) shit.

This much I recall: I was boarding the Brightworth Pier and I may have just said good afternoon to the tollgate master when the explosion occurred. In my right hand was the fruit knife with which I planned to end the life of Max Cochrane, the Founding Father, Chief Executive Officer and Editor-Emeritus of Raven's Towers Publishing International - the company that owns my Glossy International.

Max Cochrane also happens (or happened) to be my husband.

"So what were Vicki and Max Cochrane doing on the Brightworth Pier?" I hear you ask, tiresomely. It's too complicated to - ugh! -

My head's too much of a jangle right now to go into the whys and wherefores. It's a miracle I have said this much. And speaking of miracles, how astonishing it is to discover that I am here, in this place, in this...this...well, I'm alive.

After a fashion.

I know I'm still thinking, I know I'm talking to you (don't ask me how), I know I am sentient - a word I rather like and one I learned from Max when he joined the anti-vivisectionists last year. Apparently all living things - rabbits, kitties, earwiggies – they're all sentient.

Sentient means: I know I live!

Of course I have no idea where I am. If I am "dead" then I think I may have been short-changed. I certainly did not experience the rollercoaster transition here via the so-called astral tunnel which I read about in a copy of Psychic News *that I browsed through ages back at LaGuardia Airport, New York, while waiting for a blizzard to pass.*

Not for me the spangled, fairy-lit, Lilies of the Valley-garlanded and violets-scented tube which purportedly connects the now (death or "death") with before (life?). Not for me the astral straw up through which I expected to be sucked towards the embrace of my Jesus or Buddha or even that rather ample woman Mrs Blavatsky of the Theosophical Society - the things my brain picks up!

Nor for me the promised welcoming committee of passed-over loved ones. Not even my mother. Typical! Relatives, dead or alive, are never there when you need them.

Nor are husbands. Especially if they're husbands called Max Cochrane.

But then I don't know whether he is dead, whether he survived that entirely incongruous explosion on Brightworth Pier. Perhaps he was the one who lit the fuse - or whatever the technological equivalent. I am full of suspicion.

He may have had a motive.

I'm not an expert on explosives, I know little of seaside piers. It turns out I knew Max not at all. Did I know anything in your world?

And here's another thing. You'd think in this after-world place (don't ask me if it's heaven or hell) my thoughts would turn to matters sublime if not philosophical.

But no. Two images flash repeatedly across my mind's eye.

First, there's this knife or axe: I catch its stainless steel mid-arc glint as if it is being wielded against the light, followed by the spin of a flying hairstyle: certainly an odd detail, and most certainly an odder hairstyle, last seen in all its huge and waved and lacquered complexity on the head of Princess Leona Humperdink.

I never forget a hairstyle.

To me a hairstyle is as clear a clue to identity as the DNA fingerprint is to a forensic sleuth. Why would any hairstyle be airborne? I can't think straight at this precise moment.

Second - and this is sordid, so children turn away - I think of my ghastly, treacherous features editor Germaine Harper. Of Germaine's sexual quirks. What a thing to come to mind after all that I have just been put through.

Of all things.

Yes, it was my beauty editor Timothy who told me about Germaine and her strange fetish for heights. According to Timothy she can only climax while in the throes of vertigo and delights in nothing more than being thrown upon the battlements of some ancient castle, such as the Duke of Norfolk's at Arundel, and screwed mercilessly and doggy-fashion by some "stubbled scrote" - to use one of her crude yet very telling words – with her noisy head (face down, naturally) craning over a two hundred foot sheer drop. Maid Marian she is not, and as I said to Timothy at the time, I can understand certain kinks and *perversions but how the fear of falling could in any way be regarded as stimulating is beyond me.*

It sickens me to imagine that she may have introduced Max to her peculiar head for heights on the Brightworth Pier, perhaps as the tide was out. Even now I do not know what to think of Max and Germaine as a sexual item. It seems so improbable...but those pictures, sent to me anonymously. Oh yes, I remember those....

I know that Max and Germaine are an unanswered question...

But I can't put it off any more. I feel compelled to tell you more of where I am now.

Some subtle influence is at work on me.

I am sitting in a white room, on a white chair, in front of the white screen of a video or TV monitor - one of those giant wafer-thin Japanese jobs by the looks of it. Everything in the room, including the room itself, appears to be made of light, hues of white light: nothing appears solid. Yet I can touch this small white table to my left and the document resting on it.

I pick up the document.

I see that it is headed with capitalised words embossed in white. They read:

VICKI COCHRANE

CASE PENDING

VICKI, PLEASE OPEN THIS FOLDER FOR FURTHER INSTRUCTIONS

Goodness, how efficient. Someone's gone to a lot of trouble here. "Case pending": what does that mean?

I open the document to find two sheets of paper. The top sheet looks like a questionnaire, but with a difference. All the dotted lines have been written on already. How presumptuous. In my handwriting, too. It's a forgery! I don't recall filling this lot in.

One of the questions reads:

"Can you put a name to, and elaborate on, the code of ethics by which you lived your earthly life [in no more than 50 words]?"

What a dull thing to ask. The answer reads: "Yes, fashion. Fashion is the science of human mood and everything in life happens because of mood. Nothing exists but to be replaced. The right life is the one that surfs the changing mood - be it morals or angle of eyebrow. Never stay still."

I most definitely did not write that. But, you know, that answer is quite good – that's how I would have answered that question, if I had.

My eyes dart to the top of the questionnaire. The opening message reads:

"Dear Vicki, welcome to this place which has no name but which has been customised to suit your needs and expectations. As you will have deduced by now the answers below are not yours as such but are distillations of your private, unguarded thoughts upon which your earthly life was truly predicated. This approach saves time – and you the embarrassment of being found out. Your case has the status of "Pending" because:

(a) Your earthly body is only in a "near-death" condition and may yet revive to draw back your life essence which is now reading this document;

(b) You passed here while still in a condition of love for the earthly life. You had not grown tired of it. This is most unfortunate.

Please read all the questions and answers below and then turn to page two for further instructions. (If you disagree with an answer, think again.)"

Naturally I am stunned by all this. How bureaucratic it all seems, as if angels are the souls of dead social security clerks. They're right, of course. I loved my life, the conspiracy of it....

I look at all the Q&As. Another question reads:

"Name your most significant fate partner. Did you treat him or her or it honestly [20 words]?"

It?

The answer:

"Yes, I treated my husband Max Cochrane honestly. He recognised my special needs, and I his. Ours was an advanced.... [Deleted over 20 words]."

How annoying! And how odd that this automated response was unable to sum Max up in 20 words – I'd have managed it! Yet how can one fully encapsulate such an important matter as one's significant fate partner in so little space? The place is run by dead social security clerks. Officialdom won't meddle with me.

Q.8. reads:

"Did you love your fellow man and woman [20 words]?"

Answer:

"In bottled form, as definable mood-changing scented essences. We love or loathe people according to their mood effect on one."

Perfect! In 20 words. Hyphenated words count as one.

I skip through the other Q&As: everything appears in order. It all seems so curiously knowing of me, if not knowledgeable. The last item is not a question but a report. It reads:

"Serious Universal Law Infringements: "0" [Attempted murder of Max Cochrane: Credit Note mitigation due to subject's disturbed state of mind.]"

That means I didn't succeed in killing Max. Pity. He deserved to die. No mention of Princess Leona Humperdink – that's a relief. I can only deal with so many shocks right now.

I turn to page two. The message reads:

"Dear Vicki, while you remain 'Pending' we suggest you review the last few days of your earthly life using a series of specially edited astral video tapes we are happy to loan you."

I look up. There to my right, a pile of video cassettes has just appeared from nowhere. They're numbered 1-2-3 etc.

I read on:

"We suggest you play them in numerical order so that you may relive your life in proper sequence. These are not like your earthly video cassette tapes. Once operational these astral tapes will draw your essence into the screen, enabling you not only to relive certain moments but at times to witness events at which, originally, you were not physically present. The tapes have been edited so as to include all contributory elements to your demise. Perhaps in seeing the total picture of the events leading up to your arrival here, you will love your earthly life a little less and come to terms with your astral condition."

Astral? What a terrible world. Not like sentient. Astral is one of those tinkly words that mean death.

I am not dead! The Queen of Fashion lives on!

The message ends with:

"WARNING:
THIS IS NOT AN INTERACTIVE EXERCISE. ALTHOUGH YOU WILL RELIVE THOUGHTS AND ACTIONS AS IF THEY OCCUR IN THE PRESENT, AND ALTHOUGH YOU CAN THINK INDEPENDENTLY AND DISAPPROVE OF YOUR EARTHLY SELF, YOU CANNOT ALTER EVENTS NOR CAN OTHERS SEE OR SENSE YOU DESPITE THE ILLUSION OF REALITY. ONLY WHAT YOU THINK IN YOUR ASTRAL PRESENT CAN BE CHANGED."

I gaze already exhausted at the pile of astral tapes. This Is Your (Before) Life! I find it astonishing that one's whole life had been bugged in this way - not just one's office, car or home by one's friends and enemies.

Nothing is deemed too trivial for recording on a reel of plastic or ether. As if every damned thing mattered in the end.

I pick up "Video No.1." There are words on its label. These read:

"April 27, 1988: 4.08am: Max's call to Vicki: the beginning of the end."

Indeed! How pessimistic. My case is only pending. I could survive yet.

I examine the tape itself: the reel appears to be made of a band of white light run on spools of light. Then I notice for the first time that I too am made of the same substance - light.

Wrinkle-free light. If only it could be bottled on earth: the ultimate elixir from the House of Cochrane. Karl Lagerfeld would be sooo envious.

The tapes and me are one.

I peer behind me: no wings.

Well, I've time to kill. I never could resist eavesdropping. I particularly like the bit about witnessing events at which I was not present first time around.

Germaine and Max, my treacherous staff at Raven's Towers, the caprices of fate itself: all that lot needs answering....

I wonder what happens if I put Video No.1 in the recorder's slot...will I be trapped forever in a recording of my own life? I never did understand how technology happens.

I slip the tape out of its sleeve and push it gently into the recorder -

OOOOOOOOOH!

I'm being sucked into the screen.

Gross body turned to light turned to pixel dust.

Am I dreaming - yet again?

>>>

CHAPTER TWO

WOOOOOOOOOOOOOOOO! Some excitement at last. My tummy tickled then.

At the very moment I put the video in the slot my body of light was drawn into the astral video screen. And I'm now surrounded by ruched and floral chiffon clouds on the theme of peach, on a floor of pale, glossy jade-green; and the air is light with peach potpourri (in tiny hanging baskets); and on a French tasselled antique pelmet (the finest example of wool and silk passementerie – a gift, natch) there's that funny little mark I've been meaning to mention to Franca....

Good heavens. I'm in my bedroom - at my home in Belgravia.

More specifically I am lying in my canopied bed and I have the distinct feeling that the astral me is both in the physical me - the Vicki so many earthbound people love or loathe - and outside the physical me. What an odd sensation. Do you know what I mean? Probably not.

This is going to take some getting used to.

And, you know, now that I'm sort of in my body and head I'm thinking thoughts already familiar to me.

I can't stop them, I can comment on them, but you don't want the two of us talking at once - that would certainly confuse me.

I'm thinking in my bed: "The last thing I need first thing in the morning is the sight and sound of Max." Actually, it's 4.08 am so it's not the first thing in the morning but the time before.

Before time begun!

He has woken me up; he's on the videophone. Only Max can use that phone. In a half-sleep I've already clocked the clock. I clutch at the receiver to end its infernal squealing, and this action automatically flicks on my video screen at the foot of the bed so that I can see Max on the other end of the line and camera - oh, there he is, funny to see him now. He looks like that newsreader – whatisname....

You're probably wondering why Max isn't in the marital bed and why he's on camera. Well, I won't have him in my physical presence, out of hours. He lives next door in a separate household linked by our very own improvised videophone. My husband is my neighbour. They say: Love Thy Neighbour. But truly to love anyone you have to keep them at arm's length. That's what I say. For me the miracle of technology is its delivery of a vital backup to personal space needs...of keeping people at bay.

Why is Max living next door? Why do we communicate in this way? What's it like performing to camera in a real-life scenario all the time? No time now to answer these intriguing questions. I am compelled to follow the action in which I co-star.

"What...what time is it?" I moan, yawning, at 4.08am. I glance again at the red luminous digits which cast a devil's eye glow on my ice white sheets: they read 4.08am. "*Madonna!*" I shout - an Italian dialectal profanity - "It's 4.08 am!"

"Vicki, Vicki, wake up. We need to talk."

Yes, thanks to a tiny camera on the monitor, he can see me. My hair in the cap, face shiny with Estée Lauder moisturiser.

"Are you mad, Max? It's 4.08am, no, 4.09 now. I'm on television at 7.45. Now I'll drop off after this and oversleep - Franca always lets me oversleep – she'll have to go - and I always get dyspepsia if I wake up late."

"Vicki, this is very important. I have something to tell you."

Where's Franca - my maid?

"Can't it wait?" I ask wearily, thinking already that calling me so early breaks with all precedent. I feel alert to sudden change. "You're so thoughtless!" I shout. As I pull myself up the bed, I catch an updraft of pine from the pine bubble bath I had hours earlier. I remember that. The pine, after half-a-night's sleep, is a little too humanly balmy for my taste.

Pine should be cold, antiseptic. Pine is sparkling loo basins, free of germs, free of those other smells....

"No," says Max firmly. "It can't wait. I am about to do something of which you must be apprised. You will be upset, and you'll wonder why…."

"You haven't found another woman have you?" Those terrible words - if only I had known then!

I am very alert now. In all honesty Max has this effect on me. He is like eucalyptus which shoots up your nose and blasts your sinuses. He is my eucalyptus, bottled behind the glass of the video screen which is how and where I prefer him.

He looks tired, his eyes are tired, labouring under those collapsible fleshy pillows just below the brows. In fact, they're pressing down on his top lids now, giving him an aggressive eagle-eyed look - like that actress Charlotte Rampling. It makes him look fierce.

Max looks ready to pounce this morning.

"There's no other woman. But I am leaving," he announces, and lies flatly.

"Leaving? What are you talking about. You've already left!"

"I mean," he says as if spelling meaning out to a simpleton, "that I am going away for an indeterminate while."

"Away? Where? Have you finally succumbed to your various neurotic obsessions and decided to admit yourself into a lunatic asylum?"

He ignores my seriousness. "I am leaving after this call for Brightworth-by-sea. I am going to live on Brightworth Pier - no, let me finish...."

I said nothing.

"It's all arranged. In a matter of minutes I will not be living next door and I shall be a resident of the Brightworth Pier. I have already registered the chalet there as a UK additional home for Poll Tax purposes."

I sit up in bed and absently draw pillows behind me. The Poll Tax reference is alarming: the insertion of this detail is a tactical ploy of his to grab my true attention. He knows me so well.

Oh, I know all about Brightworth - the town of Max's boyhood. The best years of his life; his life-long excuse for being a bastard. I know Brightworth on England's "sunny south coast" only too well. But the Poll Tax thing added to the 4.08am timing mean he's trying to say something else.

This is not just about Brightworth. He means business.

I examine his face on the screen for signs of any uncharacteristic levity. He's clearly rehearsed this item of news: his very facial immobility tells me of the hours he has put into anticipating my shock, queries, incomprehension....

I am thinking these thoughts, there in my bed. They rush through me in a one of those nanoseconds I've read about in one of Max's *Reader's Digest*s. I am aware that the condition between us is red and that I must not do anything too predictable like ask him that old movie classic, "But, Max, what are you trying to say?"

Max gets dangerous when you become too predictable.

Max relishes an authentic surprise.

"Oh, the Brightworth Pier," I say on the skip of a giggle. "Goodness...."

"Yes, this may seem strange...."

"Well it's not every day that a wife is told she is being deserted for Brightworth Pier. I mean, as an international publishing tycoon you're entitled to your eccentricities I'm sure. I mean, Robert Maxwell has a thing about ducks...."

He does not acknowledge this attempt at making-light: what I mean is, he knows I am shocked and ordinarily he might try to say something reassuring, depending on his intention. But this morning he chooses not to make me feel better. By omission he wants me to suffer.

He says, "I have my reasons."

"I had hoped so Max. The fact that you have a reason is reassurance in itself. I mean...."

"Don't be ironic, Vicki. You are naturally flabbergasted by my news, as anyone would be."

"No!" I dissimulate, pulling a peach tissue from the box. "In fact, I think I had a premonition of you going to Brightworth Pier. Just then, at 4.07am, I dreamt you getting into your Daimler and making your way down to that charming seaside town - and Max, keep still, your fidgety movements on the screen are making me feel queasy, screen-sick, anyone would think you've got Parkinson's the way your body tics about...."

It's funny, but jelly, or anything wobbly, is emetic to me. I'm sure it upsets something in my middle ear - I read that in Max's *Reader's Digest* as well - I feel like throwing up....

"Keep still!" I bawl.

"I am still," he responds. "It's you who are moving about. I can see it myself. You're trembling, hence the effect of wobbling on the screen...."

"Don't try your old tricks on me. I know all your tricks! You're not talking to one of your little foundling lackeys at Raven's Towers. So you're off to Brightworth Pier. It's news to me that piers are residential - what are you up to? Planning to buy out the local council and become the Prince Rainier of Brightworth? Your Serene Highness!"

Max's brow hoods grow heavier. "Try to control yourself, Vicki. I have come to an arrangement with the mayoress of Brightworth, Mrs Elsie something or other...."

"I've just thought," I interrupt. "You'll be sharing the pier with that clairvoyante, Madame Smith. Perhaps she'll give you free psychic readings when the Force Nine gales strike. God help you if there's another hurricane like last year."

He shows signs of irritation at my lateral improvisations on Brightworth Pier. He is fidgeting. He always fidgets before a journey - something to do with once being a simple Brightworth boy who didn't get out much - who got excited at the prospect of a trip on a train or something.

The simple boy born and raised in Brightworth.

He says, "I just have to get away."

An obvious thought occurs to me: "But who will run Raven's Towers?"

"I have memo'd Roger Masefield that as my deputy he is acting chief executive in my absence."

"And does he know where you'll be?"

"No. Which brings me to another point. Only you will know I am on Brightworth Pier. I don't want it known that I am on Brightworth

Pier. I want total privacy, no intrusions. I don't want you getting up to your usual tactics, Vicki, of cross-pollinating various key individuals with secret information to suit your own ends. This confidence is an act of faith in you. Are you listening Vicki or is your mind off sniffing scents?"

A bolt of rage hits me right down in my lower intestine. I feel it even in my dissociated astral state. I detest personal insight used as a weapon: "Who do you think you're talking to?" I scream. "Have I ever let you down? Raven's Towers would be nothing without me and *Glossy International*. Without me you'd still be just some trade publisher stuck in Milan. I am *Glossy International*! Over the decades you have consistently pillaged and leeched on my sensibility, on the day-to-day reality that is Vicki Cochrane...."

Trouble is, the word "Brightworth" makes me giggle for some reason – don't ask me why - and I can't suppress my laughter anymore, and now it bursts out of its manic pod. My head rolls on the padded vermillion of the headboard as my body chugs with the sheer joy of playing the *monstre sacré* to Brightworth's blue-eyed boy.

I can laugh at myself. I can do self-parody. Or, perhaps it's nerves.

But I am making a serious point. That bastard has copyrighted my very soul under the Raven's Towers imprints. *Glossy International* is me made laminate, and its - my! - personality rhythms resonate down the entire empire, conceiving, shaping, giving birth to dozens of down-market derivatives.

"So don't project your own tricks on me," I conclude, "trying to cover your tracks while you embark on your pathetic trip down memory lane to Pension Paradise. How long will you be there?"

"I don't know."

So this is war, of a sort. Max never did not know nothing - if you follow my meaning. I never knew him not to know something like that: how long the journey, how long the stay.

A little sperm of panic breaks into me.

"Vicki!" he says sharply. "I'm going soon. I want to say this. At the age of 64 I think I should be free to do as I please. I don't have to be at Raven's Towers 24 hours a day. Roger is very capable...."

"And very ambitious. You'll play into his hands - especially if he finds out about your destination. He'll see you for the crazy you are."

"That's up to you Vicki."

"These things get out – Raven's Towers is not exactly the home of positive discrimination for trappists!"

"It's up to you - and Vicki, you're holding the receiver too close to your face. I can hear you breathing into the receiver...."

"For God's sake," I snap.

"It's a bad habit you have. You've never learned how to hold a telephone receiver properly. Every day it's like talking to a lunar astronaut."

I shift the receiver so that I can see the full field of mouthpiece. Typical Max and his obsessions with little noises. That's one of the many reasons why I won't share a house with him. In the old days, when we lived together, I had only to give my soup bowl a chance tap, and he'd deliberately tap his soup bowl back - in order to draw attention to the fact that yet another incidental noise of day-to-day life had upset him and his mental equilibrium. It was torture by mimicry. I won't be subject to that kind of domestic control.

"And you call me neurotic!" I shout.

"It has nothing to do with being neurotic. People have asked me whether you're asthmatic after talking to you on the phone. It's terrible having to talk into such a wind tunnel."

"OK! Look, see, the phone's there," I say, waggling the receiver at him. "I'll hold my breath if necessary. Tell me when I turn purple!"

Max composes himself - "I was saying," he says, "that Roger is fine. You get on well with him."

"I have barely spoken to him. We've not even lunched. He was your appointment after all. According to Leona Humperdink he was known as the Smiling Snake in New York and you make him your number two. Another game of yours. It's not enough that you're alive, that you own one of the most influential publishing companies in the world, that you're married to me! No, you have to engineer little games, set people against each other. Why don't you learn to sack people? Every day you should say to yourself: I am going to sack someone."

A Max sigh, then: "Vicki, you're going on and on. It's a feature of your mind that you assume the world runs according to your pattern of behaviour. You are a subjective sociopath without the slightest capacity for objectivity...."

And on he goes, pot calling kettle black: I do love those English clichés. We Italians - Max is not Italian - we, well, we don't condense our thoughts. I interrupt Max's clinical deconstruction of me.

"Max, this going down to Brightworth. Is it that you wish to get away from me?"

He is stopped and silent. What a mistake to ask such a question in the middle of battle. The raising of the question of fault in me! If only I could rewind this astral tape and change my words. My first big error of the day and it's only 4.10 in the morning.

To compound my error I then ask: "What about me, Max?"

Foolish Vicki. I relive the precise experience as if it were now but unable to do anything about it. He remains quiet. Silence is his answer. How brilliant has been his rehearsal.

"Eh!" I scream, "Can you hear me, *figlio di puttana*! I said what about me?"

He comes to life: "What about you? You will continue to run *Glossy International* and all its foreign editions, as usual; it's just I won't be in the building nor will I be available on the phone as much. I just don't want to be accessible to everybody. I want peace."

"I'm not everybody," I wail. "I'm your wife. Is this all this is about? That you don't want to talk to your own wife?"

"*Talk*?" he echoes bitterly, his already aged-thin lips turned to dashes. "I am a walking personal therapist, your dream analyst, your on-tap Samaritan...."

"What!" I think that's the word I utter. Or perhaps it's just a yelp of disbelief. "Is it too much to give a bit of moral support to someone whose whole life is devoted to our work. And what about you? Every day you ask me important questions - questions - you asked me only yesterday whether virtual reality fashion shows are cheaper than real life model shows - millions of pounds worldwide resting on my advice. You begrudge the tiny support you give my heart - the heart of Raven's Towers!"

Max sighs heavily again as I fail to weep. The tears won't be forced unless it's one of my bloody allergies. When I lose control my tear ducts remain dammed, but my brain goes.

Despite appearances I am not a good actress.

He says, "Look, my going to Brightworth is not just about you, but about me, about my life, about...."

"Your wattle!"

"My what?" he asks, pulling a grotesque, incredulous face. He was just about to get truly serious and I sabotaged him.

"Your wattle." I repeat. What a flash of inspiration on my part. Brilliant. "All that turkey flesh under your face. Look at it. You've been self-conscious about it for years. Two chins, three chins. Your face is like a face within a face or a face framed by flesh. That's what this Brightworth crap is all about. You're going away to have cosmetic surgery. That's it, isn't it?"

Max rarely incandesces but the blush on his cheeks tests the video screen's colour integrity.

"I won't even dignify..." he splutters, halted by his own fear of predictability. "You vindictive, demonic bitch."

I improvise, routinely, "The times you've talked about your wattle, flapping away as it does in conferences as you discuss the exponential growth of magazine circulation in the twenty-first century. And you should do something about those bags above your eyes while you're about it. Most people have bags below their eyes but, no, you have to go and have them above. Any minute now they'll flop down over your lids and you'll wonder who switched off the lights. Perhaps it'll happen in Brightworth. All that south-westerly wind will push them over the edge of those creased eyelids of yours - those eyelids, they look like fried bacon rind. I've noticed sadists have that fatty overhang above their eyes - Margaret Thatcher is another one, Hitler - he was an Aries, too. Or was he Taurus?"

Perversely, Max has grown relaxed in the torrid sauna of my onslaught - as ever. He knows the keener my insults the more desperate I am. That's his way in war.

"Vicki, I'm going in a moment. Who knows? Maybe I will have my wattle seen to, my eyelids too. But I have many reasons for leaving, not least to be free of your persecution. But not even that is the whole reason. I am going back to Brightworth for me - for all the personal reasons I have, which have nothing, or not much, to do with you. Nothing lasts, Vicki, remember that. Nothing lasts. Nothing. And I am not going to waste the rest of what remains of my life pretending it's going to last. I want changes in my life, big changes; I want you changed, I want Raven's Towers changed. I want us to remember...."

"I've got the message Max. You're going through the change."

It's not so much his words that are unsettling me as his tone: he is serious, he does mean to go to this ridiculous pier: he has never done this before - left me in the sense of not being there as a fixture of our respective but coordinated schedules.

Physical absences I welcome. But spiritual emigration is another matter.

"Max," I begin cautiously, "has this thing, this going to Brightworth, has this anything to do with that time we went to Brightworth - together? Six months ago - God, how time flies."

He looks surprised for a moment, as if the thought is new to him. He could be faking it. "Perhaps," he says slowly, looking away from the screen in a theatrical mode of thoughtfulness; very Gielgud as Hamlet. "Yes, perhaps all this is to do with that day...."

I had hoped never to think of that visit again. I'd better explain quickly. Last October Max insisted that after 38 years of marriage - or 39 (whatever!) - we should drive down and see the place of his birth and youth. I'm not sure why. A voyage back to his past, he said. He had this longing to get back to his roots, he said. In a moment of weakness, or curiosity at the very novelty of actually being with him again all day, I agreed.

We drove down. But I was so appalled by the seaweed stink and the complete flakiness of the place that I saw very little. Instead, I sought refuge in an off-shore astral establishment called Madame Smith's Psychic Pagoda on the pier itself. I think she was burning a strawberry incense or something - a gas heater sizzled and added a comforting fume - and I said to her, "Do you mind if I stay with you while my husband goes for a walk on the beach? Is that incense? It's lovely - how can anyone but the olfactorily disabled stand the stink out there? You can give me a reading if you like." I took out cash. "There, there's £50. Give me £50 worth of the future so I don't have to breathe the present."

Poor Madame Smith. She gave me a gormless look and said something out of the University of Life, like "Yer wha'?" Admittedly I did not bother to disguise my brutal metropolitan ways and need to escape the coastal stench, but natives like her on the whole react well to honesty so long as you're just visiting or seem out-of-it. Madame Smith soon settled down. She took my money and shuffled her cards and she prattled on forever and I didn't listen to a single word because I was enraptured by the incense and then by something else about Madame Smith - she reminded me of an ancient opiate; an intoxicating drink, the name of which....

"Vicki, Vicki! Come back to earth. You're dreaming again and your lips are moving." It's Max talking, yanking me back to his reality.

I say, "I was just trying to remember when you went for that walk on the beach while Madame Smith read my cards - if only you hadn't."

"Don't dramatise," he says. "It couldn't be helped. All that pollution, debris. Brightworth is not the town I remember."

"After your damned walk you listed all the rubbish on the beach. What pleasure that gave you. You know how badly I react to ugliness. The used condoms, the polystyrene, the oil splotches, the dead birds, all lying on the shingle. Britain's graveyard, you said. You used a funny phrase. You said the dry seaweed was like walking on poppadoms. You said you'd had a vision on that beach - a vision that ephemeral things were killing the world because everything is disposable so the sea is the obvious end of the trash chain. Not an original vision. It's coming back to me. And in the middle of all the debris you saw...."

"There's no need to go through the transcript," he intrudes harshly.

"No, it has to be said. Among all the rubbish on the beach you'd seen a torn, sodden copy of *Glossy International*, just discarded there with all the other rubbish."

"It was just there. I didn't mean to upset you."

"How you upset me! But it was what you said. You said we should have a new slogan for my magazine. I quote: 'Today's *Glossy* is tomorrow's drossy'. Unquote. That was very cruel – if lame. You said that my magazine was the champion of waste, an example of the irresponsibility of society to nature, the sea, the birds. You said Raven's Towers was as much to blame for the adulteration of Brightworth as any other corporation. You said you were going to atone for your part in the downfall of Mother Nature - you always were a bit of mother's boy! - and start-up a green magazine and save the likes of Brightworth beach. I was never quite the same after those insults. You lost faith in me and I lost faith in you. Beyond the banality of your 'revelation' I intuited what was really going on."

That's true. I sensed that our joint conspiracy on the world had ended. No time to elaborate....

Max shakes his head slowly as if to say "I give up". But he said those things. He did. Even now they echo in my head, in what Max calls, in vicious moments, my "lacquered belfry."

"God!" I shout in desperation, now on an emotional roll, "If only I'd had children, a normal life, not this freak existence."

Max smiles for the first time. "It's not so bad."

"I feel too much, see too much…."

"It's all in your head," Max adds helpfully. "What would you have done with children?"

As he speaks those knowing words I see head pictures of milk bottles shattering all about me. There and then I have a vision of flying glass, oceans of milk, engulfing me; a ghastly tidal wave of domestic dairy product (unskimmed probably). The vision is real, one of my terrible daymares (that's what I call them), those waking nightmares when stress plays wicked stepmother to my volatile imagination.

Children. Milk. Spilt.

"Vicki, Vicki - your lips are moving again…."

"What?" I say in a daze.

"Your brain, it's talking to itself and your lips are miming on – you're having a daymare. Wake up. We don't have children. At 58 it's improbable you will conceive outside the unlikelihood of in vitro fertilisation. Calm down."

"The daymare is your fault. If you didn't upset me I wouldn't have them."

"You're simply associating milk with suckling babes. This is quite logical."

"Yes, that is logical. I saw the milk bottles in my head. You know the smell of cow's milk makes me retch. Udders!"

"Gone now."

He cares at least, a bit. We haven't had sex in ten years.

"Max!" I shout. "What happens if I have a daymare while you're in Brightworth?"

"You must learn to try to cope in new ways."

"Max!" I shout again, surprising myself. Max flinches. I so alarm myself that I forget what I was about to say.

To break embarrassed silence he says, "It doesn't become you to be clichéd and pathetic. My going for a while will be a trial for us both, an opportunity to see what happens, to discover if we have the same resolve, the same capacity to deal with change as, well, forty years ago - when everything was less certain. Also Raven's Towers needs shaking up - I have many reasons for wanting to absent myself."

I know what he means. But: "I have never known certainty, Max. You can't be what I am and know certainty. My life is *Glossy* and *Glossy* is fashion and fashion is everything in life, everything you can think of, all changing, beginning and ending."

"Beginning and ending, that's what I mean," he says.

"Max, listen to me." At last I know what I am dealing with. A Max in a state of flux. A Max who I begin to suspect imagines I may be turned into an item of (transient) fashion if I'm not careful. "Max, look, I understand your need to return home. I know that feeling. Whenever I see mountains, or white cloud in the distance, I think of the Dolomites, the mountains of Friuli: I am not without feeling. I would love to return to my home town of Casarsa della Delizia. Not a day goes by that I don't hum *Come Prima* to myself - but you have to resist the longing because the past is gone. Now is what matters. Now. Now. Now."

I am stunned by this awful outbreak of wisdom: I couldn't give a buggery about Casarsa - I couldn't wait to get away from that picture postcard nostalgia tip.

"Well, I'd better be going," Max says, as if he has just politely declined the last cucumber sandwich.

Panicky, I lean forward in my bed: "If you leave Max I'll force you back. I'll do whatever it takes. I like my life and you play a valuable role in it as I in yours and nothing's going to upset this apple cart. Don't make the same old mistake of underestimating me. I know what you're up to - you want to destabilise me, get me out of Raven's Towers because I'm too old, that's it, isn't it? Trade me in. So you can find some new younger genius to surf on, to carry you on as the plumber you are.

But I haven't survived this long by chance or by being married to you. Oh no. I know how to steer fashion - and do you know where I'm going to steer you? Into an Oxfam shop. That's right, Max, an Oxfam shop. Overnight I'll turn you into an old pair of nylon slacks with the perma-crease and throw you out. I know my way round the Raven's Towers board. I put you on notice! You think that by going to that terrible Brightworth I'll be unable to cope without you. But I'll survive and you won't. REMEMBER THESE WORDS!"

Max offers me a goodbye smile, eyes crinkled: "Nothing lasts at all, Vicki, including me."

And with that the TV screen flicks to grey.

*

I'm still in my pine-scented bed and wondering what the hell all that was really about.

Astrally, I think of Germaine: all his lies for her! If only I had known then.

My earthly self shouts, "Franca! Franca! Franca!"

Then I hear movement outside. I spin out of bed and peer through the curtains. A blackbird is already twittering its song to the waking anxious. Twit. Twit. Twit. Oh God.

Dawn readies to spread tawdry rumours. Again.

I see Max in a wide diagonal below leave the house next door. He's carrying a suitcase, stained as he is by the hellish sulphur glow of a street lamp. The chauffeur opens the sulphur-grey Daimler door and clunks it shut once Max's behind has made contact with the cashmere leather. I don't hear the clunk, thanks to the double-glazing.

As they drive off I stab the digits to his car phone.

"Yes, Vicki," Max says before I speak.

I hiss, "You should have hired a hearse because I'll see to it that you're returned in one."

"That's not a very original line, Vicki. You are a first class editor, and I have a pier to catch. Good morning."

He hangs up.

*

I am tired, exhausted, defeated; it's 4.16am. Max (my sinus-blasting eucalyptus) is no longer happy in his bottle. He is spilt, like that awful kiddies' milk.

A knock at the door and Franca emerges. "Signora, I hear you screaming, you dreaming?"

"Go back to bed Franca, just go and leave me alone. I was just screaming and dreaming. Remember my early morning call. My TV thing is 7.45."

"*Si*, signora."

She looks hurt by my abruptness. Dear sweet Franca. She's about my age, looks two decades older. I often look at her and think: there but for the grace of God go I - is that the cliché? She is a reminder to me of what would have happened had I allowed my body to follow its predestined path.

She is a visual yardstick of the years I have held or clawed back. I gaze at Franca now and think of sweet oil of rose - something irredeemably romantic, but passed it. Roses to me have always had this association, of love lost and now only dreamt of; a longing – or disillusionment.

I am a reinvented rose thorn.

The part of me which is no longer the Vicki in her bed, the astral Vicki, wishes to escape. I feel again my old sense of bewilderment, of loss. My head is numb.

In my bed, stress lulls me into sleep again. I drift into a dark refuge and a familiar nightmare....

In this dream I am my old (that is to say, young) self again, Vittoria Valentinuzzi, the woman of yesteryear. The maiden me.

I am on a train, the train I used to take to work in Milan everyday over forty years ago. And once again I am tormented by the salty smells of human flesh and visual pustular horrors: the other passengers. I see them clearly now, drooling, emitting, exuding, leaking - dreams exaggerate, I know, but this is how I remember them.

I observe with terror their red-trimmed noses blown into cotton handkerchiefs mucous-stiffened to cardboard. Their white collars grimed by sallow sagging turkey necks and double chins. Then, like a poolside child in a Hollywood TV movie, I am thrown into the septic tank of gaping mouths where I swim in the lactic breakfasts - milk! - that gleam on camouflage beds of white stinking fur. And I choke on the uncouth gases of their inner tripe belched up or released through nature's feculent vents. Then, in the dream, armpit and groin liberate their signature me-seeking odours in what can only be described as a wilful assault – a desecration of my meticulously programmed inner climate. Pimple UXBs stand poised, they wobble even, ready to discharge their contents over the pristine, blameless, scented Vittoria....

And then the dream tongue looms....

"No!" I cry out.

No more please.

I am awake again, sprawled now on my pine scented counterpain (goose down). I dropped off before I could get into bed. Max is a flashed thought and a heavy slack in my belly.

He has deserted me. He is to blame for my dreams.

I reach for the bedside lamp toggle switch. No tongue, I think, not even a dream tongue, is going to make tip-long plunges into my bellybutton - which is where I feel it was headed.

I know that a rampant tongue let loose on my body, even in the safety of a dream, will conjure up the ridiculous, upsetting images to which I am susceptible. I would know what the tongue is tasting, you see; and I would taste what it tastes.

I feel fatigued.

I need water - "Franca! Franca!"

She enters again with the intuited glass of water.

"Thank you, darling," I say, propped up on pillows. I look at poor Franca in the eye - after glancing at her little black moustache - and say:

"Franca, just remember the body is a time-bomb of corruption which with careful application can be reset hourly to prevent an outburst of stink and rot."

"*Si*, Mrs Cochrane. Your interview is in about two or three hours." She closes the door behind her.

Distress makes me sleepy: I believe it's the body's switch-off survival mechanism to do with endorphins - my beauty editor Timothy mentioned something about it once...

I drift off again. In sleep the dream tongue that tortured Vittoria Valentinuzzi a few minutes ago returns. It will not be thwarted. It works its way from my neck, over my breasts, left nipple-wise, to my hip. It's wetting my body, and stops at my inner thigh where a Spiritualist séance is about to commence.

In the dream a Red Indian has come from the higher spheres of the next life to convey a message of instruction to me through the Romany clairvoyante Madame Smith of the Brightworth Pier. His shiny face transfigures her ghostly visage.

He has been conjured up in my head by a trace of what remains on (in real life) my inner thigh and which the tongue has tasted - jojoba oil. Whether in bottled or soap form, jojoba oil leaves the skin silky smooth and takes up to ten years to produce. Red Indians used jojoba oil for that silky smooth effect long before Anita Roddick thought to retail it in her Body Shops.

And these days you're more likely to encounter a Red Indian

raised up at a Spiritualist's séance than on the plains of North America.

The Indian (or native American as I prefer), his powerful body gleaming in the light of unseen fire, takes possession of Madame Smith's tongue, and a rich baritone breaks from her frail body:

"There is in a garden an aviary of beautiful birds of all colours," he begins. "And out of the trees flies a blackbird, and he settles outside the aviary and he stretches his wings because the sun is out. And one of the great beauties of the exotic birds in the aviary flutters and says to him, 'Huh, what are you showing off? You're black. But look at me. I open my wings and look at the colours I have.'

"And so then the blackbird says to him, 'Yes, but I have something you do not have.'

"So the exotic bird asks, 'What is that? I've got everything, I've got beauty.'

"And the blackbird says, 'Yes, but you haven't got freedom. I have.' And flies off.

"Now little lady, little Vicki, that gives you a clue to a new type of reality."

My eyes open gently. I feel the momentary timeless calm before the brain grabs control again. What a sweet parable with its simple little message. But what is this freedom? Freedom for me is the fulfilment of what I can do.

To be a blackbird would be a denial of what I can do - which is to spray colour on the world and dab new scents behind global earlobes.

I adore my prison. The obsessions, neuroses: these are the lively walls. The modern mind need not be underestimated in its capacity to know and wallow in its own sickness. Most thinking people understand this.

*

My head still resonates with the rich Red Indian baritone.

But the dream tongue has shrivelled away and I imagine turned into a fig.

What I need is my beauty editor Timothy and his plant oil essence, his essence of juniper berry, to clean out my mind.

To clean out Max and his bad news.

Timothy's being has that effect on me.

Did you know smells affect our mood, affect the physical, mental and spiritual bits of us? You've never heard of aromatherapy? The essence of juniper berry is used by aromatherapists to clarify a patient's head.

Laugh, but it works, believe me.

Timothy is my juniper berry. His sharp, springy nature reminds me of juniper.

In fact all my *Glossy* staff together comprise a personal apothecary of essential oils, each with its (or rather, his or her) special effect on me. Bottled. They are more than bottles of course, they are human beings, but we all bottle other people; yes, we do.

Each member of staff delivers a special mood to me; but I mustn't go on; I feel I'm being drawn away....

Timothy is not with me in my pine scented bed so I'll have to settle for coffee.

"Franca! Franca!"

But too late. I am being drawn from the old earthly me in my bed, away from the Belgravia home, from London, England, Europe, World - you know the rest....

>><<

OOOOOOOOH!

Just then, as I was calling for sleepyhead Franca and coffee, I was pulled out of my bedroom in an instant and brought back here, back to my astral sitting room.

The astral screen is blank - just the way my own videophone screen was blank when Max hung-up and pissed off. I see the parallels without seeing the point.

I hear a gentle whirring in the video recorder and out slides the cassette - Video No.1.

I pop it back into its white sleeve. No astral Franca to clean up.

But what technology! To be able to relive one's life in this way: Who held the camera? Who was the gaffer boy? It is all a mystery to me, not least my own life, not least Max whose truancy for Brightworth caused me such tremendous anguish. I shall try not to go on about Germaine, but she is a major issue: I saw the pictures of her and Max, on the pier....but, no, I must not pre-empt things.

What I did know then was that Max could be very tricky, and tricksy. It was this knowledge that unnerved quite as much as his incomprehensible self-exile to a seaside resort on the sunny south coast. My determination was to get him back before any real damage was done.

I take out Video No.2. The label reads simply: "Roughly four hours later".

I put it into the recorder

>>>

CHAPTER THREE

In an instant the screen soaks me up again and squeezes me out onto a London street, as if I were a window cleaner's dirt water. I'm in my earthly body and I have just come from the TV studios a few hours after Max told me he was off to Brightworth. I would have known this even had I not read the Video No.2 label. For my mind is buzzing with Max, with Brightworth, dream tongues and native Americans.

And with the GlossRam Virtual Reality Fashion & Beauty Show to be held next week at the Rambagh Palace in Jaipur, India.

Most of all I'm thinking: how will I survive?

This much I recall: my chauffeur Stephen has collected me from the TV studios, after my 7.45 interview, in one of the company Daimlers. Our destination now is Raven's Towers. But in the rear seat panic has overwhelmed me at the prospect of a Raven's Towers minus Max: it is a place with which I am no longer familiar.

I hear distant oil essence bottles rattling nervously....

New interests, new forces are at work within the emerald skyscraper. I can sense them, I am at a loss.

"Stephen," I cry out. "Stop here. I need air. I think I'm going to be sick."

I like Stephen because he doesn't mishear me or query the sense of what I say or throw me the sort of bloody-minded facial expressions Max does when something just emerges from my mouth.

Stephen just gets on with it. He's a seasoned self-editor, one of my preferred kinds of person.

As the car draws up to the kerb I jump out. "Stephen, just drive around for five minutes then come and get me. Be prepared for surprises!"

I can smell the morning traffic and I feel I want to sneeze. I can't remember the last time my feet actually touched asphalt - I presume it's asphalt. It sounds such an American word, like sidewalk, something you might find in the Bronx. I'm thinking *The Asphalt Jungle*.

I prefer "pavement".

Menacing grey quilts roll above me: truly, momentarily, I have to reorientate myself to the dimensions and living unpredictability of the outside world. It was the same when I went to Brightworth with Max six months ago: all that land turned to inconstant water, having no real colour at all but volatile (illusory!) moods of greens and greys, heaving back and forth in a timeless state of attack and retrenchment.

A life all its own. No wonder Max worships Mother Nature. His faith is fear.

Give me an air-con office any day with temperature control: I'm no eco-masochist. Water has its place – in the bath or basin.

*

I'm standing in the street, alone.

Only water, thank God. Not that other stuff, bird shit.

A pearl droplet is glistening in one of my tiered chiffon petals overhanging my face from an outrageous silk organza saucer in navy.

My hat.

Then another droplet appears. I make the awning of a TV and video rental shop just in the nick of time before the squall starts in earnest.

Where's Stephen?

Rain falls so hard that a dense spray hisses off the road, which then unrolls into curb-side shelters - egged on by passing cars and buses - and dampens exasperated feet and ankles. In an instant I catch a glimpse of what it is like to be on the receiving end of riot police water cannon.

This is what nature likes to do. Trip you up, fool you. Make a mess!

I turn to face the shop glass by force of habit - to shake droplets from a petal and check for a facial smudge - only to be met by an uncommon sight: my own reflection superimposed on at least five of a bank of TV sets in the window now screening my own talking head. This is the interview I gave for gargling, breakfasting viewers just half an hour ago.

And they said it was live!

I can't deny the charge of excitement that shoots through me on recognising my all-time favourite chat show person. Now I understand what synchronicity means in practice.

Beyond the veil of chiffon, in the dimming glass, I see a new version of myself: a caricature drawn in broad lines of charcoal. I see my face as an archipelago of flesh edged by a vast night-time seascape of shadow. Here is a face that has risen from an ocean floor frolic with crabs, and now bobs on the still dark surface. Water, I see, has collected in drooping grooves and gouged cavities, the highlands of rose and cheeks (not forgetting my pert, designer dimpled chin) serving only as reminders of what may have been.

My staccato movements on the TV screens behind distract me again from the spectral reflection. My facial gymnastics seem robotic and absurd in the soundless display. Teeth, smile, teeth, nod, teeth: I read somewhere that distressed chimps bare their teeth in a rictus.

This of course is what happens if you stand and stare. I've always said that even a tentative voyage into one's interior will end in tears.

Thank God for fashion which holds us in the moment.

That's where Max has gone wrong. Perhaps one night at Brightworth he stared at a cloudless sky for too long and allowed the twinkling of a star to over-illuminate the recesses of his life.

Stare for too long at the sea, sky, a mountain, church or your own reflection and you're lost to this world; useless. Any distancing from the moment renders all worldly things absurd and futile. Perhaps that's what happened to Max and he went away.

I try to collect myself. Yes, I still admire my saucer hat and its lovely petals. But it's hopeless. The reflection grabs me again, making a fog of my dilapidated exterior. The window spectre is claiming me back against the hideous TV mime show - this is how I see it. It wants back the honest feature, the organic expression, the real me! It is screaming at me to do the unthinkable before it is too late – that's what the Red Indian séance dream must have meant: to wipe away the make-up and pluck out the chiffon petals and stamp on my hat. Scowl at the world. Fart at a fashion show - an audible ripper to blow away Saint Laurent's introvert face - and cry in a public place.

Marley's ghost exhorted charity and goodwill. My spectre demands back-to-the-babe simplicity and a standing, legs-apart piss into a street drain. This is the face of death, untinted, tainted....

"NO!"

No.

A car horn stirs me from my horror show. Stephen has traced me in the storm and calls me to safety.

He jumps out and ushers me into the safety of air-con, a place which doesn't aim to make a fool of people.

"Are you all right Mrs Cochrane?" he asks.

"No! Just drive around. I don't want to go to Raven's Towers yet. Just drive around."

*

I grab the car phone and dial Max's hideously expensive Nokia something-or-other 1320 brick.

"Yes, Vicki." No impersonal hello.

"How did you know it was me?"

"Only a handful of people have this number - and only you

would call me at nine in the morning. You're breathing very hard into the phone - is this an obscene call?"

I scream: "Don't make fun of me! I'll breathe as hard as I like."

Then I say at a more sensible volume so that I don't upset Stephen: "Look, Max, listen to me. I'm in a terrible state. I've just had a terrible experience - a ghost was looking at me in a shop window...."

"A ghost?" There's a ripple in his voice, suggesting incredulous mirth.

"I looked at least eighty - it was another me haunting me!"

"Now that's complicated even for you. Everyone looks old in shop windows. It's a fact of life. You looked old forty years ago when I used to watch your reflection in shop windows in Milan while you stalked behind men to sniff their aftershave. Because you hated the smell of the city."

I could kill him."I didn't phone for idiotic history lessons. I want you to realise what you've done to me already - the pressure you've put me under. My dreams are crazy...."

"They always were," he says nonchalantly.

"I dreamt of a Red Indian after you left me this morning, and I've just seen crabs crawling over my face in the shop window - something like that, anyway. I dreamt of a séance on my leg. What does it mean?"

To my surprise Max breathes into the receiver – he's usually very careful not to. He says in a diminuendo sigh, "I told you earlier that I have come here for peace. I cannot imagine what a séance on your leg means symbolically."

"Just this once, Max. I won't ask you about Brightworth. Just get the psychic dream book out. Look up Red Indians. I'm certain Red Indians symbolise something. I won't bother you again."

He puts down the phone. I hear a rustling and then turning of paper.

I say, "So, you packed the dream book down to Brightworth. Show's you think of me after all. What's that terrible screaming noise? Have you a woman there?"

"It's a seagull crying overhead, Vicki. Wishing you a nice day from Brightworth. If you're not careful seagulls shit on you. Now, Red Indians. Ah yes, it says a Red Indian in a dream is a warning to beware business associates."

"You're making it up."

"It says so here. I can fax it over to the car if you like."

"You have a fax machine on Brightworth Pier?"

"Just if I need it."

"What are you up to?" I ask. "Why would you take a fax machine to Brightworth? You said you wanted to be free of Raven's Towers for a while. I suppose you have a whole office down there. Why don't we set up a videophone like at home so I can see you. Stop this nonsense now, Max. Come back and we can talk. We can discuss your problems. I could order Stephen to take me to Brightworth now."

"Do that and I shall have him fired. It's in your hands whether he remains in the employ of Raven's Towers."

"What a shit you are."

Inexplicably I touch a raw nerve. With exasperation in his voice he says, "You amaze me. All your life you've said to me 'nothing lasts'; 'everything is but for a moment;' 'everything exists to be replaced'; 'what matters is the Now'; '*Glossy International* picks up an interest and throws it away next month'; 'the perfect life is the disloyal life'. Now I'm doing something different and you want everything to be the same. You will have to try to understand. We've been married forty years and you want no change. You've been at *Glossy* for twenty-five years, and you want that unchanged as well. We're stagnating, Vicki. I can even anticipate your unpredictability. Even when you make up something on the spot I can foresee it. Even the phone sounds like you when it's you calling. The slightest alteration in your life and you crack-up."

"You're the one who's cracking-up, Max," I say softly, aware he has made himself naked for a minute or so. "I'm the one who's going to work this morning. It's not I who's about to turn into seagull crap on Brightworth Pier."

On that note I hang-up, the way he does as a tactic to unsettle employees who bore him.

*

I'm still in the Daimler, being driven about in the rain. "Just drive around Stephen," I say. "Pretend I am a non-English speaking tourist new to London and you're a mute."

So Max is bored by my unpredictability yet wants change. Can you understand men, or Max?

We pass Buckingham Palace - a filthy, vulgar edifice - then cruise down the Mall towards the gay hang-outs on the perimeter of Trafalgar Square which is but a stroll from the Palace of Westminster.

All human life is to be found here if you're into that sort of thing.

My dawn turmoil is giving way to the early morning cooler side of my nature. Earthly thoughts pass through my astral self like a shoal of tiny wiggly silver fish. Perhaps I imagined it but did I detect in that last call to Max a little need in him for my approval of his irrational action?

I'm not certain; it's just a feeling. That's enough for me to forge ahead and think of something that will draw him away from Brightworth. He must not be allowed to linger there, or else new thoughts will turn to habit and replace the habit that is me. Do I believe that?

It was that exasperated voice of his that did it. And taking the psychic dream book with him was a tactical error. Obviously he anticipated my calling him with my wretched dreams but hadn't the moral courage to say to himself or to me: No more.

He has made his first mistakes. I know my Max.

Nonetheless, right now he is not my husband but my enemy. He has made it clear enough that he thinks I've been around too long. But I'll be the judge when Oxfam is to call!

The battle plan:

First, I must monitor his activities. This is field work so none of my spies at Raven's Towers can be used. I need a spook in situ to be my eyes and ears.

Inspiration has not deserted me this troubled morning. Step forward Madame Smith of the Brightworth Pier.

I smell her strawberry incense as she comes to mind, and her gas heater fume, and that strange ancient drink she reminded me of...ah yes, Madame Smith.

I'll hire her to read the present not the future.

I think no more. I dial Directory Enquiries.

"What name, caller."

"Madame Smith, of Brightworth Pier."

"Madame Smith. Is that M/S or S/M?"

"S/M? I'm not phoning a bondage parlour!"

"I mean, is it Smith, Madame, or Madame Smith, madam?"

I feel like throwing the phone under the wheels of a passing juggernaut that's attempting to cut us up. These people will be the death of me with their filo-brains.

"I don't know," I shout. "Find out for yourself!"

Telepathically attuned to my victimhood, Stephen stops the car at a bus stop layby, turns to face me - I have this sudden urge to suck his fine-grained square chin for some reason - and he offers to get Madame Smith's number and dial it for me.

"Thank you darling," I surrender.

That's what I call true clairvoyance: anticipating and responding to the needs of another human being. Max has always said I wasn't fit for ordinary life. He's right there.

Soon we're back on the road again and Madame Smith is on the line. I am impressed she's already at work: ready for the early season strollers, perhaps.

"Is this Madame Smith - the clairvoyante?" I begin, in my humble voice.

"Yeah." The voice is slurred. Perhaps she sleeps in her Psychic Pagoda.

"My name is Vicki Cochrane. I edit *Glossy International* magazine. You gave me a reading six months ago - do you remember me?"

"Nah. I see a lot people. You'll have to phone later if you want to make another appointment. Haven't had breakfast yet. You're lucky I'm here at this time of the morning."

She's not what you would call customer-friendly. This is what happens when venues are council-run. I look at my watch: it's 9.22am - almost lunchtime!

"Madame Smith, I'm phoning from a car phone so if we're cut off it's because I've entered a tunnel."

There's interminable silence on the line. Then: "Yer wha'?"

"Tunnels cut off car phone signals - oh, never mind, Madame Smith. Look I want to say something to you in strictest confidence - can I talk to you in confidence, Madame Smith?"

There's another one of her infuriating pauses. I don't think she can follow normal spoken sentence structure beyond basic commands and inquiries. On the line I hear seagulls cawing and screaming. I have an image of Brightworth as a filthy bird cage in need of a thorough shaking out at the hands of *Glossy International*.

"You're talking to me already," she says finally.

I try another approach:

"Madame Smith, don't say anything, just listen. In the next hour I will have couriered down to you £500 in cash if you do something for me."

"Half a grand?"

" Half of what? This is no joke, Madame Smith. The cash will be in your hands if you do something for me."

"What? A party reading? Sure. But remember, every psychic reading is in the nature of an experiment and…." I remember reading the very same words on a legal notice in her Pagoda.

"No, no, Madame Smith. I don't want a reading. I want you to do something unusual. I would like you to keep an eye on my husband who has just moved onto the Brightworth Pier."

"Oh. Husband? No one…oh, wait a min. Not the old boy who's

just moved into the Southern Pavilion here? Didn't look too happy. It's funny anyone living there. He was walking up and down the deck. He's your old man, is he?"

"You've seen him already? Goodness." My adrenals pump harder. "Yes, he is my husband. And Madame Smith, I want you to observe him. Is this something you could do?"

"'Nother woman then?"

"Sorry?"

"Marital difficulties? You're not the first, love."

"No...."

"Bit of the other?"

To establish a workable rapport I say, "Oh, well, that's for you to find out."

"Spy on him, you mean?"

It's odd how regional morons always need to turn everything into lingo before message engages brain.

"Not 'spy' as such, Madame Smith, just tell me what he's up to. There'll be more money plus bonuses. Perhaps you could call me later if you have anything to tell me."

After a pause she says in a doubtful monotone, "Well, I'm a clairvoyante not a spy. The council might take a dim view...."

"Do our horoscopes as well," I throw in desperately, not thinking. "I can give you our birthdates. I'll enclose the birthdates with the cash."

"£850 cash and you're done. Plus bonuses."

Eight hundred and fifty pounds – plus bonuses! These street market hagglers. That's what Thatcherism has brought to Britain. In time, price labels will just be the starting point in retail trade! But I have no choice.

"You have a deal Madame Smith. But mind you keep an eye on Mr Cochrane – that's his name, by the way. I may call later."

*

I'm still in the car. We're near St Paul's. I phone my personal assistant Lee at *Glossy International*.

"Lee, that was six rings before you answered. It's simply not good enough."

"I'm sorry Vicki. I just got in. The Tube was...."

"Never make excuses, Lee. Accept you did wrong and promise to get better. It's 9.31am and you're in my time now."

"Sorry, Vicki."

"Now don't ask questions. Arrange an emergency payment of £850 from petty cash and send it by bike on a red - pronto! - to someone called Madame Smith at the Brightworth Pier, Brightworth-by-Sea. Don't ask questions! Don't even think what this is all about. Also enclose my and Mr Cochrane's birth details - talk to Human Resources – it's a sort of surprise for Max. Just do it. DO IT!"

"Right away."

"Has the GlossRam film director turned up yet?" I ask.

"Freddie Smith? He's sneaking around - I haven't told any of the staff."

"You had better not, Lee. It's vitally important they do not know they are being filmed. I shall call again shortly. I may ask you to do something else that's also extremely and personally important that will tax your sense of what's usual. Something that may affect Raven's Towers' future."

I hang up. It's an effective ploy, hanging-up.

*

9.32am and I phone Max again.

"Come back Max. I'm asking you reasonably otherwise I cannot be held responsible for what happens. This is your last chance."

"I'm about to have some breakfast, Vicki. I suggest you eat something for a change. I suspect you're hypoglycemic, could be early diabetes - I can tell in your voice."

"What you're hearing in my voice Max is a woman in a difficult situation not of her making…."

"I met your Madame Smith a few minutes ago. I thought I might make an appointment."

"You do that, Max."

And I hang-up.

Good.

Madame Smith has not wasted time. If you want something done, secure the services of an opportunist. They're all in place.

*

I rest back in the car seat. What a day. And it's only 9.35am. I feel I've used myself up already. I need to be recharged. I want a new persona to deal with Max, an unknown Raven's Towers, a hostile staff (especially when they learn what Freddie Smith is up to) and my treacherous dreams and nightmares.

My ultimate enemy is me. I must placate me. Make peace with me. I must try to keep calm and visualise armour about me against hostile essences and moods.

"Raven's Towers, Mrs Cochrane?" asks Stephen.

"No, not Raven's Towers," I say. "Umberto's! That's where I want to go."

My head doctor. My armour supplier. My hairdresser.

I pick up the car phone. "Please see me now Umberto, darling. This is an emergency."

"Oh, Vicki, Vicki, you have no appointment."

"P-l-e-a-s-e."

"An outrage! Come then!"

Now I can enjoy the journey. Umberto – another juicy opportunist.

I stare out through spinning, topsy-turvy worlds caught in the deluge's many window droplets. Peepholes to a new kind of life.

And all because of Max.

"Umberto's! Fast!"

*

OOOOOOH!

>><<

All this darting about. For a moment I was enjoying myself there. Video No.2 has run out and I'm back here, in the astral waiting room.

No real surprises so far. Germaine is a sort of non-issue to you - but torture to me. I know she is the subtext to my woe of morning April 27.

Everything is very much as I recall it. The temptation is to jump ahead and tell you more about my staff, Max, Madame Smith - the treacheries, in a word. But I shall try to follow the story as it is revealed.

The astral room is still white. The décor is deliberately boring in order, I suspect, to drive me on to feed the astral screen with my life tapes. To distract me from boredom. White is a utility colour - hospitals and museums and ghastly neo-Andalusian villas, Hampstead.

I suppose if I were a connoisseur of fine chamber music there would be an astral music centre playing Liberace.

Oh, yes I'm wise to the tricks of this place already. Video No.3 looks interesting: the label says, "April 27, 1988: 9.09am: Meanwhile,

Max on the pier."

That's odd. We've already seen what happened at around 9.20am. I was on the line to Max from the car phone. A bit of rewinding, then.

I feel excited. I am the child again who sucked licorice at Saturday cinema mornings - yes, we had those even in Pre-War Italy as Il Duce planned a new Roman Empire.

I'm putting Video No.3 in now.

OOOOOOOOH!
- >>>

CHAPTER FOUR

There's a funny smell. Some people call it ozone, fresh air. In fact it's the air of disinfected waste product intermingled with salt. I know these things. I am on a ship. No, not a ship – it's Brightworth Pier, naturally. A thing not born to float.

My belly is upside down and so's my head. And as for my mouth....

I hear the hiss of the sea. I feel I want to disgorge into the water or the cracked lobster pots draped over the paint-chipped railings next to the sign: NO DIVING.

Stretched out below is a crowd of sea-made silvery sparklers. They have assembled in dumb insolent demonstration. What do they want of me? More rights for marine life? Free the crabs!

The civil police of cloud-shadow is already moving in on the trouble-makers, cutting long grey swathes into the body of troubled sun-glitter, ensuring that boatmen and divers can go about their lawful business unmolested.

Blearily I discern what at first sight appear to be psychedelic shark fins slicing through the silver and grey. These turn out to be the garish sails of windsurfers - in their shiny black wet suits weighted against the breeze.

The air is full of sweet manufactured smells, of bodies – and it's still early season; not yet summer. Seafront Edwardian balconies smile me the scrolled black tooth welcome of Brightworth.

I have a vague recollection of sour saltiness, the freedom of rank sexiness.

Frisky foam winks a breaker's interest in a lusty groyne....

Hang on! Rank sexiness? Ugh!

Good God. Video No.3 has placed me in the body of Max. I feel I am in him, and I can sense what he senses, yet my mind is free: I am Vicki and Max at once.

What a muddle.

This is cruel. What is this rank sexiness or sour saltiness? I believe I have stumbled into a Max erotic interlude.

He's been tippling, for sure. The excitement of getting away from Raven's Towers, from Vicki (from me!), has been celebrated with a near-dawn malt glug. In the Daimler down from London, I bet.

Max has little tolerance of alcohol. It goes straight to his head. I've picked up his hangover, or tipsiness.

A large woman nearby upturns a brown paper bag. A snow storm of broken crusts blizzards across the wash. I feel I am that Tippi woman (or "Tippi" as she was credited) in a Hitchcock horror as dozens of gulls wheel and shriek about me.

Once upon a time, when I was young, a seagull splat on your clothes was taken as a good omen. That's Max's memory, not mine!

The very thought cools my face to a pre-gag tingle.

Then Max turns away from the sea and gazes at Madame Smith's Psychic Pagoda. Everything is thrillingly familiar to him, and he feels at home - this is a place where he would choose to die.

The glamour of truancy, the rhapsody of being where one ought not to be. Max is that truant.

Even in Max's teens there was a Madame Smith's Psychic Pagoda on the pier. The grandmother? The great-grandmother of the incumbent? The promotional photograph doesn't seem to have changed, he is thinking.

The Pagoda is shaped like a large policeman's helmet: an outsize dome of lead fish scales topping an octagonal (Max must have counted) kiosk in a chipped and faded blue pastel.

It's a Tardis of sorts, resting in an off-shore no-place called Brightworth. I see yellowing newspaper testimonials stuck on a noticeboard, and framed tributes from famous clients dangling from hooks - mainly small-time TV soap stars who dipped into Madame Smith's Pandora's Box during their hard years of "resting" and bottle-washing.

Why do so many English soap stars die such grisly deaths? Cancer, alcoholism, rickets. Perhaps it's the price of acting oneself for decades.

The Pagoda's thick, vandal-proof lattice windows, tinted ruby red, sky blue and soup green, tremble to the flicker of candles within. I can make out the silhouette of its occupant. She's on the phone - I guess this could be my (Vicki's) call when I hired her (Madame Smith) to spy on Max that day, April 27.

This could get confusing. I must not reminisce or speculate!

Max is about to walk away when the Pagoda's door is flung open. Can this be the same Madame Smith as the one depicted in the photograph boasting her international fame? One or other has been touched up. Her crudely dyed black hair - to retain Romany integrity - has sucked her face dry of blood.

She's sparrow-thin, in her late forties, and has the slightly gormless expression of someone about to yawn - as I, Vicki, first noticed when she gave me that reading six months ago and Max went for his fateful walk.

"Been on the toot then?" screeches Madame Smith, in her piercing voice. She's talking to Max. She latches back the door because of the warmish breeze. Yet I see she has the gas heater on.

"The toot?" queries Max. That's his drink voice, strangled and greasy.

"Yeah, the razzle."

Max won't be accustomed to boozer-argot.

"Been hitting the bottle?"

"Oh, I see, yes, well, I think the air has got to me."

"Yeah, well, fresh air never harmed anyone. Hair of the dog, that's what you need. So how're you finding life on the ocean wave? I heard someone was moving into the Southern Pavilion chalet. Saw you go in earlier. You him then? Staying long? No one's lived there in years. Funny place to stay what with all the B 'n' Bs and hotels round these parts. You must have passed a few readies to Elsie Bush to wangle that one."

"It makes a change from London," says Max. A lame response. But then international publishing tycoons are not practised in the bright banter of lowly bonhomie.

Madame Smith puts down a jailhouse of keys on her small table. I glimpse the interior of the Pagoda - a timeless zone like the pier itself. It could be Ali Baba's cave or Santa's grotto. Stained glass mandalas throw colours wildly, protesting at intrusive sunlight. Red crepe paper on the walls rustles its discontent. The gas heater's pilot light dances irritably. I spot two Benares brass dishes for incense, and a crystal ball cradled in purple muslin.

"I imagine you just work on the pier," says Max.

"You must be joking," she squawks. "The pier's just me base for passing trade and the taxman. The real money's in my private clientele. Many a city man has made his millions through me. Not that I get a look in. I'm very good on the stock market. Just like putting money on the ponies. But you've got to know the form - which is where I come in. Reduced rates for pier residents!"

"How do I get hold of you when you're not here?" A sad, vain attempt at humour.

"By telepathy, stoopid. Ta-ta!"

And she withdraws into her timeless cockleshell, keys and all.

*

Max strolls back to the Southern Pavilion, his refuge at the end of the pier. The two-storey Pavilion itself resembles a Mississippi steamboat minus the paddle-wheels. At night, as I (Max!) recall, it unveils itself as a gaudy drag queen in the rainbow lights that trim its decks like tiaras.

That's when older Brightworthians converge in the Pavilion's lower deck main hall for an evening song and dance to a Yamaha organ. Max already imagines the organ rumble shinning up to his chalet on top deck and dreading it: Max is not one for noises.

Max is doing some figure work. Was it really nearly fifty years ago when as a teenager he got his first job here cleaning the Pavilion - for pocket money?

A rags to riches story.

His heart never left Brightworth: the usual nostalgia stuff.

But in his body I sense other longings. It's not easy making sense of all the images, the sheer spaghetti of all those thoughts.

Max's outer eye in caught by the sight of lithe young men in black wetsuits swaggering by on the sands below. Armed with harpoon guns. Splattering bare feet with sandy water on their way to the sporty killing seas.

His eye lingers on the broad beams of back and ripply curve of buttock. Ghosts long lain are summoned up. Sandpaper faces chafe my neck and spicy musks of sweat and breath drag my gut….

I think Max must have gone through a homosexual phase in his youth. He never said anything to me. Oh well. It never did Marlon Brando any harm. I suppose.

Max has become his younger self and he is now to be found beneath the pier (in his memory). He lies in the dank, brackish alcove just before the promenade junction of ascending shingle and pier deck; hidden away. There are other figures in this dark man-made and made-for-men cave. Anonymous tongues wet anonymous pelts, and fingers wander freely into secret unseen places. Bodies plying blindly at each other in frenzied moments.

Molten bodies flowing seaward.

I am filled with exquisite mouth yearnings: to suck inner thighs and cheeks, to joyride my tongue on big dipper bone and sinew, to bury my face in humid pits.

What a greedy mouth!

A mouth magicked out of nowhere in Max's head: the Max Cochrane mouth that I see now as a disembodied giblet, floating out of the past and into the present like mist, floating over images of people I recognise as certain Raven's Towers staff whose faces are licked and private parts tantalised, earlobes nibbled and breasts sucked.

All by this unseen, unfelt, ghost mouth.

His invisible tongue rolls them as a pastille, turning them this way or that, for the layered flavours to tingle, whose bodies are sipped as a wine for the tartness of unripe knee or the flowery fruitiness of finger or light astringency of neck or the faint suggestion of vanilla in a wet mouth.

They are pastilles of the mind, the fate of people in his imagination. I do not think Max has ever literally sucked or licked a member of staff....

Then in his head he visualises me as I am now, at 58. A tallish woman, blonde, forty-something-looking, a little broad in the hip.

The Max Cochrane tongue hovers over my image, uncertain, and just as it is about to lick me it....it flicks, like a serpent's, out of sight.

It simply disappears like a magician's handkerchief. Clearly I'm not to Max's taste. No wonder we've not had sex in ten years.

I want to be out of Max's body. How terrible is the traction of the past in his belly. In Max it's all bound up with an unfocused hatred for his life now, with its plots, restrictions, its finite time.

Plots? Max is thinking of Roger, Leona Humperdink, me – Raven's Towers itself: Max is thinking that we are plotting against him; but there's something else, a wish to see what happens – he's gambling, toying, calculating, wishing for something he cannot have, knowing he cannot lose - all these things swimming in the same sea.

There is no lighthouse in this sea, no land, no boat. And as for me, Vicki? I am just part of the swell of his life, the part which makes him lift and fall while his mind is in another place, another time, but somehow in the present all the same.

I (Vicki!) would drown him now if I could.

>><<

The relief to be back in this astral place. I never thought I would see it as home. I'm going to have to stop all this chopping and changing. It's dizzying. Of course that's the astral intention. They'd like me to announce that I'm staying here and abandon my poor, crumpled body lying between two groynes on the beach at Brightworth.

Not once did Max think of Germaine. This does astonish me, more than anything else. I saw those pictures of them both. Yet you would think she'd figure somewhere at this moment in his erotic, mental interior. Oh God!

What is truly shocking to me is the three-dimensional quality of his life. It's all his own life. It has nothing to do with me. I really am just part of the swell. Perhaps that's what we all are to each other, part of the swell, while real-life carries on in each individual head.

Come to think of it, Max was part of my swell. What does swell mean in this sense? I'm not certain precisely, but I know what I mean.

Was/Is Max a closet gay? I shall have to think about that, and Germaine. I'm more fascinated than appalled by evidence of his deviant libido – my capacity to surprise myself is just one of my power virtues; and I say this with a certain humility. If it turns out that he was homosexual all along, this will help to mitigate my own wifely deficiencies to which he has alluded. And if not (in the final analysis), such information of youthful indiscretions will prove useful in our ongoing ding-dongs, should I survive "death" and live again. Every cloud, etc etc.

It's funny about all these tongues. I always used to say to Max that *Glossy International is a huge tongue. Nothing in the world of Glossy exists but for the transient charm of its flavour. The flavour could be a personality, a frock, a film, a type of chimney stack – anything, anywhere; anyone but not everyone.*

Glossy is unafraid to dip its tongue into the huge banqueting table that is the world.

Nothing and everything forms the rich parti-coloured patchwork of human experience. Every day a Belle Époque; every reader a peri-wigged grandee.

The trick is to taste and then throw away. Taste and throw away. The essence of fashion. The trick of life.

And the essence of Max if I am to believe this tongue of his. What a strange attitude he has to Raven's Towers staff. He's worse than me.

But people are flavours. Then one day they go off.

Video No.4: "April 27, 1988: 10am: Vicki at Umberto's".

Now where did we leave off before the Max downer? That's right, I was in the Daimler with Stephen, I'd just phoned Umberto after calling Lee about Madame Smith.

- >>>

CHAPTER FIVE

Humid lemony and piny fragrances enfold me....
"Vicki! Vicki!"
Umberto, sweet Umberto, my head doctor, my hairdresser, outstretches his arms to me, beseeching his prodigal client to come to daddy.

"Are you ill, Vicki? Has there been an accident? Have you been taking those multi-vitamins I gave you last?"

"No, Umberto. My husband has left me."

"Come in all you jesters, enter all you fools..." growls Grace Jones from the speakers into the ancient Roman salon, neo. Her timing displeases me – almost worthy of a discount for my injured feelings.

Umberto has yet to recover from my news when I say in my own less contrived contralto drawl (which may trickle to purrs if he's very cute), "Umberto, *dahhhling*, please switch that bitch Grace off."

So typical of today that Grace's words should greet my entrance. Umberto snaps his fingers at a gofer - "pronto!" - and then closes the door behind me and takes my hat and coat - "Eh, take these, then switch off the tape," he commands the gofer.

"This is terrible news, Vicki."

"I don't wish to discuss it. Let's talk about multi-vitamins instead. All tablets give me indigestion. Headache tablets, malaria tablets, vitamin tablets, they all give me acid and I burp. I'm on malaria tablets for India for GlossRam - do you know about GlossRam, Umberto? Vitamins are no good for me."

Actually, I could be talking about vitamin Max.

My voice has gone up an octave in Umberto's presence, like a schoolgirl's. I feel whimsical with him and so I make things up on the spot. Perhaps I'll faint and see what he does. Unlike many Italians in London he does not drop his aitches, not like my maid Franca.

He knows his role without fussing.

He ushers me to a private cubicle. White fluted columns with acanthus-leaf capitals rise out from the floor and halt midway to the ceiling as if marble suddenly ran out.

Disconcerting to me, even after all these years, are the busts of Roman emperors - Nero, Tiberius, Augustus - from whose nostrils viscous dollops of shampoo and conditioner issue on the pull of their tasselled earlobes.

"It's not every day a woman loses her husband, Vicki. No wonder you sounded distraught on the phone."

"He ran off with a pier," I say for effect.

Dear Umberto. Judging by the lift of his eyebrows he thinks I said "peer". I wanted him to misunderstand. I have a sense of humour.

"Oh, goodness," he says. "And you never guessed he was that inclined earlier in the marriage?"

"One doesn't ordinarily think of a pier as a rival, does one?"

"No," he says. "There was a time when they were better bred."

I half-smile in the mirror at my contrived double entendre. Hairdressers are earnest people. Umberto is shaking his head at degenerate English aristocracy today. I have yet to meet a witty hairdresser. It's all that conditioner – gradually softens the head.

An odd calm has come over me. I imagine Madame Smith is taking receipt of her swag of £850 about now. Perhaps she's counting it all out in her Psychic Pagoda.

I think of my personal assistant Lee: yes, I have another mission for her. All at *Glossy International* - Timothy, Glenda, and any of the rest of my essential oils - must be enlisted in the task of bringing Max to heel.

At this moment, regaining control appears to be almost in my grasp. My machinery of supports is warming up.

Around me I hear the sibilances of indistinct confessional whisperings and hairspray. I am in the hair temple of Vesta.

Umberto strokes my head.

I hold his gaze in the mirror as he stands behind me: "Why do you think Max has left me?" I am Shirley Temple.

Umberto's face is the Big Bang in microcosm, every broad feature flying outwards in the dawning of a new expression. He's saying: Search me!

I notice again that his small head fans out into a huge bull neck. His cinched chest billows out into a bean bag pelvis - somewhere just behind me. Hips to accommodate childbirth. His nose, too, starts on a thin bridge which then flares out wildly. Everything is triangular about him. Like a Christmas tree.

Perhaps his willy is triangular too.

My head is sandwiched in a pyramid of his huge hands. In a massage. I'm elsewhere.

"Do you love your husband, Vicki?" he asks. Making conversation.

"Love?" Good heavens. What a naked word. "Love."

I repeat the word over and over again: "Love, love...." It's as if the word has hit me like a policeman's cosh and I feel nothing. The word smashes me to the ground, and still I feel nothing.

"Love...love...." I know the word should evoke some response of sentiment. For perspective I imagine love as a grape - black grapes are my favourite fruit. I stamp on the grape, it seems squashed, yet the moment I lift my foot it pops back into shape as if it were a rubber ball. There's no life in this grape, no juice. The grape simply bounces about my head leaving no impression except the echo of meaningless thuds.

Who's playing squash in my head?

"That's a confusing word, love," I say to Umberto. "I don't use words like love."

"But everyone loves, Vicki. Of course you love your husband." Then he sings some hideous tuneless lyric for those in need of sedation, *"Love makes the world go round....in happy harmony...."*

I stick out my tongue in a downward curl to signal illness.

"Umberto! Stick to hairdressing," I rebuke. "Love, love..." I'm trying again to feel the word. "There's something better than love," I conclude finally out loud. "Mutually assured destruction. No, listen. Finding someone whose purposes suit your needs and whose needs suit your purposes: the symmetry - no symbiosis! - of two manic egos suckled within the illusion of caring. If one side withdraws the two sides collapse which is in no one's interests. I can understand that. That sounds honest. It sounds like life. It captures the grasping trait in us all. The service of self with its incidental giving bits. Max gives me structure and I give him life. He likes surprises and I like to surprise; but I hate surprises - yet I married Max. Perplexing. There's a feature there somewhere for *Glossy* – I'll mention it to Germaine."

Poor Umberto. First peers, now my judgement on love. "If you say so, Vicki," he says lamely, all Latin romance thrown out the window.

I am sure he would wish to drown me in the solitary wild place of the washbasin.

After the shampoo suds, the climax of the rinse. Umberto turns on the tap and all the froth goes away. A pleasing thought: perhaps this froth will end up in Brightworth as scum on the beach: the sort of bubbly stuff one sees on the lips of a loony. My mood is warming. This at least is what I'm thinking at Umberto's.

After towelled purdah I decide I want a simple minimalist cut for the no-nonsense approach I wish to adopt for the coming challenge of retrieving Max. For battle a shiny flat helmet is requisite.

"Short, Umberto."

Happily, he is no virgin to the caprice of powerful women.

"Not at all! Not in my salon."

I retreat a little. "I want a new cut, a new look for a new me."

"A cut is different from a cut," he says imperiously. "A chignon wig! That's what you shall have. You need bulk, extra strength, for the week ahead. Nothing can be done with short hair except turn you into a boy and grow a fringe, and you're not a fringe person, Vicki. A chignon with the muscle of extra!"

"Chignons can be so heavy...."

"Nonsense. More hair will be like Samson's beard."

"I should be a bearded woman?"

"It will be your back-up. When all around you fail you, your bulked-up chignon will come to your rescue. I have hair from the Dolomite mountain people, pure unpolluted hair, from people who go to their graves at the age of one hundred and ten yet look fifty."

"I come from near the Dolomites. Very well, Umberto."

I can resist no longer. I am satisfied. Fate's true intent must be sieved through acts of childish wilfulness. Umberto has clearly interceded on behalf of God in the matter of my hairstyle, and made a providential decision for me. This was meant to be.

I can no longer see the soft grey quilts beneath my eyes. I am on the mend.

The chignon!

The chignon look: a serpentine orgy, vipers forever knotted in passion, at the back of my head to the nape of neck. I like it. From the front there is the effect of severity because of the drawn-back hair flattened into a hard polished finish. At the rear, another Vicki reveals herself: a flamboyant Vicki who at the end of the day knows how to relax and enjoy herself. Who knows that too much stress can cause coronary disease or arteriosclerosis. She knows that laughter and cuddles release happy hormones.

The chignon hints at the other me, the me that other people need to think exists outside *Glossy International*, if they are to respect what they see at the front.

Why, the chignon wig may yet make a comeback at the GlossRam Virtual Reality Fashion & Beauty Show next week. Thinking of it makes me a little anxious. The first fashion show without live models. In association with the Rambagh Palace, Jaipur. All the international society queens are expected to attend - Nan, Babe, Loll, Lauren, Doris, et al; and New York's current Queen of Chic, Princess Leona Humperdink - oh God, Leona!; but not I pray Imelda Marcos who is just an embarrassment with the trials and everything. We just can't allow her to come. Perhaps Leona will dissuade her.

But I don't want to ruin this moment at Umberto's in cyclic anxiety.

After the hairdryer's whoosh I feel so coddled. And perfectly skittish. No more daymares. No more imaginings in shop windows. Red Indian - back to your reservation!

I can think again of Freddie Smith, my naughty GlossRam film director who I'm afraid is at this moment shooting my staff via the Raven's Towers security cameras. What fun he must be having.

I hope he can catch Germaine performing one of her disgusting sexual acts. I want her out. Sacked! Even my earthly self, trapped in this other present, knows she has her eye on my editorship - well, dream on, Germaine.

I think of Roger Masefield, and Lee, and of course Max. I *feel* that I have a plan of action which will reveal itself to me in its precise detail when it's ready.

I giggle. And Umberto smiles, not knowing what I think, not knowing whether I'll put the bill on account.

*

"Raven's Towers," I say to Stephen. "But take the scenic route. Let me linger and gloat." He complimented me on my new hairstyle as I stepped into the car. Unprecedented in a heterosexual male.

*

In the car I phone Lee.

"That's a lot better, darling," I say. "It only took you three rings to answer the phone. One day I may have you plugged to the exchange!"

She giggles. She knows that actually I have no sense of humour.

"How's things?" I ask. "I've just been at Umberto's."

"You haven't forgotten conference is at 11.45?"

"What time is it now?"

"Eleven minutes past eleven."

I'm astonished. "How time flies! Any trouble to report? Did Madame Smith get her money?"

"Yes. And the troops are lively, Vicki. Timothy's hit his secretary and had a row with Glenda. Something's going on between Timothy and Germaine, and…."

"No more details," I say quickly. "And Freddie Smith?"

"No sign of him now. He's up in security operating the cameras. He phoned earlier to say he had some corkers."

I don't know this word - "Corkers?"

"Presumably some promising material."

I decide to get to the point of the call.

"Lee," I begin. "How old's your mother?"

Understandably she's taken aback by this question.

"Uh - oh - woo! - 49, I guess."

"And you love your mother?"

"Sure." Lee's so sweet. No care home dumping for Lee's mum.

"And," I add, "if you swore on her life to do something as promised, you would so swear?"

She pauses for a second, nervous in the dark. "Sure."

"I'm about to tell you something in strictest confidence and then I'm going to ask you to do something of great importance. Promise not to betray me?"

"Oh Vicki," she moans. "I would never betray you. I swear on my mother's life."

I tell her that Max is on Brightworth Pier and that no one is supposed to know about it. "Don't ask questions, Lee. Just listen." Then I instruct her to call Roger Masefield - her lover, by the way. He's married, of course. She is to tell him she has vital information about Max's whereabouts.

"You'll find him receptive, Lee, because he will have received a memo from Max this morning making him acting chief executive in Max's absence. Obviously don't tell him I told you to tell him. Act the traitor! Betray me with conviction, Lee. Roger will be most interested to know more about the circumstances of his fascinating promotion - temporary as it is! God knows what he will do when he hears of Brightworth Pier. And tell Roger I'll lunch him today. Book the Notre Dame for 1.15pm."

Lee is normally cool but even she is making strange asthmatic-sounding noises.

"No questions Lee. Not now. I'll see you in ten minutes. Contact Roger now!"

*

We are in sight of Raven's Towers. Another five minutes and I shall be at its electronic portals. In the car I marvel at my muckraking.

God knows what Roger will do. That's what I said to Lee. But nothing is what it seems at Raven's Towers. I just happen to know that behind my back Lee tells Max *everything*. Take my word for it. No question about it: And Max will have told Lee where he's staying. Lee is his special spy. She will now tell Max that I've instructed her to tell Roger where he (Max) is to be found: Max will have to make a very quick decision as to whether he allows this to happen - if he wants to keep his precious privacy! And of course if he stops Lee she will have to answer to me. In which case I'll fire her - Max wouldn't want that.

This will irritate the hell out of Max; I'm certain of it.

Max has his spies, I have mine.

And yes, Lee will by now have also told Max about my call to Madame Smith.

What truly matters is not these intrigues as such but that Max will feel the powerful tentacles of *Glossy International* coiling about him before his second night's sleep in Brightworth.

Raven's Towers (as personified by me) is jealous of its Founding Father.

>><<

I have no comment to make on my earthly self right now. Vicki knows what she knows. We shall see what she (I) knew.

I pick up Video No.5 whose label reads, "April 27, 1988: 9.45+am: Meanwhile, at Raven's Towers...." So we go back in time again that fateful day.

"9.45+am" indeed! They never got into work before 10.

>>>

PART TWO

RAVEN'S TOWERS

CHAPTER SIX

I am soaring. Flying over London. The moment I played Video No.5 I was sucked into the sky and am looking down on battleship grey. The city of London. Normally, heights give me vertigo. The sight of a ladder loosens my knees and dampens my palms. That's why, among other things, I cannot identify with Germaine's fetish for heights.

Today I fly like, well, like a raven, an appropriate simile given that I am now gazing at the splendid edifice of Raven's Towers, home of *Glossy International* and forty other titles besides.

Suck away the fug, allergens and other airborne pollutants that make up the London biosphere and on a clear day you will encounter an emerald, and its name is Raven's Towers.

To many people, at a distance, Raven's Towers resembles a fabulous waterfall passing through clouds of rock magically suspended over a wicked fairytale city. Day and night the Towers' sheets – frozen froth-free oceans! - of opalescent glass blush alternate between hues of aquamarine and turquoise, depending on the light, as if it were a moody Piscean (Pisceans are very temperamental Madame Smith informed me during my pier consultation. I'm Pisces).

I shall describe the building because even in these early days of globalisation (what that means precisely) I wouldn't want it assumed that we are all familiar with the capital.

If you trace Raven's Towers from the outside just up to the twelfth floor you'd think it another common or garden skyscraper that brings false dusks to cities worldwide. Beyond the twelfth floor and you are witness to a great architectural adventure. Beyond the twelfth floor you are forced to imagine that you are in the Rockies - because supported on great cantilever beams of various length, shooting out into the city skyline, are boulders and rocks supposedly extracted from coastal and mountain regions; all arranged in a cemented tumbledown - or tumbleup, if you prefer - for at least another twenty floors. (These rocks and boulders are of course manufactured from some light synthetic material that needn't detain us here.)

I see them now as I swoop past. Those great beams rushing out in all directions: often they remind me of pins in a voodoo doll.

Happily there are staggered gaps in this rock arrangement, not only to admit legally- required light but to afford editorial staff an inkling of what it is like to see the sun rise or set in a naturalised environment. In fact the "rocks" are so patterned that at any given moment of the day (subject to cloud, solar eclipse, Hawaiian volcanic dust eruption, etc) some place in Raven's Towers is experiencing dawn or dusk whatever the Greenwich Mean Time.

Max was determined that Raven's Towers should pay some homage to Mother Nature in its design. Staff time-keeping was one price we paid for his reverence.

If you stand at the foot of the Towers and gaze up, you feel like a skier - or perhaps a yeti - about to perish in an avalanche. By the way, it is I who gave Raven's Towers its name - after the ravens who still occupy the Bloody Tower and whose wings are clipped to ensure there's no slacking in their mystical guard over England. I read some place that their grating croaks would have been the last thing the condemned heard on the gibbet.

I liked that. The co-mingling of magic and feathery shininess, tinted with threat: an imaginative conspiracy of images.

And a thing or person does so become its name.

My only complaint is the number of professional climbers who risk their lives every year trying to scale the home of the world's finest magazine, as if Raven's Towers were just another Everest or Hilton Hotel. Weekly they arrive, soldier-like in flak jackets usually, parties from America, Austria, Japan (etc), with their picks and crampons, rope and salmon paste sandwiches wrapped in silver foil, bladders full for a mile high urination. They are usually prevented from making an ascent.

*

Now something strange is happening. I feel a pull on me as I fly. Some magnet draws me towards Raven's Towers as if I were a rare golden eagle being sucked into a Boeing 747 turbojet engine.

I am helpless.

And as I make my approach I sense that I am the Towers. I can hear its breath in my bronchial lift shafts, its beatless heart in the hush of my ventilation systems. I am the staff who scry their lives in its mirrors and who are suckled on the teats of my many vending machines.

In an instant I sense that lights may flicker and editors come and go, but one single constant is that lullaby hush.

The soundscape to the screaming, groaning, weeping and whispering of its - and my! - human charges.

*

A moment ago I was everything and now I am just one again, standing on the marble concourse of the Raven's Towers atrium.

I am astral Vicki in my earthly work home.

I feel the urge to board one of the four escalators from ground to first floor, each of which ascends through an authentic "rose walk" lit by trailing fairy lights - more icons of Max's worship of nature, as he sees it.

On the escalator I glimpse through gaps tended places which make me sigh. These are the Towers' fabulous atrium gardens which flank me in terraces of green and abundant bloom.

I would normally show my pass to one of the security guards on the first floor. On this occasion I float on unacknowledged. I really am a ghost of sorts.

Though this is the morning of April 27, I also feel that today is also a compilation experience, a melding of the many times I came to work, all those years, every morning; a generality fixed in no-time.

I'm going to work and no one sees me.

I call one of the six lifts that serve the Towers, step in after the sound of air-rush, and check my face in the wall mirror.

Another day for me. Another defeat for others.

I am taken to the twentieth floor, the station of *Glossy International*. How very odd to see it in this way, both present and absent at once. I am keyed into the collective mood immediately. There is the familiar buzz of expectant busyness, and a hint of menace in the air.

It is as if spirit world tricoteuses of Robespierre's guillotine are arriving unseen, clicking their needles already, delighting in their own soundless cackling.

Today an editorial meeting is the highlight of the morning agenda. No one here quite knows when earthly Vicki Cochrane will summon her staff en masse through the person of her personal assistant, Lee.

As usual phones are courting each other with unanswered mating calls. I hear sedatives and laxatives at work in lavatorial cubicles. I bristle at asthmatic sounds of percolating coffee - for how else to kick-start jaded endocrine systems?

I drift through the maze of corridors. Years ago the Towers' board, against my will, introduced open-plan offices in an attempt to deflate self-importance and high redundancy packages. But over time, as I predicted, self-importance has grown up again like weeds on a motorway, with each new star appointment and the bribe of premium privacy.

The human animal cannot stand to be observed all the time and no-one knows this more than I.

Through this labyrinth of door-less sanctuaries I float (no I'm not floating. I must not exaggerate. I am walking normally) until I am stopped by an objectionable little sign which resists tearing down by the cleaners:

"BEWARE: GAY CARICATURE ON THE PREMISES!"

This is the work of my beauty and lifestyle editor Timothy Timms - and there (between two pot plants which have become bent and twisted like lepers in their attempts to catch those all-too-brief moments between a Raven's Towers dawn and dusk) he is!

Such a darling, wish-bone thin, Maypole long: he is so real, so solid, I can scent him even, his inevitable carnation, bottled, mixed with something else; an odd odour, one that is horribly and strangely familiar to me, what is it now?

Still, today he has opted for the Regency look - boots, tailcoat: the beaver hat sits like a badger on a desk. He could be talking to his secretary Sarah - one can never tell with Timothy as he is inclined to look at inanimate things while engaged in monologue. Which reminds me. At a party for - oh, I forget who – but anyway, for someone – I heard him snarl, as he looked hurriedly at me (perhaps by chance; perhaps not), "Poppy-wearers! My work will be done when I have disposed of these Ypres-creepers." I have never worn poppies, either the Remembrance ones or Mary Quant's, so I failed then as I fail now to understand his assault on the poppy and its wearers. But I assumed his remark to be a declaration of war.

Sarah as usual at this time of day is attempting to apply lipstick in between lipless bites from a chocolate bar - Mars I think.

"Lordy love a duck," Timothy is saying, in what I assume to be his real-life satire on caricature. "Goodness knows how I *winched* myself out of the Radox."

He scrutinises his gorgeous face in a mirror balanced on his rarely used VDU. A cigarette smoulders on a floppy disk. Once again that curious feeling of total identification as I had with Max and Raven's Towers itself: I feel I am Timothy: I am half-inclined to solicit myself, which is what Timothy is thinking.

I admire my - his! - high cheek bones, the full red lips (raw I sense from a night of sucking and kissing) and the melting embrace of his lapis lazuli gaze.

"Oh *gawd*," I hear myself rack on his rich drawl. "No rictus can rive my mug looking like this."

He applies a stick of neutral moisturiser to his lips. Then flicks away balletically a single flake of scurf which has thoughtlessly nestled itself upon an eyebrow, having lost its footing in the fringe to his ponytailed, chestnut locks.

He is thinking that he must somehow glue together the dead

keratin scales on his facial skin surface as an emergency measure. Whether to use Estée Lauder's cerebrosides or Chanel's ceramides. Questions, questions.

Why is life so fraught? He thinks: perhaps hyaloid liquid (extracted from the eyes of cows) will clear up the small dry patch on his forehead.

He talks on to Sarah via his mirror: "Went to the Casa Nostra launch the other night with Ol' Lady Lottie - so I dropped a curtsey and a few clangers."

I notice his reflected eyes do throw sharp glances at Sarah who has finished painting her lips and is now removing a headband from her long shiny blonde hair.

"Such a lovely mane Ol' Lottie has. You know, it should be made law that we have to bequeath all our good bodily bits to a beauty bank for recycling - but she's so *creped*, and those eye bags of hers - enough to give anyone a stoop just with the weight of 'em. Why these women won't use all that cellulite accreting round their waists to fill in their solar-cracks I don't know - raddled crones. And I am getting quite tired of middle-aged women going on about their hideous thrush: makes me think of furred-up kettles. And all that honeyed giggling and hooking her tresses over those jug ears of hers as if she were a light comedy ingénue or something. I thought to myself I thought, if only she'd walk backwards on my arm we'd make the most fabulous party entrances in all...."

Instantly he pouts at what he has spotted in the mirror. "And what do *you* want?"

I turn to see *Glossy*'s reflected mousey-looking yet shrewish chief sub editor standing in the threshold to the beauty department. I personally cannot bring myself to look at her face-to-face just in case my gaze falls to her two top incisor teeth which strike me even now as grouted together by some foul substance, the colour and consistency of smegma.

"I jus' wanna knorr when we can expect the return of t' Auric Colour Coordination proofs," she says in her hideous accent. "And corrected. We're five days late."

Timothy rises to his feet disjointedly, like a string puppet. "Away with you!" he bawls. "I am not interested in your wretched tick-tock schedules. I answer only to the inner call of my biorhythms. Sarah, when's my next peak?"

Sarah puts down her chocolate bar but does not know what to do with her headband.

"Get a move on Sarah!"

She throws the headband on the floor in a panic.

"Oh pick it up," screams Timothy, "you bovine dollop." Her forefinger guides her to his biorhythmic chart on the wall.

"Three days' time," she reports. "At 8.03am"

Timothy throws his eyes up. "Not possible. I never rise before 8.30. When's the next peak after that one?"

"Um, not for another ten days and then you'll be in Papua New Guinea shooting Schwarzkopf with Demarch...Demarcha….."

"Demarchelier! Say it after me, De-march-eli-er."

"Demarch-um."

"Hopeless! So there we are," says Timothy, addressing the ceiling, waiting in vain, I suspect, for the chief sub editor to detect his irony and thereby indicate a modicum of smartness. "You'll have to cancel the issue," he concludes.

The chief sub retreats."We'll see wharr Vicki has to say about that."

Funny to hear the chief sub speak of me like that - she mentioned me by name, "Vicki". I should have expected her to say "old cunty" or "the bitch". I am touched by her respectful familiarity, to be spoken of as if I were someone close to her like a friend or even a sister.

And if I say I "love" Timothy it is because I know his type so well. He is indeed my juniper berry - I smell him now, along with the carnation, and that something else.

Sarah says, "Blimmin cheek her talking like that. Gets up my nose she does."

How tiring is the underling seeking to make common cause for capital.

"'Nother coffee?"

"Thank you chuck," says Timothy.

How I deplore this Northern affectation, "chuck". He is now attempting to prise a crust embedded between eyelashes.

"You make me 'nother coffee - you really must try to drop that ghastly launderette-speak of yours, Sarah, I blame your mother - while I tell you what I heard about Lady Lottie…."

Already the novelty of my situation is beginning to dilute. Lottie is perfectly irrelevant to my story.

"So, Lady Lottie introduces me to no less a personage than Vicki's telephone friend Her Royal Highness The Princess Leona Humperdink…"

Oh!

"…who as usual is on the arm of that clapped out sit-down comic P.B. Jones."

"Amazing, that," interrupts Sarah. "Fancy a man going round with a glove puppet."

"For heaven's sake, Sarah. That's just one of Vicki's little jokes. To catch out silly little munchkins like you!"

I notice the kettle is steaming. Appropriate.

He adds, "Now don't interrupt me, child. I am not going to discuss the Princess' person until I have completed this anecdote."

Sarah huddles close.

"Princess Leona told me something so terrible about Lottie. Now even you must have heard of the suspicions surrounding the death of her husband after what was quaintly termed in the press a short illness....Well according to Leona, Lottie was bonking her chauffeur Salvatore...."

Not bonking, as such, dear. In fact, Lottie would give blow jobs to Salvatore in the time it took little old ladies to toddle across bad Big Apple avenues. Naturally her husband had the car bugged and videoed and each night, instead of *Carson*, he'd watched his wife's late show, growing incrementally depressed. It was on their yacht moored off Capri - oh! my head is screaming!

"For heaven's sake Sarah what's that whistling - switch that kettle off. Anyway on the yacht she did something so terrible - just put the coffee there. She prepared a Greek salad - yes, there - for a marital lunch à deux...."

"That's the one with olives?"

"Olives? Oh yes, Sarah, Olives. And onions."

"And those lovely big tomatoes, sliced."

"Big tomatoes Sarah - and don't forget the cucumber. Why don't we make one up now before conference."

"And that other stuff."

"Lemon sherbet, Sarah?"

"Nah! Now you're taking the piss."

"Tip non compris, cherie."

"Yer wha'?"

I am staggered that such a conversation should be taking place at *Glossy International*. It is like the servants' quarters in *Upstairs, Downstairs*.

"Now do you want to hear of Lottie's outrage or dress a salad?" demands Timothy.

"I'm all ears."

"Right. So Lottie was preparing a Greek salad with that cheese, what's it called...."

"It's on the tip of my tongue."

"That's no good is it?"

Well that does it. Clear the house. It's fromage to eternity.

"So yeah, go on," says Sarah.

"No, it's impossible. My rhythm is broken. I sense the moment has passed and we can only wonder what did happen. You've ruined my foreplay and so I play for you no more."

A small miracle. We are spared the details of yet another banal soap opera.

"The tales of high society pale by the side of cheese names, Sarah. You had the chance to shine but instead you stalled on the tip of your tongue and faltered on feta - there, now I remember.

"Oh Tim…."

Happily the curtain comes down with Timothy's Madame Yale's Blush of Youth, a tiny bit of which he is applying to his face. I always did wonder at his colour. Odd he has not yet noticed a strange odour in the office; stranger still mixed with his carnation.

He applies refreshing calendula to minimise under-eye circles. "You know Sarah, there's an odd pong in the office."

At last!

He gurns his face, stretching it into grotesque shapes to maintain epidermal elasticity.

"So what else can I tell you Sarah? - find that smell would you. I was stomping up the street to this place when this hunk of redhead gives me the glad-eye. God, I was all aquiver. My girdle was killing me. They say redheads have the biggest cocks, not that I would know. I'm a Virgo still intacta, as my aunt used to say."

In my experience big-boned men of short stature are the best endowed. But then I never was a size queen.

"My Pete's, y'know, well rewarded in that department," volunteers Sarah.

"Really. You dark horse. A redhead?"

"Ginger with…."

"Freckles?"

"Yeah. And green eyes."

"Hazel more likely. The classic type. How many basic complexions are there in the world Sarah?"

"Five, Timothy," she says wearily.

"And they are?"

"Blond, brown, dark, er…."

"Yes."

"Er, ginger and…."

"And black Sarah. Try to memorise these things. One day you

will have to write my letters for me in my mode, God help me. Big you say?"

"Wha'?-Oh, Pete? Well not exactly long but, y'know, really thick."

"Ooh. You are a down-to-girth girlie. As thick as Gibbon's *Decline and Fall*?"

"Dunno, but he's hopeless in bed."

Timothy makes a face. "Oh well, anyway. This redhead gives me the glad-eye, a humble road labourer, a grunt. Then the flirt bends down to his asphaltic task and half its rear pops out of its belted jeans. What a Hottentot! Lovely bum cleavage, really. Just like Vicki's up top."

Grazie, Timothy.

"Minus the bum fluff, of course," he adds, gratuitously.

"You and Vicki ought to settle down and get married," says Sarah, evidently not listening to Timothy and unwrapping 'nother chocolate bar.

"There's a thought! I should say mad Max would have something to say about that, Sarah. Just a nice test tube baby for me which I can raise in the Raven's Towers crèche. Just me and poppet. I don't want some ghastly uddered she-bull cramping my style, all yin and yoghurt."

Does he mean me? Thank goodness I am familiar with camp hyperbole though the day must come when women have to address the problem of gay men's misogyny and their mockery of femininity - a subject I suspect I shall return to.

"You're a real chauvinist you are. I'm sure the mother would have something to say about that," squeaks Sarah.

"What mother? My child shall be chosen from a mix "n" match looks catalogue: the hobbled and discombobbled need not apply. I shall sire the perfect child courtesy of a quick hand job and micro-technology. My looks, my brain - her womb. You don't have to marry the oven to bake the cake, as I'm certain my great uncle would have said had he the wits."

"Honestly!"

All this low comedy. What about that smell!

"So I arrive here in a bit of a state I can tell you," says Timothy, returning to the subject of his early morning lust. "I was in need of a bit of brow-mopping and naturally I retire to the Men's out there." He waves a long skeletal hand in the direction of the nearby corridor. "And this day being what it is, I encounter this gremlin midget caretaker mopping the floor. ''Ere laddie,' it says in some ethnic dialect. 'See wha' arm doin' 'ere?' What the English language has to contend with since we became a federal outpost of Europe! His simian orifice could scarcely form the simplest words without atonal garbling - I say Sarah, is it you who smells? Perhaps you, too, have thrush?"

She is indignant. "No! I've noticed it myself. I think it's coming from your cupboard."

Timothy swivels his head with such epileptic violence that his ponytail lashes his left ear. "What? That can't be, unless...,"

He unlocks and opens his beauty sacristy of collected scent flacons and soon spots the cause of all our morning sickness. "Sarah! We've got crabs!"

I can see the crab myself as I bend down by the side of earthly Timothy. There in a corner, between Lauder and Nina Ricci, lies the putrefying corpse of last February's conscripted crab model - employed in its freshly dead mode for a jewellery piece I believe we called "A Paella of Shells for Belles".

Timothy's right ear is lashed by his ponytail. "This is the absolute limit Sarah. It's not enough that you always fail to leave me telephone messages or type up my letters or misspell 'necessary' - even if I scrawled it on a blackboard you would revert to your illiterate type, mouthing and blabbering. Now this! Why on earth didn't you throw the crab away when I told you to - this is awful, *awful*."

Sarah melts to the ground in tears, her hair falling over her face like collapsed Venetian blinds.

"Don't try your lachrymose tricks on me, you wretch. Go get a bucket from that anthropoid in the bog and get that fucking crustacean out of here."

*

"Now Timothy, stop that," says Glenda.

Her voice is a sedative to the histrionics a moment ago. I can actually smell her voice. It is the soothing undertone of aromatic camphor that does it for me. Many's the time I have called Glenda into my office after a trying day just to absorb her personal, perhaps spiritual, essence of lavender.

She is my bottled lavender, my peace of mind.

She exudes lavender - in my head at least - though she insists on wearing some sweet bumpkin perfume on her actual flesh.

"Sarah," she says calmly, "stop blubbing and go and ask Mr Caretaker up the corridor to lend you his bucket. And if you're nice to him he may offer to take the crab away. And Timothy, come along and have a mug of rosehip."

Glenda is also my country homes and interiors editor. God, she's plump, and her airy floral skirts and billowy white blouses do her no credit. I do wish she would cut her heavy auburn hair which she has to hand-ladle back every minute or so out of her face.

And is that a crouton I see embedded in the right shoulder of her rusty red poncho?

Timothy utters an "Oh" of relief that he no longer has to deal with Sarah, the crab or the caretaker. He follows Glenda to her office.

Here, to my shame, I see the strange tableau that Glenda begged me to have installed next to her desk - a wax model of an Eighteenth Century farmer, a hand-me-down from Madame Tussauds actually, standing up to his ankles in straw, with spades, hay rakes and wheelbarrow close by: her icons of olde, free-range England where apples were once *scrumped.*

Or so she insists on believing. Staff call the wax yokel Benny after some TV soap character.

With relief I home in on Timothy's frayed wing collar, then his kohl-like thick eyelashes. He is indeed an oversized Bambi of a man. How wonderful to be able to observe him from the safety of invisibility, from another dimension.

"This is an omen," Timothy says, crank-starting one of his monologues. "An omen! You don't have my problems, Glenda. I can't possibly use my office again. It will have to be fumigated, sterilised, pasteurised! I'm sure I can smell that crab on my jacket. Year in, year out, I travel the globe, disrupting my body clock and upsetting my menstrual cycle and making metaphors of bottled spa water for age retardation, depriving myself of my birthright peace and quiet while that door-stop of a secretary of mine can't even administer a crab's Christian burial."

Glenda pours steaming water into mugs, each hung with herbal teabag string and tag over the rim - paper anchors in the modern tempest. She is lost in some rustic fantasy no doubt.

"When are we going to automate secretaries, Glenda? They're devolving out of any practical use. They can't write, can't talk, can't listen. What's their role in life, Glenda? I look at Sarah sometimes the way I look at Emma and Vanessa's Strudel kitty cat and I think: what's going on in there? Is anyone at home? I suppose she won't have the sense to ventilate the office. The Paco Rabanne scent! Some use for it at long last. I suppose I should tell the indolent dolt."

"Now there we are," says Glenda, handing him his mug of piping hot goodness, deaf to his juniper berry's unpleasantness, as a true lavender essence should be. Juniper berry can leave a nasty taste in the mouth.

"Allow the bag to steep a little longer," she says.

"You're a treasure," says Timothy with a smile that springs too quickly to his face, deepening embryonic crow's feet and adding five years.

"And while you're waiting for it to cool," says Glenda, "why don't you calm down and tell me what you're planning for November."

She means our November issue. Being a monthly, *Glossy International* is planned six to seven months ahead. We celebrate Christmas at your Easter.

Curious. I can hear everything - as if I were Max. The rasp of the teabags as the water spills out. The rustle of clothes, the sticky pop of dry lips parting.

Timothy sits upright at the thought of November. "Well, since you ask, m'dear, I've just found this incredible photographer, a wide-angle merchant par excellence. And for ages now I've been thinking of doing something truly big before I end up as the Firbank of beauty writers. Ignored in life. In death, too. A Cecil B job. With the whole cosmetics range of La Casa Nostra in one unifying image!"

"The *whole* range?" echoes Glenda, twinning query with hint of doubt. "Surely other beauty companies will think you're on the take from Casa Nostra."

"On the take? Honestly Glenda, you sound like a character in one of those police propaganda TV series. Any minute now you'll be wearing black stockings and calling me guv. What other companies may or may not think of me is of no consequence. Everyone knows that the aerial roots of my notoriously purple prose will curl about all their goodies - eventually. I'm no pauper! My new idea is tailor-made for La Casa only because they are where it is at. And I have no control over the at."

I study Glenda. It's strange how a fulfilled life can be so ageing. Have you noticed how happy people, people who've been in love for years, invariably look their age, or older? I suppose it's because their metabolism gets exhausted with all the tit-for-tat sex and compromise which put a strain on the body's resources. Basically they use their bodies more than miserable people who are somehow preserved in the stillness of woe. It's the one example of divine justice in an unfair world. Stress and misery, on the other hand, burn up all that fatty tissue; and tears are a wonderful moisturiser.

I fancy that Glenda's face is made up of two lineless buttock cheeks vertically and seamlessly glued together. She has the face of an oversized baby that has grown and wedged itself into its pram.

"I don't expect you to know this as our house editor," continues Timothy, "but 'house' is the word du jour. And what is 'house' in Italian, Glenda?"

"Oh, be quiet!"

"*Meraviglioso*! 'House' is La Casa in Italian, and the entire world currently revolves round the concept of 'house', just as it was spinning round Waugh's *Brideshead* only a few years back. There's the Acid House craze and all those wonderful raves where Biggles used to park his aeroplanes; and the growing interest in astrological houses as opposed to mere sun signs. People are talking about working from their house rather than going to work in the future and there's the controversy over Poll Tax and the like which will liberate the house from the tyranny of rates…."

Glenda throws up her eyes.

"I hardly need tell you Glenda that the very name La Casa cleverly anticipates the ascendency of the house concept and subtextually encapsulates all the converging social whatnot in La Casa Nostra's comprehensive range of cosmetics."

Glenda puts down her mug on a desk. "So, you are on the take."

"Oh fiddledeedee! If La Casa wish to convey a chateau in my name - which they are not - then there's nothing I can do about it. Let not wan youth trouble itself with adult particulars."

"May I just add here," says Glenda, holding her head in both hands, "that I am the house editor, thank you very much." She squeaks the last word. Then she notices the crouton in her right shoulder and plucks it out.

And pops it in her mouth.

"Now don't get all territorial - not with me," says Timothy, as seriously as he can be. "My inspiration cannot be contained by Raven's Towers job descriptions. After all, who'd have thought to use actual gormless animals for a beauty feature before I? I mean, these days you can hardly pick up some third-rate copy-cat glossy without coming across a dog with red blusher about its whiskers. And who before I would have thought to make-up the little street urchins of Bombay and put the latest line of straw hats upon their impoverished heads? The world is truly my canvas - nowhere does it say that in my employment contract, worthless scrap of paper that it is. And beggin' yer pardon, ma'am - and old Benny over there - but who precisely gave birth to George and Gilbert?"

Not Timothy's tortoises! No time to explain now.

"So you see Glenda, 'house' is the thing right now, the concept I mean, not some particular thatched variety or any gabled particular that you might feature in your pages, but the very idea…."

Well, even Timothy can be boring sometimes. I am relieved that I can cut off for a moment from the events. It's a luxury and a novelty for me to be able to listen to people at all. In life one is always on one's guard, avoiding eye contact, listening for coded meaning, and basically being deaf, dumb and blind for survival's sake. Look at Timothy now, semaphoring away like a Latin octopus.

"In any case I shall select a detached house, and I suppose I shall have to uproot the privets and any other déclassé vegetation in the foreground. Then I will do a make-up job on the front facade of an actual, real house! Using La Casa cosmetics!"

Glenda presses her teabag against the inside of her mug with a spoon. She looks troubled.

"I think the door shall be the lips," Timothy premieres, standing now in a ramrod-straight-John-Gielgud sort of way. "And the lips I shall paint with Rouge à Lèvres Satiné, or clear ruby - I can't decide which - but certainly something to match the real intensity of the new season's look of the mouth…."

Glenda catapults her used teabag in the bin with a flick of her spoon. Good aim; no finesse.

"The guttering I think can take the role of eyebrows which I shall paint a silky jet. And immediately atop the upper level windows I shall improvise almond-shaped eye-shadow in a pell-mell of lovely but muted jades, mosses, forest greens, silvery tortoises - turquoises, I mean, silly me! - azures and midnight blues. Won't La Casa Nostra love that! Especially for late autumnal November and Santa but a bankruptcy away. I'm not sure whether to go so far as eyeliner - what do you think Glenda? - but I suppose the window frames might serve a useful simile. Naturally the brickwork must be powdered. Porcelain is out and rose tints are in - or perhaps even beige (that would get them at *Vogue*!) and then I shall apply cheeky terracotta blusher beneath those self-same windows - casements would be utterly wonderful. For a witty climax I shall suspend a selection of jewellery from the guttering - Ken Lane's freshwater pearls for starters - oh no, those are the eyebrows…."

"TIMOTHY!"

Goodness. My heart jumped then. Glenda's on her feet at full stretch which is five foot eight plus extra for psychic impression, as Timothy puts it.

"This is a mockery," she rages, rose apple cheeks now plum. "A mockery of me and my work!"

I zoom in on Timothy's reaction. In caressing one side of his face he has just discovered, to his presumed annoyance, a glade of unshaved bristles in the lee of his left jaw bone ridge.

"Oh don't be so silly," he says in his goo-goo voice. "As if I would...."

"Don't patronise me with your..." She pauses for thought and a rummage in her tiny arsenal of nasty words "...your dinky words."

Wrong word. Timothy maybe exotique on occasion. But never dinky. Timothy gives good stretch to his six foot frame plus extra for psychic impression - considerably more than Glenda's - and....

"How dare you sink to the *ad hominem* attack, you wretched drudge," he screams. "I trade in abstractions and impressions, not literal surfaces and your twee-ness-by-numbers. How dare you even think of my work as a variant on your mundane exposures. I am soul, you grouter. You might as well think of Mapplethorpe and Turner in the same breath, or Constable in your case. I'm surrounded by eructing air-heads. The lot of you!"

And with that, trembling at his own effortless articulacy, he storms out to the clarion, "And now to deal with that other dollop!"

Poor Glenda. Her lavender essence has temporarily deserted her for my purposes.

Her large frame is still for a moment.

Then it begins to expand and contract like one of those award-winning wobbly cartoons from Canada, or Hungary, and then she starts blubbing.

I'm not sure but I think that one of her contact lenses has been swept off an eyeball by the tears, because she is now on all fours, rootling around in Benny's straw. Between the blubs she is whispering to herself as if at vespers - something like "The shaft of sun suddenly flashed on a distant bit of prospect...." I can't hear the rest. And then: "The rhododendron empurples the woods and the leaves of the woods shine...."

This is all a bit too deep for me.

Now look at her. Her body appears to be racked by spasms of grief. Then she shrieks, "Drudge!" to the walls before rearing onto her knees like an alarmed pit pony and making the most pitiful sounds. I can see that all this unusual activity around Benny's base may well dislodge him from his mount - uh! As I feared. There he goes. He falls on four-legged Glenda, bounces off her quilted back ("Oh!") and dives with much clatter into the adjacent wheelbarrow.

*

"What the fuck! For Christ's sake, Glenda, are you calfing or what?"

Germaine speaking! At last she appears. She caught me unawares. She is in her characteristic pose: arms crossed, body leaning against the office door's petalled architrave in her all-black Gaultier.

"Jeez-us. You're pathetic, Glenda. To allow some unreconstructed, iron-lunged faggot dinosaur to do this to you - Jeez."

What a despicable thing to say to poor Glenda in her present condition. I bet Germaine's been standing there gloating for at least a minute. The pit pony looks up at Germaine and wails afresh.

Oh, the racket. Germaine half-lids her eyes in fake exasperation before shrugging herself off the door frame and strolling over to the pathetic figure flat upon the straw.

"If you think I'm going to bend down and pick you up Glenda - forget it! Now get the fuck up before I kick you in the ovaries. Come on, up, up, up, UP!"

"Well, there's something to be said for the National Service approach. Glenda rolls onto her back before jacking up part of her top bulk with one arm.

"You're just like Timothy. Hard and without compassion," splutters my house editor.

"Stop mooing like a cow and get on your feet and behave like a woman for a change. What are you?"

"You're vicious! You don't care. Everyone's the same here. Hard and - ugh!"

Germaine has grabbed hold of her just as she gets her balance.

"That's right, straighten up," barks Germaine. "Come on, get this straw off you, come on Worzel."

I could kick Germaine myself. Those shocking red lips stuck in that pubertal pout of hers, painted on a bloated white-powdered face - she looks like a parrot fish that's seen a ghost. Or Julie Burchill. I should say here that, among other things, Germaine is my features editor if I've not mentioned it already.

Then she surprises me by handing Glenda a tissue to mop up. Glenda, evidently mistaking this act for sympathy, honks again. Well, why not. A good wail is good for the soul, and since she's started she might as well as finish. And she wouldn't want to embarrass Germaine by not matching the proportion of her unlikely concern.

"Come on Daisy," says Germaine to Glenda. "I'll make you a black coffee and then you can tell me what that walking drag act did to you."

"Rosehip, please." wrenches Glenda from hiccups.

"Rosehip," repeats Germaine, flatly.

"Oh, and Germaine, please switch off your tape recorder."

*

The rain's beating against the cliff faces of Raven's Towers. This must be about the same time as Stephen dropped me off in the street and I had my shop window daymare. And there's another sort of beating, this one taking place within Raven's Towers.

"Ouch, oh."

"Stop bawling! Seven, eight."

"No Timothy! Ouch."

"Nine...."

Timothy is administering an illegal smacking to his secretary Sarah. She lies over his lap like a royal's plaid blanket.

He's quite mad, the darling.

"There. Let that be a lesson to you," he says as he pushes her away. "It's for your own good and perfectly in line with right-wing MBA dogma. Now, when you yield to secretarial indolence and incompetence, you will think of pain. In consequence you may end up earning more than I. Think of me when you do your will."

Poor Sarah runs out to the loos, whimpering.

He strides into the corridor - and almost bumps into Germaine carrying mugs from Glenda's office.

"Making little girls cry, Timothy?" she says.

To my surprise he grabs her by the arm and frog-marches her into his office.

"Careful, Timmy," she says flatly, "Don't break my skin. I hope you've been tested lately."

"So," says Timothy, unfazed by her malice. "Little Miss Nightingale administers to the needy."

Germaine sighs: "As if being Glenda is not already a heavy enough cross to bear. Isn't it time you worked on a men's magazine, Timmy - you could cruise the corridors then."

Germaine places the mugs on Timothy's desk and plugs in his kettle and asks, "Mind if I use this? I did warn you last night not to tell Glenda your dumb 'house' idea. She is after all the house editor. Makes much more sense to take her by surprise in conference – that's the way she is, not quick."

I notice her tongue rolling and lashing against her teeth and palate as she searches for an appropriate accent. She's quite schizoid, psychically stratified.

"Don't lecture me you wraith!" shouts Timothy, "You had no

business going through my notes. I should have dealt with you last night but instead I'll let you stew awhile wondering what terrible revenge I have in store for you."

"Well, you could start with a slurpy French kiss. Then we could spend our last days together in a coastal hospice."

Timothy pulls his face into one his ghastly ironic smiles. "Despite your promise to me last night not to tip Vicki off about my wonderful La Casa project, what did I overhear but one half-hour later, by the photocopier, but old Mata Hari here in her aspiring executive mode?"

I think Germaine gives a look of amazement but it's difficult to tell under all that porcelain foundation.

"Fuck off, Oscar," she says, assuming the Esperanto of contemporary accents, the transatlantic drawl.

"Yes. Did I catch you out!" pursues Timothy. "Twice in one evening. Definitely not the Germaine of old. It's all that bottled black in your hair rotting your brain."

"Phew! I can still smell that crab. Or is it you, Timmy-poo?"

Timothy looks into space, his hands outstretched like a preacher's. "I see last night as if it were now. There was Vicki, still here at six-thirty in the evening and the rush hour in its prime, and we all know how much Vicki detests loitering mid-London in her Daimler. She's just hanging around..."

I never just hang around.

"...waiting to happen upon some glistening blob like yourself to engage in some inconsequential chit-chat to pass the time. It could be any blob. It could be Strudel. Benny even. But no, it's Germaine, poor possessed Germaine and her tongues; Germaine, still in her Punk clobber, circa 1979. Vicki says, 'Any gossip darling?'"

Yes, I did say that. He does my voice very well.

"Well you couldn't help yourself, little Miss Facial Tic. 'Anything to tell me darling?' repeats Vicki. 'Nobody ever tells me anything.' So you tell her about my La Casa idea, compulsively disordered as you are, in your Julie Andrews voice if I recollect - even I can't keep up with all your latest retro-cultural references. And then what do I hear? You say to Vicki my La Casa idea could make for a problem in conference. You say I am trespassing on Glenda's territory and in any case I am becoming too conceptual by half. Then you go too far, how you let Vicki off the hook."

Did she?

"You play devil's advocate and suggest that, on the other hand, perhaps Glenda should think laterally for a change and not be literal.

'After all,' you said, echoing me, 'the house is not just about deeply swagged pelmets.' Well, that wasn't very bright. I suppose you thought you might kill two birds with one stone. But Vicki could see you were out to make trouble…"

Did I?

"…and you should have remembered that she does so hate being presented with problems because then she is forced to think about them, whereas she prefers to respond on the hoof, as it were, and tune into spontaneous Fate's waveband for an instant, uncomplicated judgement."

That is a cruel simplification.

"So, what did Vicki say to you? Well, why settle for reportage when one has the precise words to hand."

Timothy takes out a micro-cassette tape recorder from his jacket pocket in a clearly rehearsed move and presses a button. God! It's my voice! I sound so tinny:

"Thank you, Germaine," I say. "You seem to have a thorough understanding of the problem. So much so that I want you to knock Timothy's and Glenda's heads together before the planning meeting tomorrow - darling, there's a smudge on your teeth, yes, it's fine now - yes, and knock their heads together and sort the matter out. One day you'll be an editor darling and this is just the sort of trial you'll have to deal with. I don't want a row. No unpleasantness. God! This photocopier does give off fumes, I feel quite…."

Timothy switches me off - strange nails he has, like toe nails. How dare he spy on me like that!

Concluding, Timothy says, "Oh dear, Germaine. Glenda or I or both of us have only to create a fuss in conference this morning and it's bye-bye career ladder for you. Oh well, perhaps you could take up auxiliary nursing - in that coastal hospice you were talking about. It would be good for your soul."

He flicks her right cheek, failing to stir up a small white cloud as from a chalk duster.

And then he goes over to the steaming kettle and pours water into the two mugs, dunking Glenda's rosehip teabag in one of them.

"Mind it steeps, chuck," he says. "Now take this back to Miss Moo and do your bestest to persuade her not to thwart La Casa. Quickly now, there's not much time."

Timothy gooses Germaine as she makes a stony exit with two hot mugs in her hands. She doesn't flinch. She's a cool customer, though I hate saying so.

Sometimes I wonder about Timothy's true sexual orientation.

*

Heavens! What was that awful noise?

Even Miss Cool herself, Germaine, flinches in alarm, dropping a powdery spoonful of coffee onto her patent black leather shoes.

Glenda has just sneezed in Germaine's office area, one of those unapologetic expulsions in which certain types of passenger on public transport specialise. But it is the crack from Glenda's nose-blowing which has sent a shock wave through Germaine, shattering years of hip refrigeration in a nuclear-nostril moment.

"You needn't have come through," says Germaine sharply. "I thought I'd make myself a coffee while your rosehip soaks."

"*Steeps*, Germaine. I try to keep to the traditional herbalist words. The tea does taste better as a result. Coffee is very bad for the adrenals - oh, Germaine, your shoe!"

"Never mind that. Here's your steeped rosehip. I've added Canadian honey as you like."

Bridget, Germaine's secretary, gets on bended knee and with light, skilful strokes, using a dry cloth, transfers the instant rich roast decaf from shoe to polypropylene carpet.

My two editors tinkle their spoons in their cups, sounding like Sally Army triangle players. Such a noise would drive Max to murder.

They gaze absently through a gorge in the Raven's Towers mountainside and out at London's dampened pall of carbon.

"Timothy is so foul-mouthed, so vicious," Glenda says finally. "The things he said to me. He called me a drudge. Wouldn't you think it outrageous that he plans to do a makeover on a house? What will my contacts think? Tortoises, yes. But a house! Houses are my patch and I'm going to have to raise this with Vicki."

"It's disgusting," concurs Germaine.

"I mean...."

"Did you find your contact lens?"

"I didn't lose it after all," says Glenda. "It just slipped behind my eyeball."

A tinkly pause. Then:

"Glenda, I have a confession to make." Germaine has turned away from the window and is facing Glenda's profile...."Vicki is not unaware of the problem."

Glenda faces her. "What? You mean she knows of Timothy's house proposal? Oh well then...."

"Hang on Glenda. You see, Timothy told me about his ridiculous La Casa idea last night and I thought I should mention it to Vicki."

"He told you before me? Naturally! I'm only the house editor. Why didn't you tell me first?"

"You had gone home by then, and I thought I could avert trouble by tipping off Vicki. I did it for you. You are in the right. I wanted to see what I could do."

The lies!

"That's really sweet, Germ."

"No. It's just that circumstantially I was put into a position where I could see a problem brewing. Timothy is pretty wild...."

"And no doubt Vicki took his side. She always sides with men."

"Well, she certainly has a fondness for him. I suggested to her he was getting too clever by half with his conceptual makeovers. But then she made a point that had not occurred to me before - it may alter your view of things if you want to sabotage Timothy."

It amazes me how Germaine is now talking just like Glenda - a vague, nearly-gone west-country burr-y sound. And as for Glenda - seconds ago she was inhaling rosehip as a post-tears decongestant. Now she lifts her head and is breathing clearly.

Germaine continues, "Vicki said that La Casa must surely be his last conceptual makeover because novelty ideas of that sort have a limited shelf-life. She said his philosophy is like a hologram which seems real but is in fact an illusion, and readers will soon tire of it. She said your features, in contrast, were timeless fixtures of the magazine."

"She actually said that?"

No.

"Yes. As I'm standing here. She said timeless fixtures. She said let Timothy have his last fling. And then...."

"Not redundancy! I'd hate to think that he'd lose his job because of this silly row."

"Well, his sensibility is redundant. The post-feminist woman maybe comfortable with traditional expressions of femininity, but she's also looking for assertive role models so that her freedom from feminist dogma is not misrepresented by certain types of opportunistic men...."

"Speak English Germaine."

"Timothy is not Madonna. Agreed?"

"Oh no, well...."

"Timothy is not Madonna, Glenda, and shut up for a moment. Post-feminism is OK so long as other women espouse it - not some hormonally-disturbed queen finding refuge on a women's magazine."

"What has this to do with La Casa, Germaine?"

"Jeez-us Christ, Glenda!" she shouts, in her ad-rap mode. "What have you got for a fucking brain? Mulch? You know what your problem is? You've got the hots for that drag act, haven't you?"

Rosehip spurts from Glenda's mouth as if from the head of an exhaling sperm whale in a herbal sea.

"Germaine! You're disgusting!"

"Come on now. Tell Germaine all. Even I as a girl, when I fancied a boy, would claim he was the most horrible boy in the world. And, you know, I'm not so sure you're wasting your time."

"Germaine!"

"The way he contrives little hostilities with you. What better way to maintain contact. And how he loves to get physical with women when he's angry. Just because he's a faggot doesn't mean he can't have a soft spot for you, Glenda. And I mean a hard spot."

Clever Germaine. The operative word here is "women". I guess Glenda must be flattered to be included in the women tribe after that private sense of exclusion all these years due to her plump quasi-autism; I presume.

"Don't make fun of me Germaine. I don't have to be buttered-up in this insulting way so that I won't kick up a fuss over his stupid La Casa scam. I've decided not to say anything. I shall take your word for it that Vicki said what you say she said. But Germaine. Why were you recording my words, earlier?"

"I record lots of things," Germaine replies smoothly. "I'm thinking of writing a novel but I'm unsure about dialogue. I need to understand natural speech patterns."

"I hope I don't end up in your novel! You could write about Timothy taking bribes from La Casa Nostra - that would be a good read."

"Bribes, Glenda? Do I know about this?"

"Well, I can't prove it. But why else devote an issue to one cosmetic company?"

"Mm."

*

This is odd. I, astral Vicki, am now standing behind Glenda who appears to be inspecting her drinking mug, empty now of its rosehip tea.

It's dazzling and glazed, and if I am not mistaken, part of the Wedgwood White Collection. I notice a tiny copper stain near the rim.

Her fingers are surprisingly attractive: slim, tapered; well-manicured nails in muted silver. I deplore red nails, especially smokers' red nails. The juxtaposition of red nails and a cigarette is fundamentally common. Certain types of powerful women think red underscores power. It doesn't in my view. It simply draws attention to their ignorance of taste and their inexperience of power. I have fired people because of their red nails.

But, anyway. Glenda is gazing intently on her mug. This is interesting. I crouch down behind her to see what she sees. Ah, I see. In the shininess of the mug I see two people reflected. In fact Glenda has positioned the mug just above her shoulder as an improvised spy mirror - she is spying on Germaine and Timothy around a corner.

How curious the two of them look in Glenda's mug, all arched bodies and pinheads and hunchbacks in the curved distortion. I hear their muffled voices. Glenda hears them, too.

"So?" says Timothy.

"I think that solves your problem," says Germaine.

"What did you say to her?"

"Didn't you record it then?"

Timothy sneers, "Capturing your treacheries last night exhausted my batteries. So?"

"I led her to think that La Casa was your last great indulgence. I said Vicki thought your idea of beauty was a redundancy to post-feminist woman, blah, blah, blah. That sort of thing. Basically you should be allowed to put yourself out of your misery."

"Oh, yes."

"I said to take pity on you."

"That will have to do for now. You'll have your work cut out when…." I can't hear the rest. Both have dropped their voices.

"I was right, though, you…." Missed it! Something about redundancy.

"Is that so?" says Timothy.

In the mug I see Timothy clasp Germaine's head as if studying it face-to-face.

"What an interesting specimen we have here," he says. "This is what beauty semiotics tells me about you. Notice the neo-Nouvelle Vague whitened face to signal the glamour of a sleepless life and First World food guilt. And these safety pin earrings and leather micro-skirt promise a controversy that you never quite deliver. But the black leggings and gold swirl embroidered jacket reassure your betters that you're a good girl at heart. Post-feminist female! You're just another power-crazed con trading on whatever's to hand."

Then in the mug's reflection I see Germaine raise one hand to his face, almost to caress him one might think, before grabbing his crotch with the other in a reflex move.

"Come on faggot," she's shouting, "rise and shine for me. What you need is some sexual harassment. Up, up, UP!"

Timothy's reaction is not what one might have expected. "Oh, squeeze harder Germaine. You've got just the right touch - ugh!"

Suddenly the couple fall away from sight. Poor Glenda has dropped the mug in shock at these sights and sounds. Her hand is left trembling in space.

*

Oh dear. I can understand now why she was so upset in conference later this morning - oh, perhaps I shouldn't have revealed that.

Still, what an ingenious form of espionage. A mug! I would not have expected it of Glenda.

But why am I being forced to relive all this rubbish?

Am I to deduce that all my subsequent troubles stemmed from Glenda's improvised espionage with a Wedgwood White mug?

*

Glenda's mug has barely stopped spinning and rolling about on the office carpet, dispersing rosehip remnants here and there, but a new drama unfolds at *Glossy International*.

My film man, Freddie Smith, is breaking cover to my staff.

He has just barged into the office where Germaine and Timothy were fondling each other in mutual hatred. Freddie is followed by a nice young man carrying a video camera.

"Now settle down folks. Gather round, please," he is announcing. What a powerful voice Freddie has – I suppose exercised by having to shout at thickhead egotists of TV, stage and screen.

Germaine and Timothy (whose crotch is now free of her grasp) are united at once in a joint gaze on Freddie of uncomprehending contempt.

Others in the semi-open plan forum are trying to ignore him as one might side-step an evangelist with dental problems in a shopping precinct. What a middle-aged mess Freddie is. I notice Timothy glancing at Freddie's pee-bleached scrotal bulge which is as heavy as a weaning mum's breast.

His tensioned jeans really are a living keepsake of youth's snake-hip virility - but he is a love.

"Come on now, are we deaf?" he's bellowing. "Yes, follow me please, yes, you young lady as well, come along follow me. No, sir, I am not mad, I'm here on the instructions of your good editor Vicki

Cochrane. I have a very important announcement to make and there's very little time. Please, move it!"

He strides up the corridor to the art department, a Pied Piper of sorts. "Follow me, everything is about to be explained. This is all legit, believe me. Please down your tools and follow me."

Freddie's face is even redder than usual, and in consequence his hair seems whiter, pure lamb's wool on an old ram's head. Harvested from their desks and cubicles, *Glossy International*'s elite corps are baled amid art department light boxes and page planners.

Then to everyone's consternation and giggles, Freddie mounts a desk like a randy bull-seal and stands on it.

"Thank you ladies and gentlemen," he begins. "QUIET! My name is Freddie Smith, film director, and you're probably wondering what I'm doing with this video camera here held by this young man. Good question! As you know in a few days' time you hold your GlossRam Fashion & Beauty show in India. What you won't know is that before the show proper there will a short film of *Glossy International* staff at work in their day-to-day environment, a fly-on-the-wall docudrama of everyday chic people - and that's why I'm here. Just think, ladies and gentlemen, your chance to shine for Ivana, Gloria, Nan, Babe, La Belle, Princess Leona and all those other international society pussy cats."

At this the *Glossy* lynch mob metamorphose into a rhubarb-rhubarb Proms audience.

"Now," continues Freddie, "Here's the bad news. For the last hour the security cameras in your offices and corridors have been recording you all on special film and we've canned some very odd sequences indeed...."

A collective intake.

"These include a woman crawling about on all fours covered in straw, a crab in a bucket, a man putting a woman over his knee and smacking her bum, a woman gazing at her drinking mug with a mad expression on her face and a wrestling match in which a female is sexually molesting a male colleague...."

"Outrageous! It's Big Brother!" roars Timothy.

"Quite so," say some.

"Shocking," say others.

"You two-faced Jezebel," whispers Glenda to Germaine.

"Sorry, Glenda?"

"Traitor! I saw you with Timothy. Just you wait!"

"But there's some more good news," adds Freddie, lowering his head and crumpling his three chins into one fleshy cascade. "I don't think those international society pussy cats will want to see all that. So we're going to start again. You're all going to return to your offices and get on with whatever you do, and my cameraman here" - a big-boned lad with a crew cut. Pity - "will walk briskly from one department to another for a fly-on-the-wall whole ten minutes in the life of *Glossy International*. So, make sure you're doing something interesting; otherwise it's pay-docking time! My assistant Sally will make-up those who've had a long night, but I want you all natural, OK? Any questions? And if I am happy with your performance I may just bin all that naughty footage before Vicki gets to see it!"

"Well, that's just typical," says Timothy to no one in particular.

He makes back for his office - he of all people will know the importance of looking one's best before the critical likes of Princess Leona, Babe, Nan, et al.

En route he is side-tracked by the astonishing sight of Unity Hall's banquet, all laid out for a special shoot, in her food department.

"So, you knew what was going on," he deduces, cleverly.

"Well," Unity responds coyly, "Vicki told me in confidence about the filming. She said to keep it under my tea cosy. She said that some of our older readers actually imagine themselves living with us at *Glossy* and we wouldn't want to disillusion them. She said some readers take it for granted that I marinade my teriyaki steaks or whatever over a desk-cooker. I was surprised. I said to Vicki, 'But surely the likes of Princess Leona Humperdink would not be so naïve.' And Vicki said, 'You'd be surprised.' So I prepared all this last night and drove it up this morning - a real slog. If you're a good boy Timothy you can have a little lamb and pineapple kebab after the filming."

Timothy smiles and leans forward to give her a peck on the cheek. Unfortunately she moves at the wrong moment so that his lips smack her left earhole. "Thank you, Timothy. I'm now quite deaf."

Unity had no business breaking my confidence to Timothy. Unity is too sweet - even now my mouth feels stuffed with meringue just seeing her. I could only ever take a teaspoonful of Unity.

I follow after Germaine. She's the one to watch! She rushes to her office, her red lips fuller in the pout; almost breathless.

"Tina," she says to her assistant. "I'm clearing off for a while. If that old scrote Smith asks where I am tell him I've pissed off because of a heavy period."

"Germaine…."

"Don't argue. Have you finished transcribing Meryl Streep?"

"No. But why don't you want to be filmed Germaine? Vicki will be furious."

"Fuck Vicki. I know what that slag is up to...."

Now this is the Germaine I can relate to.

"She's out to humiliate me because she thinks I'm too big for my boots. Trouble is, she doesn't know my boot size. But she's already got me on that fucking film squeezing Timothy's balls."

"Germaine! Why would you be doing such a thing? Timothy of all people."

"Do be quiet," snaps Germaine, lighting a cigarette. "It certainly wasn't foreplay. Now I've got Glenda on my back. This is a real mess if she goes nuclear in conference."

"But the scrote has already said they won't be using that film."

"Don't be naïve. They'll film me working all prim and proper at my desk and then splice in a brief sequence of me in Timothy's crotch for a GlossRam laugh. Vicki will do it. So that the society cunts can have a laugh at my expense and make me look ridiculous. Then I'm sure never to be editor when word gets back here. No. I'm off to the thirteenth floor where the security cameras are operated. I'll get that film if it kills me."

"But Germ...."

So that explains her non-appearance on the official film. I remember that now. Trust a professional paranoiac to suspect rightly a plot and then get the rest all wrong. Does Germaine really think I would imperil the reputation of *Glossy International* by inserting embarrassing sequences of my staff in our promo movie - in front of international aristocracy?

That was always Germaine's problem. No sense of proportion - or propriety. A feral female - talented, but talent alone is quite useless. In fact, to jump ahead a bit of the action, and by way of explanation, I can tell you that I did intend to show Freddie's film of Germaine's assault on Timothy to the Raven's Towers management team at the next knees-up. There would be laughter, certainly, but also the feeling that one destined for higher things - such as the editorship of *Glossy International* - should not allow herself to be caught looking foolish. Managements expect a precognition of danger in aspirants to the throne. A street-wise and supernatural gift for survival which tells them that they, the management, will be safe by association with their sassy editor.

It's a dangerous world out there.

Germaine rushes from Tina and the office and crashes through a fire exit before a cape of nicotine smoke.

Light on the cold grey walls rushes away from us in a thousand trickles as we pad down the staircase. Her little gasps grow to sordid puffs up and down the well of the Towers; whispers building up into full-volume song. Conspiracy finds its true ambience here as noise assumes the music of echo and breathing and shuffle.

She reaches the deserted thirteenth floor fighting for breath. I recall that the last occupant here was the music rag *Jam Machine* which I insisted had to be evicted because of solvent abuse among its staff.

In my astral state I'm not exhausted at all. Clog-lunged Germaine however leans against a corridor wall and quietly resists death.

She must be wondering at the twists and turns of Fate. She's loose now in a soulless place. Sadly, what she doesn't know is that Security was moved to the eighth floor a little while back.

Regrettably, I am in no position to advise her of this.

As I watch her - do your ears sing, Germaine? - I am aware (as she is) that the soundtrack has altered subtly. The rapid breathing we hear is no longer hers.

Gentle regular sighs are enlivening the south side of the floor. She creeps towards the new sound. Through the glass panels of the swing doors, interleaved with security mesh, she can observe south south-east a plundered site of carpet space except for a lonesome telephone on the floor.

Drawn by another gasp she turns her head south-south-west.

Well!

There, lying face up on a desk, is the moaning and mewing figure of my young personal assistant, Lee, being rather vigorously pumped, screwed, shagged - I am searching for a word to convey the loveless urgency of the spectacle - by the obese and standing figure of Roger Masefield, Raven's Towers acting chief executive officer.

When I instructed Lee to talk to Roger about Max I did not have this in mind!

Poor Germaine squashes her nose against the glass and she looks appalled. Certainly Roger's arse is an appalling sight - it really is an arse rather than a bottom, or even a prim behind. It is truly massive, as large as any of the boulders clinging to the side of Raven's Towers. It is cumulus-like in its heaped roundedness, its flesh wobbling like an earthquake's after-shock with each dog thrust (or lunge, as movement hinges on knees rather than pelvis).

In fact the wobbling is having its usual unfortunate effect on me. I feel a bit queasy - like watching Max trembling on our videophone. Nonetheless I am fascinated by Roger's navy-blue Pierre Cardin silk handkerchief, flowing unfashionably from his jacket top pocket, waving hello, as if beckoning Germaine to join the fun.

But that arse! It's actually a colour chart of his foreign activities in the sun, striped like a tutti-frutti, in three shades ending in an ambient chocolate tan. The first is a narrow strip of fish-belly white flesh -

measled with acne - running midway across his buttocks. This hints at the skimpy briefs I imagine he adorned for a mistress he may have taken to Skiathos or wherever - oh, but there isn't time to speculate further.

We are witness to a quickie.

A sudden quickening of his bobbings and jiggings turns the tutti-frutti into something resembling an optical Mulligatawny soup. One would never expect athleticism in such a fatso. This reminds me of those heart-rending seizures of freshly caught tuna off Sicily. Like a bystander to an assassination, one cannot believe one's good or bad luck at witnessing a little bit of history in the making, which here is the launching of little anorexic Lee as editor material.

I can only wonder at this moment what Germaine is thinking, the ex-Presbyterian turned proto-punk, who I suspect has hitherto never faced up to the actuality of what promotion really means in the real world - for some.

Roger's body jerks and shudders as it might in the electric chair and then he slumps, sort of, on Lee, his blubbery belly melting over her in thick folds like a duvet of volcanic lava.

She says something but I don't catch it. Germaine posts an ear to the thin gap between the swing doors - "I wish you'd use something," Lee is saying. "It's difficult to clean up in a place like this."

"Sorry, hun," says Roger. "I was desperate for a fuck and you're so gorgeous. Hope it wasn't all one-sided."

Lee giggles. What she lacks in body she makes up for in hair. It's big and it's blonde and she's Barbie.

"Silly you," she trills.

Roger pulls up his zip and grins.

"Now," he says. "Are you going to tell me where Max is like you promised or do I drop my zip again?"

Lee giggles again. She's dabbing herself with tissues. How on earth did the ancients survive without Kleenex?

"He's on a pier," she says.

"Pier? Who's on what pier?"

"Max, of course. I'm sworn to secrecy, you know."

"Max, on a pier?"

"Roger! Max is staying on a seaside pier. The Brightworth Pier if you must know. That's where he's holed up."

"Max Cochrane...."

"Is a resident of the Brightworth Pier, along with Sooty."

"You're having me on." Roger pulls down his zip again in an act of bravado.

"I'm not!" squeaks Lee. "He's actually on the Brightworth Pier.

That's where you'll find him. He's rented a chalet or something and Vicki knows where he is and I think she's really angry with him. I think she's using some fortune-teller called Madame Smith who works on the pier to spy on him. She told me to send £850 from petty cash to her this morning - by bike! - enclosing their birthdates."

"What?" roars Roger. "Fucking lunatics both of them. A fortune-teller? What is he doing in a dump like Brightworth? He was born there, right? I read that in *Who's Who*."

"Yes. But the pier is worrying."

"I'll think about convening an extraordinary meeting of the board. The Brightworth Pier," he repeats to himself, absent-mindedlyzipping himself up again. "This is my moment to get them both out. This is an international publishing quoted company in 1988, not some private fiefdom from the Middle Ages. You know he just left me a memo saying he wouldn't be around for a while? No explanation. Anything could happen while he's away. The board would insist he go if they knew - and that crazy wife of his. £850 to a fortune-teller! Out of petty cash no doubt!"

"Be careful Roger. You know how Max works - it could be a trick, to catch you out."

"You think so? Yes, you may be right," he says, placing a hand into his trousers and rearranging his genitalia with care. "Those fucking Cochranes."

Germaine pulls her nose off the door glass leaving a white smudge. She's whispering to herself three words as if trying to memorise them, "The Brightworth Pier."

She seems genuinely astonished - I can't think why. She must know already where Max is. I saw the pictures of them together. Yet she's putting on a credible performance of bafflement. Now I'm baffled. But no, I have to consider that Germaine is schizophrenic. She's probably momentarily forgotten that she knows – it'll come back to her when her brain switches to some other identity, or whatever happens with these medical conditions.

She walks quickly towards the lifts.

Just as she is about to press the call button, she - we - are frozen by a low protracted groan.

This is not a Roger groan but the groan of a young man, I assess. It has the duck's timbre of male youth; and something occurs to me at this point: the unreality of Roger's fucking: his virtual silence. Not once did he groan, or yelp as most men do like puppies when they come; or even sigh. As a teenager Roger probably had to accustom himself to silent masturbation so as not to rouse the suspicions of (presumed) narrow-minded parents quietly rotting away in connubial bliss on sofas downstairs. I should have been a novelist.

No, this new groaning is a groaner's groaning that will grow into a howl and wake the neighbours and end up in a nuisance case in a magistrate's court. The groans emanate from the north side of the floor.

Thank God Germaine has curiosity. If Glenda were in her shoes we'd still be steeping our rosehip teabags.

Germaine squashes her nose against the glass of one of the north swing doors.

Well, there's an odd sight. A postboy, Matt, I think he's called - he can't be much more than seventeen - is standing with his back against a pillar.

He appears to have donned a sporran for size where his briefs once were. On closer inspection I see that the sporran has a life of its own, and could very well be the titian-red tresses of one of Roger Masefield's harem of assistant publishers.

Like I said at the beginning, I never forget a hairstyle.

Matt's designer-ancient denim rests concertinaed about his ankles, and his head is rolling this way and that against the pillar in expressions of exquisite torture. As her titian head nods and shakes like a domestic tabby wolfing down some chunky goodness, Matt can be heard singing these words:

"Oh uh oh no wait a sec so then uh uh Vicki was running late and arghhh and she's supposed to be having this meeting no wait a sec don't put your tongue in there and uh uh uh Vicki phoned her secretary she was having her hair done and oh no oh no oh no and there was a riot in the magazine Jesus Christ I'm gonna gonna any second and that Glenda was rubbing herself against oh Benny and Germaine was cor! sneaking around with her tape recorder eeeeee eeeeee eeeeee oh ah yum yeah and that poof Timofy hit his secretary and then Germaine grabbed his balls yah lummy and Glenda was screaming her head off oh no oh no oh no then this geezer came out saying he had filmed everyfink uh uh uh uh uh uh uh uh ARGHHHHHHH."

I marvel at the sporran head's dedication to duty. It remains perfectly still as Matt raises the roof, her gold-plated triple-leaf earrings (from Van Peterson, I'd wager) glinting.

Germaine reels away from the door. Another frightful episode witnessed as part of her education!

Gross.

She doesn't bother with the lift. Instead she bolts back up the staircase, crazy white light clawing back what little life it has given to the dingy walls.

My own mind replays images of bare flesh and red hair and dripping mouths and those glinting earrings. I feel Germaine's hollow belly and her headful of erotic treacheries.

*

Germaine stumbles out of the fire exit at the twentieth floor. She's heaving with exhaustion in her flight from the thirteenth. If only she would collapse and die now. If only Lee Harvey Oswald had slipped on a squashed grape and broken his head.

If only!

She leans over the ventilation grill to inhale some negative ionised air. She must be still thinking of the sporran. And Lee. And Roger....

"Germaine!"

Well, well. Look who's arrived. It's me at last. Earthly Vicki Cochrane. I've arrived at *Glossy International*'s offices from Umberto's. I've re-powdered my face, admired my new chignon hairstyle once again, and have just stepped out of the Ladies. I look very good, very reborn.

"Are you quite well?" I ask Germaine. "You do look pale - but then you always do don't you darling."

"Morning Vicki – I'm just catching my breath. I walked up to lose weight.

Liar. But I didn't know that then.

"Goodness. What weight is there to lose? Don't go and have a heart attack - try to think of me when you put your body at risk."

"You never leave my mind, Vicki."

"That's what I need to hear. What does my horoscope say for me today I wonder? We Pisces always suffer. Have you seen Lee on your travels? She will insist on leaving me in the lurch. You do look distracted darling - period troubles? I shall have to give Lee one of those bleepers doctors use in medical TV dramas, won't I. I must look up Pisces."

"Lots of surprises for Gemini," gasps Germaine. She's a Gemini – the Twins!

"I hate surprises! That's why Christmas is a pain. And birthdays. I always say to Max: Don't surprise me. And of course he always lets me down. The Glenda-Timothy business. Is it sorted?"

"Er, yes. Glenda's being a bit difficult and Timothy is hysterical about La Casa...."

"This is not what I wanted to hear, Germaine. Sort it out, and you haven't long. Why I'm lumbered with these problems I'll never know."

I turn to the corridor mirror, a tactical swivel by way of dismissing Germaine. I catch my slightly pursed smile, a waspish purple butterfly sunning itself on my mouth. Then I remember Freddie Smith.

"Did you enjoy the filming, Germaine? Freddie is so good. I hope people weren't too put out."

"The wha' - yeah, that was a gas, Vicki."

"I asked Freddie for a touch of the cinéma vérité for the GlossRam show - I mean, the Leona Humperdinks are so easily bored and they're all so used to the PR line and cosmetic jobs. So I thought: be bold and show them the way it is at *Glossy*. Well, within reason. If I had warned you, you would have all dressed up."

"Timothy said he would resign."

"He resigns every week. If he didn't I'd have to sack him. That way he negatives the negative. What do two negatives make, darling?"

What am I on about?

"Was Timothy spitting?" I ask quickly.

"Frothing!"

"Love it. I do adore him frothing. He's got a lovely little bum, I only noticed the other day during the fire drill as I was struggling down behind him on the staircase. I hope he doesn't misuse it too often. Was he quite cross?"

"Apoplectic."

"Life has its moments," I say, palming my chignon.

My earthly self can't quite catch Germaine's pine needle spiritual essence this morning - normally sharp and zingy.

I should feel even sharper and zingier now because of something about Germaine, but my earthly self senses that her mood is subdued, confused. I recall this now. I hated Germaine on sight when I first met her, but she did electrify me - unlike today. Normally, she's by far the liveliest of my apothecary of staff essences.

My mood-swingers.

"You like my new hair Germaine? I love to catch you youngies out. Keeps us all on the ball. Never allow anyone to feel relaxed or else they will let you down as surely as I stand here now. Remember these words from an old bird when you have attained the dizzy heights and are sitting in an editor's chair. God, I'm so old and I know it all. Anyway, tell everyone that I shall be ready shortly for conference, that's when I can find that wretched Lee - oh, there you are!"

Lee is emerging from the same staircase fire door Germaine used, with much clanking of iron. Her hair is a little more tousled than usual. Thanks to lover boy Roger - if only I had known then.

"You're not trying to lose weight as well are you?" I ask in all innocence. "No one's using the lifts any more. I shall have to tell Max and we can save on the running costs. Lee! Smarten up and get to your desk. You can lose weight in your own time. And Germaine - Glenda- Timothy!"

>><<

Poor misguided me! Perhaps I oughtn't to have told Lee to talk to Roger. It's always better to handle these things personally.

I have Video No.6 in my hand. I don't like the look of it. The label reads: "Vicki's seminal breakdown."

I should hardly call it that! It was a response to the pressures building up around me at Raven's Towers in Max's absence. Superficially, I seemed to have recovered from Max's news. I had Madame Smith in my pocket, Lee in Roger's (so to speak) and I had my chignon for strength.

But I was volatile.

Vulnerable.

You've met my staff essences. My lavender, my juniper, my pine needle. Bottled all of them in my head. But sometimes an essence wants to escape its container and become something else. Bottles begin to shake with revolution. The oils start dreaming of the cocktail shaker. Max was my eucalyptus - then he didn't want to be my eucalyptus.

He wanted to be the dead, stinking air of putrid seaside nostalgia.

I've said it before (and I shall say it again) but we all bottle other people in our lives. I'm not the only one. It's just I have formulated a language to communicate this commonplace. The presence of some people makes us happy or sad and we don't know why. The only difference between you and me (in this respect) is that I put a name of these effects on me.

And that morning, April 27, 11.45am (the time's on the video label), all my bottles were restless, all wanting to be something else. Oh God....

- >>>

CHAPTER SEVEN

I've just left Germaine in the corridor and am standing outside my office at *Glossy International*. A moment ago the absence of her pine needle left me somewhat flat after the fun of Umberto's chignon.

A new mood has taken possession. An old familiar tension has returned.

It came up on me that morning around 11.45 - the time the November conference was set to start – in the way you can feel an assassin appraising you from behind your back.

Standing there I am visualising barbed claws looming over the thin lining that holds me together. I hear once again in my mind's ear the weird distant clink of glass that I heard earlier this morning when Max told me he was deserting me, and I had said that I should have had children, and then I saw all those milk bottles in my head, and then they all exploded.

Now I hear the spectral milk float on its morning round. Except I don't think it's delivering milk at all, but other types of liquid. I'm certain it approaches (yes, it does approach) and I know - then and now - that I have reason to be unsettled.

I feel that my staff essences are not very happy with me and this is not what I need on a day such as this. They're not happy about Freddie Smith. And I sense other things besides. Sense of mischief has absconded.

Once in my office I head for one of the formal unquestioned signifiers of seniority, my huge black ash desk – "utility furniture" Max calls it, dismissively. I take out a canister from a vanity drawer and, without aid of mirror, discharge a number of short sharp sprays at my hair. Umberto's artwork already requires renovation.

This ritual serves a dual purpose. The one I have just itemised. The other: multiple hairspray hisses is code to Lee to call the troops in for conference. Vicki Cochrane, editor-in-chief of *Glossy International*, is ready to hold court in her office and be enthralled by editorial submissions for the November 1988 issue.

Except I know Lee is not within earshot. She's still in the loo, I'll be bound.

I put away the hairspray canister. I remember deciding there and then to teach Lee a lesson. I will not spray my hair when I hear her return. Everything will be silent when she gets back to her desk. The tortures she will endure wondering whether I've already sprayed.

Then I'll inflict yet more punishment. I'll tell her eventually that she has missed the spraying and cancel her lunchtime breaks for one week.

Responsibility carries with it few pleasures.

But this is one of them.

Actually, I tell a lie. There are other pleasures. Ways to escape my current unease in my office. I peer into a secret compartment of my desk to fish out my numero uno scent, a bottle of earthy Chanel No. 19, a dab of which *extrait* - no lowly *eau* at *Glossy* - I love to dab on each of my (I must be wholly frank) nipples.

For that naughty erotic tingle.

I watch myself do it now, and I feel my breasts aflame for a few seconds, but what seconds! Is it this sensation I love most? Or is it the delicious incongruity of private self-pleasuring in my sacred office?

One does not know the answer to everything.

But what would people think if they knew of my secret vice? My teeth chatter with delight as tingle dilates into warm body glow.

My hand moves away from my bra cup and a whiff of iris escapes its mammillary home; and the scent conjures up in my mind the peasants I observed years ago in Provence, at the foot of the Maritime Alps, who hand-pick the May rose - the middle resonant note of Chanel No.19 - only at dusk.

One particular remembered young peasant catches my fancy (once again): uncouth corduroys no longer belted at the waist; his lips on my cheeks, my eyelids, my neck; his flicking tongue lightly teasing my earlobes; his compact body incidentally caressing my every particular, untouched by Max in a long while. Thank God.

It's vital the lusty rustic *mounts* without much regard for me: in this Chanel-driven scenario he must be oblivious of boringly balletic or "sensitive" foreplay - or of orgasmic control. Sex education goes against Fate: spontaneity is Fate's true spur. The pathologising of premature ejaculation in modern times has, in any case, not lengthened duration of the actual copulatory experience for most couples (three minutes is the average endurance according to a piece I read in the ever-reliable *Daily Mail*). Marathon porn film-sex is this century's principal creator of unattainable expectation, aside from newspaper agony aunts and sci-fi. And I loathe Masters and Johnson who initiated peeping-tommery on a global scale!

But anyway. My peasant should be totally unconcerned with my pleasure, which is my business; and I'm tired of these men who want to do everything sexually. I am going to make a bold statement: let the male have his all in one incontinent half-minute. Rather that than half-an-hour of sex manual rehearsal. I'll do the rest.

Then again, perhaps such a thing is just for fantasy, where one can rewind the cock, as it were, like a clock....

His stubbled face negligently chafes my breasts with each thrust and fevered osculation (bit *porn-filmy*. I prefer short fat cock, btw), a pink petal of the May rose balanced precariously upon the silky pelt of a buttock (a nice fragrant crack, thanks to the continental bidet so absent in the UK)....

So it is that his beard of laziness scrapes my tender flesh, and his mouth sucks my face; and I run my soft purple lips across the brittle hairs of his throat; and I smell the May rose afresh. And in a fantasy switch-about, my tongue is now teasing back....

Oh! As my eyes flicker open for a second in Chanel-rapture, I see that I'm being observed in my own office. There, standing in the doorway, is my cookery editor Unity Hall, spectating at me with mouth agape. She must have opened the door in a stalky-creepy fashion. She certainly didn't knock.

Naturally she looks astonished at the outward facial display of my own mental sex movie; no doubt shocked by my soundless tongue darting about in my open mouth, in the fashion of the late Mary Millington; appalled by my trembling dark lilac eyelids....

"Vicki, Vicki! Are you all right? Is it epilepsy?" she asks, not with conviction and a little too late.

Short fat cock, May rose petal and dream stubble vanish in an instant from my head. I am open-mouthed and boggle-eyed, gawping at the ruddy cheeks of Unity.

"I'm quite fine," I say, in a purr of recovery. "I was just exercising my facial muscles - good for ridding wrinkles, or so Timothy says! He calls it 'going for a gurn-burn'."

With that we both chuckle and a crisis is averted. But that was close. I made up the gurn-burn thing – it's quite a good idea for a feature.

Even at this moment I do not forget my suspicions of Unity. I overheard only the other day, on my driver's radio, a taxi call for Unity to take her to the address of a lesser glossy magazine. Is it possible she's planning a career move, she who can stuff but not say boo to a goose?

After the girlish giggles I look hard at Unity and lower my eyelids, giving her my mild dark lilac treatment.

If she were to desert me now, this would be just one more treachery of course, in the ongoing assault on Vicki Cochrane.

*

So it is time for the November editorial conference in my office.

I have punished Lee for not being at her desk when I sprayed my hair.

My staff bottles file in, nodding at me, wishing me good morning: not all exhibiting the usual signs of career-enhancing deference. Hi lavender. How are you clary sage?

As usual, because I'm *tolerant*, they're billowing coffee steam and cigarette smoke, a misting tension that's deepening into a pall above our heads, like the smog in our lungs.

Normally, I wouldn't miss all this for the world. But today....

"Hello, darlings," I begin lightly. The glass clinking in my head grows a little louder - can they not hear it? An odd echoey sound - I hear it now. "Is it really the November issue already? It only seems yesterday we were discussing the last Christmas issue. How tiresome for those who've been here too long." Giggles.

Yes, yes. How I remember it. I spot a few glazed, drop-dead expressions which really do unnerve me this day. I palm my chignon for support. I can deal with coke-sniffing, sexual deviation etc: these are the toss-side of talent in my view. A grave personality defect is a sure sign of genius. But what I can't abide is hostility, and I sense it today.

Clink, clink.

Then before I say another word, and to my great surprise, Glenda stands up."Vicki, before we begin, there's something I want to say about Timothy's beauty proposal."

Lavender has never done this before. This is not very soothing.

So Germaine has failed me. Her pine needle has failed to deliver thrills.

Lavender means to fight.

Before I respond, my eyes tactically glance upon my collection of office decoration: the ornamental jade elephants, the pink quartz Buddhas, the Thai butterflies, the masks from Senegal and Bali, the Japanese warrior helmets: an optic whistle-stop global tour which says: Did I really acquire all this to end up being troubled by the likes of...*you*?

"Good morning - or is it early afternoon? - Glenda," I say, lightly. "And, yes, I'm fine. Thanks for asking." I widen the address: "I hope you were nice to Freddie Smith. That goes for all of you. As you know, The GlossRam Show is the most important event in our calendar so I don't want to hear churlish moans. As usual, Glenda, we will begin with the fashion proposals, then features, then you Glenda."

"This is important, Vicki. It's a matter of principle."

"Principle, darling? How melodramatic."

"Timothy is attempting to sabotage my department."

Sensitive people should never lose their temper. Their like end up in terrorism.

"Nonsense," shouts Timothy.

"Not nonsense," shouts Glenda.

"Now calm down, Glenda." I say. I throw Germaine a look that assures her punishment.

"No, I will not calm down. If Timothy goes before me I will face a *fait accompli*. You never turn down his ideas!"

Vanessa, my fashion editor, and her associate Emma, titter like schoolgirls. I suppose the use of *fait accompli* presupposes a formality of thought with which they are not familiar.

"How pompous," says Vanessa, taking out another cigarette.

"Be quiet Vanessa," shouts Glenda. "And stick to what you know."

"Well, that's put you in your place," says Timothy to Vanessa.

"Oh, I know," croaks my fashion ed. "Any space left in the badger's sett?"

Glenda stands up to face the fashion duo. "It's pathetic the way you two can't do a thing without each other."

"Oh, you're such a bore," drawls Emma, southern counties. "Loner!"

"Glenda...." starts Germaine.

"This is all your doing," screams Glenda.

All eyes now burn into Germaine. She is pine needle no more - more like sleepy camphor.

"I might have expected Mrs Danvers' shadowy presence," helps Timothy.

Vanessa lines her brow. "Who's she, Timothy?"

"I'm the house editor," shouts Glenda.

"But not at home today," laughs Vanessa.

"We all know your fashion ideas are agreed in advance," spits Glenda. "Very convenient!"

"Oh heavens," Emma picks up. "It's a plot against Glenda. Sound the alarm."

My neck is beginning to ache with the to and fro.

"That's enough of that Emma," I say, attempting a little strategic solidarity with Glenda, pathetically cornered by her own lack of guile. Now is the time to isolate Germaine. "Now Glenda, how can you possibly know what Timothy is about to propose when he has yet to speak?"

"Because Germaine told me in confidence and she told you and she said you said Timothy is redundant."

The office falls about at this exposition from the nursery.

"That's right, Glenda, you reveal all," says Timothy.

"Shut it faggot!" hisses Germaine, her red lippy skates slipping on her icy alabaster.

"QUIET!" I bark.

The office falls silent. Time now to rout the enemy. But that odd sound of bottles grows louder - I try to ignore it. I shall deliver one of my notorious sermons to try to bring order and stop the bottle noise. I breathe deeply.

"May I remind you all that this is *Glossy International* and not the Raven's Towers crèche. Now, Glenda," I say, lowering my voice to establish a degree of empathy, "whatever you may have heard from Germaine, or even Timothy for that matter, what may or may not have been said by so-and-so - is that right Germaine? - nothing passes into this magazine until it has been proposed in conference and considered by me in relation to other proposals, and a decision is made by me.

"As I have said time and time again, my job is not an easy one, and not made easier by what has gone on this morning - or even by a certain member of staff creeping off for job interviews at this difficult time. Yes I know about that.

"My job is to achieve the correct editorial mix, the salt with the pepper, the sugar with the spice, the fact and the fiction, the heart and the world (or subjective truth as against objective truth) - everything can only be in relation to its opposite. Have I not said this time and time again? And I have to do this because *Glossy International* is the ultimate me magazine. We do not address roles and titles but the selves of our readers, their unreconstructed psyches. We do not say husband, wife, employer, taxpayer: we say you you you; and we say that you are an intelligent person who wants to be informed of ways to make your life even more elegant, beautiful: in a word; livable.

"Our purpose is to give the reader sufficient conversation fodder for at least a month, at her dinner parties. The test of what goes in is: Would our reader want to discuss this topic over the consommé? We do not have special interests. All interests are special to us. We have no hobby horses, no bees in our bonnet. We have no manifesto. But we have an attitude and we are no age. And our readers are not so deep that they bore or so lightweight that they easily bore.

"We believe in nothing other than what we choose to publish each month. We are a feeling, a mood, a sensation, a bit of this and that, which brings me back to my role: it is my role to recognise and marry these bits and bobs.

"And sometimes I know you get angry with me and call me an old bag who's out of touch, but I have to look at *Glossy* holistically - is that really a word, Timothy? *–io sono italiano –* or as a whole. And from where I'm sitting, darlings, I inevitably, as a matter of course, can see things from a different perspective, while you lot have the luxury of your little departments, your passionate beliefs, which simplify your perspective, which is good and right and how it should be, but you all have to remember that it is I who must decide what is right for *Glossy*, which is a unique identity, competing in an unstable market against all those other unique identities.

"For *Glossy* is not unique in one regard: it is not excepted from the laws of the market. I'm sorry to go on about it but none of you has made my life easier at all, not one of you has bothered to put yourself in my place. Why don't you all pretend to be me for a change. When, for instance, Germaine, you propose for the umpteenth time a piece on male rape victims interviewing their attackers, ask yourself: Where would Vicki put such a piece? Next to the fruit cordials advertising? Next to the loo roll paper? Paloma Picasso? You see my problem? I could place a piece on male rape next to these ads if it felt right, but it is difficult to know when that will be.

"Even Max has to be lectured on these things. We're the glossy with heart. As I always say, magazine readers aspire to success which for most people is the substitute for success itself; but an aspiration has the quality of a dream which means it must have the detail of reality and the proportion of a fairy tale. Please, all of you, try to think in these terms. Harmony, harmony, harmony. Light and shade. Robin Hood and the Sheriff of Nottingham. Know when the moment is right. Feel it."

I sip water, my head spins. Just listening to myself (again) has exhausted me.

I am an oracle of outlines. I know what I want when I see it. If I were to tell my staff exactly what I wanted then what room would there be for the unexpected? For Fate's contribution?

I am the taster not the chef.

If the price of that is staff exasperation, it's a small one for the greater glory of *Glossy*. A hieroglyph is far more interesting than a mere word.

How brow-beaten they all look, my children, my essences. My sermon has flattened them. Robbed them of their will to live. I share their ear-splitting tinnitus of ringing silence. No! Not tinnitus. It is the ear-splitting song of many glass bottles shivering against each other - I remember it now.

All staff heads are bowed with shame or boredom. All except one.

Germaine's.

She has held it insolently high throughout my speech, glaring at me with undisguised hatred. She is the principal cause of the psychic glass chatter!

Emboldened perhaps by the thought that her career at Raven's Towers must be nearing its end, shocked by what she saw on the thirteenth floor (of which I was at this moment ignorant), trounced by Glenda and Timothy and ritually humiliated by me - in fact I was merciful - she rises to her feet, stomach torn no doubt, holds my cold eye, and says in a sweet, hi-babe voice:

"You know Vicki, you're so full of crap."

*

I am stunned. The word "crap" rebounds in my head. I am not good at dealing with insults - I have never quite come to terms with the notion that words might be directed at me for the purpose of injury.

Only when I have registered the appalled expressions on other staff faces and the gaping mouths, the "omigods" and the gleeful "That's-Done-Its", do I begin to absorb the scale of Germaine's horrible words.

Then I react.

The echo of her words - "you're so full of crap" – does not diminish away but grows louder in my head. All this and glass chatter too.

Germaine's specific insult - *crap!* - invades me and, as I feared, is turned to flesh (so to speak) in my head: I see crap fall into my hair - I feel and smell it - into my chignon, onto my clothes, arms, legs.

Everything is messed: my Bois de Rose Blush Eclat, my faux ruby, my coin and crystal earrings - all smeared and clogged with shit.

Only a life-long devotion to self-control reins me from heaving over my staff.

The bottles have stopped their dance. They'll start again soon and then the final daymare. I know it!

In this terrible lull I take an opportunity to punish my revolting staff. I withdraw from them. This I do by wordlessly closing my eyes to expose the two full crescents of my dark lilac eye shadow, my head trembling with a supposed inner tension, like a spin dryer.

To the horrified bystander the overall appearance is that of a quivering dayglo skull, an effect achieved by my socket-emptying eye shadow and the blaze of harsh fluorescent light striking my high cheek bones.

This morbid very rare sight, together with the certainty of my extreme displeasure, is - I have been told by Max and many others, and which I see for myself now - is truly awesome to behold.

My brief counter-attack is thwarted by the return of the shivering bottles in my head, as expected. Not only do I hear them shiver, I actually see them now, I see them in my head, jostling each other. Even in the safety of my astral condition I relive them - brown little bottles with rubber droppers full of explosive essence.

They're jumping up and down in my head, singing their song, like excitable tots; not so much a song, a mindless chant, glass on glass. All because the bastards have withdrawn their support from me.

Because nothing is going right today.

Because each essence wants to be free to be something else.

Lavender is struggling to be pine needle, pine needle to be pure arsenic! Glenda behaving like Germaine, Timothy like - who? Everyone a traitor to their assigned being. Therefore a traitor to me!

Now - and this is a first even for me - I see the tiny bottles crack open. An earthquake convulses my head and glass and oils are thrown everywhere.

Scent oils are spilling into each other, forming meaningless puddles or streams, of confused essences, dangerous cocktails of undefined emotion and uncontained character which by some black magic I imagine are being worked into my flesh as if I were on the massage table.

These polluted essences are now in my body, in my head, and there they turn into demons: red, barbed monsters that begin to tear away at the thing which means most of all to me, the pages of *Glossy International* which is standing in space next to my heart.

A tornado from my breath sweeps up demons and magazine. And from its pages fly out chain and pearl necklaces, gold sunray pleated skirts, a purple hat steeped in fresh oyster chowder, and so many words, words, words, chains of them, the words of celebrities, the words of beauty, words blurred to railway lines by the spin of the tornado, meaningless words, nonsense, rubbish, word-rubbish, and numberless pictures of teeth and gleaming watches.

In the rush, everything speeded up, nothing matters any more, all is a smudge and a stain, and the tornado collects all this crap into its spiral arms for the final death hug, arms spinning faster round the shredded nucleus of *Glossy International*.

Then in the eye of this storm I see a dark distant object approach to the sound of ribald laughter - Leona Humperdink's laughter - and soon I recognise this "object".

It's me! My disembodied head smeared in, well, I'm not sure: either it's shit or dark lilac eye shadow.

The hallucination ends. My eyelids shoot up like unhooked roller blinds. No more dark lilac.

The people in the office flinch as one.

I scream at unprecedented volume: "WHAT MAD PLACE IS THIS?"

Then I say something but no-one catches it.

When no-one moves I repeat my words as an invocation.

And when all I am met with is the pitying expressions of my disgusting, worthless, filthy, disloyal, bastard cunting staff, I launch to my feet and shriek with all my reserves of accumulated panic:

"GET OUT GET OUT GET OUT."

God, do they beat a hasty retreat. Germaine tries to apologise - "OUT OUT OUT".

Thoughtlessly they leave behind their cups and whatnot on the floor.

In the emptiness I collapse over my desk. My chignon a ruin.

Now I relive those TV screens again flickering behind my spectral horror face, the one that was in the shop window reflection earlier.

*

My heart's beating fast. Astrally, I have left the office and my earthly self and am now drifting in a corridor nearby where staff are milling about after my extraordinary eruption. How animated they look, as I could have imagined they did this morning - *that* morning.

There's nothing like someone else's disaster to renew the spirit. Destroy ninety per cent of the population and the other ten will found a religion and praise the Lord.

It's human nature.

We want others to die so we have something to talk about. If I crack up they all shuffle up a bit - at least that's what they think.

Suddenly I'm in the fashion department, as if by magic.

There's Emma, hand-brushing back her long blonde hair with one hand, petting Strudel with the other.

I should explain that Strudel is a pale blue "stress" cat, designed to comfort the troubled mind, made of nylon or something, and about as alive as Benny - or Leona Humperdink, come to think of it.

If only I could teleport Strudel to me now. Emma holds Strudel up by the scruff and face-to-face says to it: "Who's a little poppet then, you gorgeous lovely little thing, and who likes his bread and jam, and oh you've got such lovely little ear flaps, you furry bundle of fluff and you've got a little button nose that's dry and you're the loveliest sausage that ever was...."

"Oh, Emma," says Vanessa, whose desk faces Emma's, her saucer-eyes full of longing. "When are you going to let me cuddle Strudel?"

"I wish Strudel could purr. Men on the Moon and Strudel can't purr."

"Well it would if you got the batteries – pity the PR firm didn't have the gumption to include the batteries. Why don't you pop down and buy some while I cuddle Strudel."

"Oh I can't. I'm in shock!"

"I *know*. Now what was that all about in Vicki's?"

"Don't ask! I wish I were a cat instead of a fashion journalist. I don't think I can stand the idea of GlossRam after today. I mean, what will there be to do? It's a virtual reality fashion show."

"Make coffee I suppose. No ironing to do. I think it's a bit much that we have not even been invited to a screening of the show - I was quite looking forward to wearing the VR helmet. Very *Flash Gordon*."

"In fact, I don't think I can stand another fashion show. I'm bored witless. Cats just live their lives for a few years, coddled to indecency, and then they get run over. It's a kind of life."

"Oh I *know*," says Vanessa, rounding off a chipped nail with a file. That's one thing I cannot tolerate. Inhaling other people's nail dust! Vanessa's "ohs" are pitched like a randy tom cat's groan. "Give me a cat's life any day of the week - well, not every day. I'm seriously thinking about applying for this job in a vet's."

I see a copy of *Pet's Weekly* on her desk. "They want somebody. I wouldn't want every cat's life. Not since I nearly hoovered up my Tino's tail." She slacks her jaw in self-disgust. "To think of it!"

"Don't! How awful it must have been."

"I threw the hoover away. His tail is still limp and lifeless."

"Not in front of Strudel. Poor baby." Emma presses her lips into Strudel's head fluff.

"I think Vicki could do with Strudel."

"Or even Germaine - no, they're all mad! They'd put Strudel in the microwave or something. It's the sort of thing they'd do."

"Well, I always thought Germaine was bonkers. The way she goes on. She looked awful in conference. That mad mouth of hers - all that lipstick - makes me see dots. End of her editorship plans!"

"And where was Germaine during filming? Freddie Smith was quite cross."

"I can't imagine," says Vanessa.

"It's amazing how cats communicate, isn't it?"

"I always know what Tino is thinking. I've only to look in his eyes...."

"Especially if he has no tail!"

"Oh Emma! Now you've upset me. Now you've got to give me Strudel."

Emma concedes. She passes the pale blue kitty to her supposed superior.

"There, there," coos Vanessa. Her blonde geometric bob needs a trim. "What a little cutie you are, aren't you. And if you're a good boy you'll get a biscuit. And when Emma and I go away to India we're lock you out of harm's way in the cupboard otherwise you won't be safe in this lunatic asylum."

"I couldn't agree more," Emma says piling up colour transparency frames. "To think, we've got Glenda, Timothy, Vicki, Germaine, all on one magazine."

"With Max at the top."

"It's more than our fair share. I've heard a rumour Max Cochrane has disappeared. The man's a maniac. And did you hear what Unity was saying about Vicki - caught her having an epileptic fit a few minutes before conference. Vicki denied it. But I'm sure she had another one just now - dressing it up as her dark lilac routine. The woman's a maniac. I wouldn't be surprised if Max has run off. I'm sure she's cracking-up. We'll have to shove a hair bush between her teeth. I blame Diana Vreeland."

"I blame Helen Gurley Brown. All that oral sex. I mean, it's bound to drive you mad."

"How revolting," says Emma, screwing her face. "And in front of poor Strudel. He's only a cat. I didn't know about Helen Gurley Brown."

"Mm-mm," Vanessa mews on two notes.

"*Cosmo*'s got a lot to answer for. Strudel doesn't know about such things. I don't think I can handle lunch."

"You must. I want to see Valentino's face when you tell him about Vicki."

"Good God, no! He'd tell someone who'd tell his PR who'd tell a Raven's PR who'd tell our ad department who'd tell Roger Masefield who would tell Vicki. Then we'd be in the dog house."

"With Strudel. I suppose you're right. Cats can't tell tales. They see all sorts of curious things as they stretch out on rugs but they don't say a thing. The most loyal of creatures. Did you notice Benny in the wheelbarrow and his straw all over the place - looked as if there had been a fight."

"Fighting off Glenda's advances!"

Both girls emit suppressed hyena sounds.

"It's sick," says Vanessa. "If Vicki had any marbles she would have put Benny in his compost heap a long while ago. It drives you to drink."

"Still, Glenda does lovely spreads."

"That's true."

Pause.

"Vanessa," Emma starts slowly, "do you think we might smuggle Strudel to India to get us through GlossRam?"

"We can't. Vicki would immediately think we're drug smugglers. Remember the time she saw a bit of chalk fall out of that wrap shirt?"

"Oh God, yes. Then Strudel would be ripped to shreds."

In unison: "How awful."

*

In an instant I'm out of the fashion department and in my body in my office. I (earthly I) am in aftershock from my terrible hallucination.

"Vicki, I've made you coffee. Two sugars this time." It's Lee's voice. Lee once trained to be a nurse. I associated her with chamomile when I first met her.

I withdraw my face from a cave of hands, glinting with the rubies, diamonds and emeralds of my Russian rings of gold, spangled now by damp eyes - not tears. I can still see those horrible demons - legacy of a Roman Catholic childhood: I know that.

Of all my breakdowns that had to be the worst because it had an episodic life of its own, its own momentum. Just what I need on a day such as this.

I am actually in my body, reliving every second, unable to stop or alter anything....

It is imperative that I never suffer such an hallucination ever again. My feelings against Max harden.

I study my life-line for a moment (as I did that day – I remember), where it curves round the mount of Venus - which is plump: a sign of an active libido, I'm told - and grooves into my flesh bracelets at the edge of the wrist. It's a long one, my lifeline; I shall make 110 if I'm lucky, if I'm unlucky. But a palmist - not Madame Smith - once told me that 110 is only potential. I dislike the word potential.

"Thank you darling. You can have your lunchtimes back," I say in the hope of more tender loving care from her. I need it more than ever. "You're a treasure, Lee. I suppose you heard everything."

"Difficult not to," she says quickly, neutrally. Her life rests on getting the nuances right. "I thought I'd keep out of the way for a while."

"You're so aware," I say. "What I could do with a few more like you. If only I could phone Max!"

I pick up the Dorset Delft mug with rabbit and duck prints and bring it to my lips. What I like most, even in my despair, is the hot steam first, to savour it almost to the point of a scald, on my upper lip; before the first tentative sip.

Luke warm and the drink is aborted.

I feel my eyes are milky with fatigue.

"There are quite a few messages - " Lee starts.

"I can't talk to anyone right now. Tell them I'm at a fitting or something. Anything. Just keep them away. Have I a lunch?"

"Roger Masefield. I booked the Notre Dame for 1.15pm as you instructed this morning."

"Oh shit. Cancel him for God's sake. Did you tell him about Max and Brightworth?"

"Yes. We met on the thirteenth floor."

"What did he say?"

Lee throws back a dislodged blonde wave with a long head sweep: an elegant move, practised. "He was, um, incredulous and amazed. I think he thought I was having him on."

"At least he knows now. If I know Roger he won't be able to resist sniffing out Brightworth Pier - just in case. He'll do something stupid to flush Max out of his lair and get him back to his duties. Did you have sex?"

"No." Only her lips moved.

"Don't lie Lee."

"We fucked."

"That's more like it. I deeply disapprove but what you do beyond the call of duty is your own business so long as you tell me everything. Roger is a useful fuck, not that I would know, but then I fucked the boss once upon a time." I look hard at Lee - "I *can* trust you, can't I?"

She gives me an almost imperceptible hurt look, nothing too dramatic or I'll detect protest-overkill. In my earthly state I hope I *can't* trust her completely. I hope she's had the sense to double-cross me and tell Max what I asked her to do.

"Princess Leona Humperdink called," she says, reading her pad.

"She or her office?"

"No. She phoned herself and was a bit put out that I wouldn't put her through."

"God, what does she want? Has to be about Imelda Marcos."

"She was phoning from New York."

"She's back there!"

"She didn't leave a number."

"Imelda's. She's staying with her."

"She said she'd get back to you shortly. She said not to call her."

"You know, Lee, if you were to kill me now it would be classified as a mercy killing. Like switching off life-support. You'd be given the George Cross or whatever it is."

"Also Pierre of *Glossy International* France...."

"No. He's being phased out. Be extra sweet and don't return calls to him. He'll soon get the message."

"Also that Madame Smith called twice. First, she asked us to pay the VAT on that £850 we sent her. Then she phoned just now to say she has something to tell you."

Madame Smith! I look up at Lee with hope, a fresh expression doubtless on my face (I wish there was a mirror at this point), Lazarus raised. Curdled optic milkiness skimmed away. "Madame Smith!"

I'd quite forgotten about Madame Smith in all the office trauma.

I say with restored, relative froideur, "Get her on the line. And close the door behind you."

I look at the clock on the wall: it's 12.46pm.

Less than a minute later the phone rings.

"Madame Smith! I'm so relieved, I mean, pleased to hear from you - so...soon. I'm sorry you couldn't get through earlier. I had a hair appointment and it's been a terrible day. I can't begin...."

"Mars in Aquarius," interrupts Madame Smith. "It's the same for all you Pisceans at the moment."

On the phone she sounds 12 years-old yet that time I saw her on the pier six months ago I was certain she must have witnessed every appearance of Halley's Comet since 240 BC. I said so to Max later in those terms and it was he who gave me the year.

"Is it safe to talk?" she asks.

How wise. So knowing of the ways of empires. This so becomes my (let's be honest) spy in Brightworth. Certainly many of the Raven's Towers' phones are bugged and with Max away I shouldn't be surprised if Roger has taken a few extra precautionary measures.

Still, risk is Fate's way of getting things moving.

"Yes...it might be risky," I say changing my mind between thought and next breath. "We can meet very soon?" I ask. "Are you mobile? Could you come to London? I understand you have some, er, information."

"Yeah, your horoscopes."

"Oh, so soon!" I am astonished; deflated.. "We only talked about two or three hours ago. I imagined these things take weeks."

"Nah. I just bung the birthdates into the computer and hey presto! Course, the art is in the interpreting of the charts and for that I like to sit down with the client and mix it with me other clairvoyance like a bit of mediumship, a bit of palmistry - depends on what I get."

I had hoped for a bit of pure and simple espionage. Then another thought occurs to me: I'm not doing anything tonight, Max won't be accessible, a whole evening and no company - and perhaps Madame Smith's horoscopes will shed new light on my present difficulties and the enigma that is my husband.

I believe in keeping an open mind.

"Madame Smith, I absolutely insist you come up to London to give me my reading and talk to me about Max - I mean, Mr Cochrane."

"There's a lot to discuss," she says as a teaser. "And for nothing I'm throwing in a special Romany weather forecast. You'll understand why when I see you. I can tell you now that your problems are very near the end."

The addition of the weather forecast is too much to bear. It feels so right in the circumstances. I could just imagine all my problems being solved by a Romany weather forecast. Sometimes an unthinkable absurdity is the solution to an unthinkable absurdity - such as Max! I could hug Madame Smith. Umberto did his best with the chignon but it wasn't enough for the sheer weight of pressure I have had to endure this morning. I think Madame Smith will be the definitive fixer in my life.

While I await Madame Smith's reports I will be on hold, so to speak, surfing on hope; excused from worrying.

Already I want to shower my seaside guru with goodies.

"Madame Smith, get on the next train. Fly up if you have to. I will pay for whatever lost fees. Stay the night. I'll put you up at Blakes – Anouska's a dear friend - did you ever see her on the telly? Naturally, you must have a suite - and I will pay; and maybe we shall have dinner first at L'Escargot, then we can talk. Is this reasonable?"

There's silence. Perhaps she's stunned by my generosity. Or making a quick mental calculation of "lost fees" plus extra for "the bother" plus VAT and plus a bit more for the Poll Tax.

I can't stand it. I feel desperate. "I'm sure you'd love to look over some items that I would adore giving you in gratitude. A Gucci handbag, a Windsmoor hat...."

"Nah. You don't want a hat in Brightworth with the wind," she says. "But since you're offering, I wouldn't mind a bottle of Elizabeth Taylor's new perfume, what's it called, y'know, Passion, that's what it's called, if you've got one spare."

I lower my eyelids as the ghost of frightful Lily of the Valley hits my nostrils. I develop a sore throat just thinking of Elizabeth Taylor's Passion. "No sooner said than done," I say. "I'll send my car to take you to Blakes when you arrive. Try to wear black if you can. Anouska adores black."

"Sure."

"I'll put you back to my PA Lee who'll sort out your travel and hotel arrangements - OK?"

"K!"

I replace the handset. I was a little uncool. On second thoughts, I should have waited at least until I heard what she foresees before bringing forward her Christmas.

Still, her call has its desired effect. I feel sufficiently renovated to repair staff relations. I feel I can afford a breather from stress.

I tell Lee that the lunch with Roger Masefield is on again. "Tell him I'll be a bit late."

I may as well try to get the measure of the man if he's going to be of any use in my Max campaign.

And I instruct Lee to buy everyone who was present at conference this morning a bottle of champagne - "No magnums darling."

To each bottle I shall attach a general note. "Lee, some very quick dictation before you go out."

She rushes in and I dictate. "To all: 'Darling, what can I say? We all behaved a little out of character this morning. It's in our horoscope I'm sure. Let's put it all behind us and start all over again. *Glossy International* is only brilliant because you - in the personal, collective sense' - underline personal, Lee – 'are brilliant. Love Vicki. Three kisses.' That's it."

I decide to attach personal postscripts to certain staff notes in order to add piquancy to my lunchtime reverie. I'll write them myself in green ink and loop my dots: I read somewhere that creative, emotional people loop their dots. Perhaps it will have a subconscious effect upon their attitude to me. You never know.

To Glenda:

"As always, darling, I adore all your suggestions and I love the wood grain spreads. But I am concerned at the apparent ages of the models in the Old Rose interiors piece. They all look 22, and frankly I can't imagine 22 year-olds bouncing about under an Old Rose quilt unless they're enjoying a dirty weekend at some inn in Arundel. And *Glossy* is not about dirty weekends in Arundel. Do try to remember who our readers are my sweet. As for Timothy's controversial 'house' idea - well, I'm sure you would agree that 'house' is very much the buzzword right now, one of my Nows in every sense, but I agree with you that we must tread cautiously in our interpretation of 'house', which as you will gather is not a domestic dwelling for our purposes but a concept-in-vogue which may well be appliquéd to anything we choose. In a very real sense you are the trustee of 'house'. So please get together with Timothy and by the end of this afternoon submit to me an idea which combines 'house' with house and personal aesthetics. Perhaps a doll's house is the answer, who knows. It must be conceptual and I don't have time now to put into words precisely what this means - perhaps Germaine can help you, now that she has taken it upon herself to lateralise her role on the magazine. I expect resolution today. Please do not go home until you have submitted your proposal with Timothy."

That should do it. What's the time? It's 12.58 pm. I'm running a bit late. Never mind. It will do Roger good.

To Germaine:

"We had better discuss your feature package for November. A pre-natal profile of Jackie O is all very well but who would be your sources and could they sign affidavits? Anything the lawyers could grasp? Of course I realise you are being 'deconstructive' and 'postmodernist' in your approach to the very concept of celebrity, but where's the heart? The warmth? Perhaps you need a holiday. Extra to your entitlement. Let's talk."

To Timothy:

"Well, who's been a naughty boy then. See Glenda for my instructions. Liaise with her. Any more rows and I will hold you personally responsible. I like the 'house' concept and I think we will lose nothing by following close to your original chosen route. Your challenge then is to deal with Glenda. By the way, by 4.30 this afternoon get a bottle of Elizabeth Taylor's Passion to me. More urgent than anything. It's for a friend. PS I have another idea I want to discuss with you for ridding the face of signs of ageing. I'm calling it 'Doing the Gurn-Burn.' Tbd. PPS Do not mention this to Unity!"

*

I switch off my hairdryer and sniff the nozzle: I love the scorched aroma of red-hot coils cooling: a private joy.

On my desk a hinged triptych of mirrors covers every eventuality for the job in hand: to restore my classical ruin to its heyday in ten minutes flat.

The phone rings.

"It's Freddie Smith," says Lee.

"Put him through." Pause. "Freddie!"

"Hello Vicki, how are you today?"

"Change the subject. You want to film me don't you for GlossRam - could we do it tomorrow?"

"Sure. No problem. The staff filming went very well this morning."

"Good," I say, trying to repaint an eyelash. "Were the children good?"

"Eventually. But your features editor disappeared. We've got verboten pre-filming footage though. Crazy incriminating stuff. She's a girl."

"Good. Turn that into a little film and keep it quiet darling. I'll pay you separately for that." I hang up.

I buzz Lee. "Darling, phone my reflexologist Anna. Ask her to come round after lunch, about 3pm."

God, the time. It's nearly 1.15pm. Roger will be half way through the main course if I leave it much longer.

>><<

CHAPTER EIGHT

Video No. 7 >>>

I – astral Vicki - am back in my physical body. Buy one get one free. The car is pulling up outside the Notre Dame. I worry about Lee. I'm hoping, there in the backseat at 1.32pm, April 27, 1988, that she took precautions while bonking Roger.

What on earth do women see in Roger Masefield? I'm thinking these base thoughts as I step out of the Daimler - I still have this urge to suck my chauffeur Stephen's chin for some reason.

I imagine about Roger that there is a certain crude energy, an uninhibited advertisement of need; one of life's seducers who always alerts you to his missing element which it is your assigned role to fill. It's a power-knack. But then there's the gross rest of him.

I'm a little tense as this is our first lunch together, ever. I am only going through with this because of Max. Because Max is not here.

The bastard.

I dive into the Notre Dame - a basement restaurant as deep as any archeological dig I'm sure. I have never much cared for the wall tiles. Make me think of a public latrine. A full house today, so many munchkins - my name for other magazine editors - present. Had I known I would not have come.

"Hi Vicki!"

Scarcely credible. Roger is actually on his feet waving at me as if we were those adulterers in *Brief Encounter*.

The maitre d' bowls him a queeny side-glance.

As a result of Roger's attention-seeking faux pas, more fanfare than usual attends my advance as hands are waved and lips puckered at me. I have to admire my own majestic brevity of movement. Not once does my head swivel. But I allow my eyes to dance with my lips. Faces, both familiar and not, open up like the mouths of a Venus flytrap as the sunlight of my smile blazes on a here, a there, but not an everywhere.

"Roger! You big boy," I welcome. I steel myself for his air kisses about the locale of my blusher. Jackie O and her sister have much to answer for. Perhaps we'll do that pre-natal profile of Jackie after all.

As Roger pulls back from me I am rendered insensate by the sweet heliotrope in his aftershave; and I fall dazed into the Restoration Louis XV reproduction chair, upholstered in deep burgundy damask.

"I'm sorry I'm so late," I say. "I see you've had a starter." I pull at each white gloved finger-tip *à la* Audrey Hepburn who I have decided on a whim is due a comeback, Now-wise. Be certain that this time next week every woman and transvestite in London will be tugging at her hand gloves, white, at table.

"You're never late Vicki. I'm always early because I like to eat."

Chivalry has not died with the duel to be sure. Particularly since he has had no experience of my time-keeping: I'm usually punctual. I look smilingly into his eyes - the only alert feature in a face hewn from coldest lard.

"Order me a glass of champagne darling," I gurgle.

Instead of just getting on with it he practises his viva voce French in the valley of the wine list. A waiter passes - "Darling," I say to the side-burned cutie, "a glass of champagne, now. And then ortolan - for both of us - and a Pouilly-Fumé – you decide which; nothing over three years. Trust me Roger."

I made the mistake a few weeks ago of nominating the Notre Dame as the canteen of the Now in a London newspaper. Hence the munchkins and their acolytes today. As much as we all want to follow fashion, and despite the joy of watching those caught on the trip-wire of its caprice, there is something lamentable about fear-driven obedience. Fashion is a moment, not the Highway Code. All I can smell today is the odour of munchkin fear - the fear of not being noticed, the fear of not being somewhere else.

The waiter soon returns with a flute of fizz.

"Thank you. Quicker than asparagus can be sodden," I say.

"Madame?"

"Never mind, young man."

Roger smiles, a surprisingly attractive one given what it has had to fight through to see the light of day - "I've never heard that expression – 'Asparagus can be...'"

I correct him quickly: "'Quicker than asparagus can be sodden,' Roger. It was one of Augustus' favourite sayings - I think he may have been rather impatient by nature given the necessity of speed in the expression. He wanted everything from the payment of taxes to the rubbing of his back to be done quicker than it took to soak asparagus - preferably a lot sooner. The ancients could teach us a thing or two. Think what public transport could learn from a floppy asparagus, Roger. Quite the Thatcherite was Augustus. He once gouged out a man's eyes with his own hands. Brutal, but at least you knew where you stood."

"Well, well," Roger says chortling. Yes, chortling is the word. Will he have the intelligence to connect the punch line of my asparagus and eye-gouging story with Max? And with his state of mind? Roger must be about thirty-eight. Looks forty-two. Coronary to come at fifty. I see already a pink expanse of pate beneath the thinning sandy thatch.

"I didn't know you were the Roman scholar," he says stupidly, failing to pick up on my gambit. "Or perhaps it's your Italian heritage."

"Neither," I say briskly. "I love dipping into books. Max is the same. When I was young I would pluck a book, any book, from the shelves, open it anywhere and just read a page or two. I am certain I have never read a book in my life. But I can safely say that in all probability I have dipped into every book extant. To read a book from cover to cover is a Dickensian habit, and would make me depressed. I predict that one day all of us will simply skim books. I don't want to be enslaved. It's the same with everything else. If I know I must see a film because everyone says it's a smash, I can't bring myself. For years I have resisted *The French Lieutenant's Woman*. I will alter my evening plans if it's scheduled on the telly. I will actually cross a continent to escape the city where it is advertised. Nothing will induce me to watch it. But the *Andy Warhol Diaries* - I just know I will *love* them when they're released next year! My spies tell me they're designed for skimming and dipping and random surfing. Perfection!"

"Gee, really?" says Roger. That's a very good Andy voice. I've heard that Roger is quite the mimic. He giggles easily, has an easy responsiveness about him, he listens - Max said he listens like a doctor. - I like the measured tread of his native Virginia. Did I mention he's American? I can't recall. Well, he is. I quite like the suggestion of caution in his aura. He's laughing now, a touch of the shoulder shrugs, as if an old engine is chugging away. He's laughing at me, I'm sure.

"Tell me, Vicki, why is Raven's Towers so-called? I never asked Max because I didn't want to seem ignorant."

"Oh Roger! How terrible that you of all people do not know the provenance of Raven's Towers. You must know of course that I deplore the apostrophe in the title, even in its possessive case as a rule, because a secretary left out an apostrophe in the original letterheads. I took the absence of the apostrophe as an omen of good luck - I mean, apostrophes are such piddling things, aren't they? No, I made that up. I just thought at the time that apostrophes messed up the logo. And they do – except of course I am ignored by everyone."

"But why Raven's Towers?"

Single-minded Roger! I tell him the story, the story I've told a thousand times. "It was my suggestion. I picked up a London tourist guide one day and it opened at a section on the Bloody Tower. The tortured and condemned only had the croaking ravens for company. It also said ravens have a mystical power, that's why to this day their wings are clipped at the Tower, so England can remain truly great. Not that I've noticed any difference. It described the bird as black and glossy: I liked that. The marriage of sheen and magic."

"Well, I would never have imagined," says Roger, playing with his glass, to himself. After a staged pause he says, "This must be a tough time for you."

That was painless.

Perhaps the asparagus and eye-gouging gambit was a bit premature.

I was wondering when we would get to the Max Thing.

"Perplexing might be the word Roger. Are you coping?"

Roger leans back to my cross-return question, stretching his spine in a feline way against his chair. "Oh sure. It's just...well." He massages his face and squeezes his eyes. "How many publishing tycoons do you know who just disappear? I mean, is he well?"

"Ah, our ortolans," I say. A timely distraction. "Now don't be frightened Roger. Drink some wine. You hold it by the beak and swallow it, guts, bones and all, after you've bitten its head off." A private joke.

His reaction is one of curiosity, not hoped-for disgust. "And the feathers?"

"They're roasted darling. Optional. No, I'm teasing; you can see they've been plucked."

With consummate skill I take the bird by the beak and...put it back on the plate. I never had any intention of eating it. "I've changed my mind. It's the Armagnac in its lungs used to drown it – don't fancy the taste now. Sometimes, phantom-eating leaves me feeling just as full."

"You don't mind if I eat mine then," he says. It's a rite of passage for Roger who could swallow an ostrich if he put his mind to it. He actually manages to down the ortolan after decapitating the creature with his teeth and just a few perfunctory munches – gourmands usually need a quarter-of-an-hour to chew their way through the body - and then burps.

"Goodness Roger."

"That one got away."

My ortolan strategy has not worked. Roger has risen to this occasion and not lost face to a tricky dead bird. Never underestimate gluttony. We are still equals.

I say, "You're not drinking the wine. It's lovely and smoky."

Roger takes the glass by the stem, sniffs and sips. All his movements are shy at this moment, self-conscious. The hand is too big for the glass yet it is the hand which looks vulnerable. Perhaps the glass will shatter and break his skin. I glimpse his palm. Palms are intimate, closed places, like diaries. I wish I could read palms. Someone out there knows Roger's palm. She'd recognise it even if it were shown to her disembodied.

The first sip and almost at once his lardish features turn buttery, softening as if melting on an inner furnace. Will he liquefy into a puddle before my eyes?

"It's a tremendous pleasure talking one-on-one with you at long last, Vicki."

"Thank you. I only wish the circumstances were a little less confused."

"Nice wine. It's the obvious question. But do you know where Max is?"

He knows I know and I know he knows. But does he know that I know that he knows? (Astrally of course I know that he doesn't - or does he?)

"Darling...." I begin.

"Shareholders get very nervous when CEOs just up and leave."

I concede, "There is bound to be curiosity about Max's whereabouts, certainly."

"He must have said something to you, Vicki. Is he returning?"

I like his straight questions. I am in the dock.

"I am sure he intends to return - I do not know when. What he might have said to me has no bearing on what has happened. I really am as perplexed as you Roger. Did he say nothing to you. You are his deputy."

"Nothing. Except he left a note to say he was going someplace for a rest and that I was to run things."

Roger has moved quite forward, conspiratorially, belly flopped over the table, tie a little askew. He pinches his nose from time to time, a masculine thing to do, and then often looks away as if on the alert for assassins. His soul is male. He was born with his legs apart, both hands clasping knees. A painful birth surely.

"Something has to be done, Vicki."

"I agree."

That surprises him. Does he think me the housewife? He must be allowed to think I am on his side, basically. I cast down my eyes on the glass which both my hands cup as a crystal ball to gesture the imminence of a shared confidence.

"As his wife, you can imagine I feel more than anyone the peculiarities of the present situation. I've tried everything to understand what's going on. Max's absence unsettles us all. Poor Germaine had a breakdown in my office only this morning, for example. It's a test of character, Max's absence; and the unlikeliest people crack-up."

"Is that why Max has gone? He's testing us?"

"I only know that in all the years of our marriage Max has never done anything without reason. In other words, we should not lose faith but we must show our best under pressure."

Roger nods to all this nonsense. "Just between us," he says, "but certain directors who know no better have queried Max's health. We have to talk bottom line - if we can't then it would be unhealthy."

A bold admission. Roger really does have his eye on the crown. Perhaps this has something to do with Max's absence. Too protective and I shall be accused of subjectivity. Too objective and I shall be suspected of complicity - of one sort or another. The trick must be to keep my options open. So Max (and therefore I) will neither benefit nor lose from this conversation.

As I deliberate, my glass suddenly flares with light from a match struck at a nearby table.

"Torch him," I say involuntarily. My imagination on auto-pilot again.

"Sorry?"

"I said...." Why did I say that? "Perhaps you should employ a private detective agency," I add, improvising.

"You would condone that?"

"My first loyalty, ultimately, has to be to the interests of Raven's Towers, Roger. I co-founded Raven's Towers. Were it not for me Raven's Towers would never have happened. It was through me that Max thought of Raven's Towers, even before I gave it its name. *Glossy International* is my invention and template of most of the Towers' core activities. I adore Max as you know. Naturally, whatever you do is your business. I mean, how do you find working with Max?"

For the second time Roger holds my gaze. It's a give-me-time tactic of alarm. Others might um-and-er.

"There is no better," he says cautiously. "He's secretive. Which is good. He has odd habits but he is alpha."

"Odd habits, Roger?"

"Only small things - nothing important - I can't think of any examples off-hand."

"How did he recruit you?"

"Don't you know?"

"If I did I wouldn't be asking. Max and I rarely discuss Raven's Towers' business on the telephone. Of course I know he can be cryptic."

Roger folds both arms on the table: draught-excluders in any other context. He says, "I really have told no one this - except my wife since, er...."

"Yes."

"Well, you know that I was at Condé Nast in New York when he first approached me. He phoned me one day out of the blue. He introduced himself. Said he was in town. Would like to meet me. Had heard great things about me. Thought it was time he put a face to the name. We met at his suite at the Plaza. I was expecting a drink, a few nibbles and a chat about magazine publishing - to see if I was happy with my lot - you know the routine sort of thing. Instead the first thing he asks me is if I'm carrying a tape recorder. I told him that I wasn't in the habit of carrying recording equipment on my person. And then you know what he said? He said: Did I mind if he body-searched me."

"How amusing. And did you allow him?"

"Well…" Roger looks away, half his mouth pegged-up by recalled bewilderment, "yes, I did allow him. I mean, it was a very thorough search. Like at the airport. An intimate body search, if you know what I mean. Arms up, legs apart, pockets thrown out, valuables on the table. And then do you know what he did?"

"You have to tell me Roger."

"He thanked me for coming and wished me a nice day. No drink, no nibbles, no more questions, and no explanations. I was tempted to tell him what I was thinking."

"And what was that Roger?"

"I thought he was nuts. Or something."

I giggle.

"You're taking this very well Vicki."

"I'm married to Max. This is all in confidence, by the way. I've heard *much* worse! And so what did you do next?"

"I thanked him for calling me. And he said have a nice day. And a month, one month later, he calls and offers me the number two at Raven's Towers."

Sounds like Max.

"Did you tell anyone of the body search before Max offered you the job?" I ask.

"No, just my wife. Afterwards I thought it was the Big-I-Am tycoon trying to be the big dick, to humiliate an employee of a rival company for some private revenge. I know you both worked for Condé Nast once. I guessed he took me for a flake and wanted to play a game with me. I was too embarrassed to tell anyone about it. I have never asked Max about that."

"A test, obviously. I suppose he was testing your discretion. Had a paragraph popped up shortly afterwards in *The New York Times* or some such place about Max Cochrane's peculiar mental or sexual kicks he would have known that you were the source and learned in a fairly harmless way that you tittle-tattle and are not fit to be number two of the world's greatest. Well done Roger. Max has sources at Condé Nast, and other places, as you may know."

"You're saying he was prepared to forfeit his reputation to test my discretion? I find that kind of hard to swallow."

I think of l'ortolan – virtually intact in his belly, but headless - and smile indulgently at his surprising innocence. "I don't know precisely why he did what he did, Roger. But what the world thinks of a man like Max is really largely quite an irrelevance. Most people don't believe what they read or hear in the media and what little they believe they tend to forget by the next day's news. And Max is not some politician or TV game host who has to worry about the micro-judgements of sedated sofa-people.

"Max has to know that his workers are *his* workers and his little tests are his way of sifting the wheat from the chaff. It's not logical. He values certain qualities in people that others might miss. You took the body-search quite calmly. Maybe it was that which secured you your job. The average man would have become all uppity and indignant. He likes to surprise people. He likes to be surprised. I hate surprises. It was always a very eccentric thing that the two of us should have married.

"Once, I spied Max approach a secretary waiting for a lift, in the Towers. He went straight up to her - no-one else was around - and said to her apropos nothing: 'Who can we trust, young lady? Who is beyond suspicion? Can you trust your mother? Can I trust you? Come to my office one day if you like, if you can answer my questions.' A perfectly absurd encounter. But he was testing her ability to deal with surprise, not her loyalty. I could tell immediately she would not pass when she raised a bimbo-ish curled forefinger to her nostrils and giggled. She responded in a natural way of course. But that's precisely what Max cannot abide. Normal day-to-day responses. Or noises for that matter. He wants people who deviate, calculate, have a turn of mind to deal with the unexpected. Roger, we could invent a board game here and now on the whys and wherefores of Max Cochrane."

He unfolds his arms and props up a chin. "I have to ask this Vicki - forgive me for asking - but has his disappearance anything to do with any problems, in your marriage?"

"Roger!" That's a very good question. "Let us imagine he returns this afternoon. And let us suppose for argument's sake that there are problems. What would happen then? You would know too much about us. Our marriage is singular in some ways, everyone knows we live separately next door to each other. We talk to each other via the videophone linkup. But then you've heard all this. We know all the gossip - I put half of it into circulation myself! It's our way of dealing with each other. But we have done so for many, many years. We couldn't have stayed together otherwise."

Then something terrible happens. In a velvety move he places his hand on mine. I am shocked - by my response. A cool electric charge shoots up my arm and then plummets into my lap as a hot bolt. There, in my lap, in a flash, I feel something grow, something quite alien, a tremendous surge of pressure that is both in and outside of me, it feels insatiable, feverish, and I long to plunge it in cold water to douse it; I crave to plunge it anywhere for relief before it explodes. I drop my head to see what it is - I relive this so vividly - to see what is in my lap. And there, for a moment, I see - actually rearing out of my dress which has not been designed to withstand such a thing - actually standing from my pelvis as if I were a man myself - I see an erect penis - a see-through penis, a hologram penis.

I shriek and jump. A mousy-shriek, so that only one or two other fellow patrons notice. My heart pounds. Not even Roger can be so well-endowed as to take responsibility for this - not across the table. He half-rises to his feet - "Are you OK Vicki - shall I...?" His fly is at eye-level and I see the unmistakable pipe-bulge of an erection, almost up to his belt, but safely leashed by his grey pressed flannel. "No, I'm fine Roger, Please sit down."

"Are you sure Vicki? Have some water. What alarmed you like that?" He pours the aqua-minerale. I'm certain of it: his brazen sexuality psychically infected me for a moment, so much so, I instantly connected with his feelings when he touched me. I think it was a libidinous telepathy - my awful imagination again - a libidinous telepathic transference to me of his own mental picture of his over-active phallus.

Roger gently rubs my arm, I'm sure I don't care for him at all, but I see now the attraction. He physically takes control of you, he assumes a fleshly dialogue, and the sheer size of him - it's different-ness. Is that a word?

"I think the ortolan came to life inside me," I say smiling. "I swear I felt a fluttering in my tummy."

"But you didn't eat it, Vicki. There's, it's on your plate."

"Oh, yes...."

"Basically you're under pressure yourself," he says. "You're amazing. You never let the side down. You come to work looking a million dollars. Not once in all the time I've admired you from afar have you ever looked anything less than the global fashion icon that you are. You cherish the company - and Max. You're carrying an incredible load Vicki - I just want you to know that as Max's deputy, I know, this company would collapse without you - but see me as a friend as well. I also need support. That's an aggressive board we've got, and they want answers. I don't have all the answers. I'm alone myself in this - trying to assuage expected City concerns, shareholders, snooping financial editors. Even staff on the floor are murmuring. If we act together we can keep them at bay and Max can sort himself out."

His pink napkin has noosed an index finger. He is the little boy again in a fix. Or a CEO deputy consolidating a perceived advantage over fragile Caesar's wife. Ha!

"You have my total support Roger. If needs be I would nominate you as chief executive - I would support such a move. I am your friend too."

*

Roger's chauffeur has arrived to collect. I agree to return in his car. I don't want to upset Stephen but I should make a show of my new alliance. Behind the black glass Roger rests his large head of my shoulder.

"You're a horror," I say, with Lee in mind if not on tongue.

"I love that scent."

"Chanel No.19."

"It's a turn-on."

"Roger – I'm an old woman."

"I hadn't noticed." He stokes my neck with his lips.

"Velvety - your lips. Yes, you're quite velvety. The only feminine thing about you Roger."

He raises the arm rest.

"Roger, if this goes further, if you tell anyone, I'll find out the address of your mother in Virginia and have nuisance calls made to her morning, noon and night. I'll have her told that you consort with male prostitutes."

"I'm an orphan."

He unbuckles himself at great speed and drops his pants - a parachute on the basis of quantity of fabric. I had hoped to be saved this embarrassment on the astral video!

But to be entirely honest, in the car, I have only one interest. I am curious to see if his cock looks like the one which teleported into my pubic region - the hologram cock, I mean - I need to know, to know whether there was a true sympathy between us at that moment. If it is not the same then it was just my imagination, prompted by a freak moment of transferred lust - his. If it is his...then, perhaps I can trust Roger.

I know this may not make sense but life is not logical. We all have our little superstitions.

Which brings me back to Roger's cock which is in my hand and I'm studying it as we're shunted about down the Strand. I'd forgotten how hot cocks are. The trouble with cocks is that they need no nurturing. They are all nature, no matter how nurtured the male owner is in modern times.

Off-puttingly Roger tells me that he has no diseases, that he has to do this, has been meaning to for a long while; he'll be very quick but we'll have the chance to do it properly on another occasion. He says.

I am disappointed. Very disappointed. It is not the cock I saw in my lap. It does not have the freckle where I remember it. Roger is not mine. The cock I saw was, I deduce rapidly, just a phallic exemplar brought to life in my head by some mysterious excitable energy in Roger. It was not a sympathetic mental transference.

"Roger, no, get off! I've changed my mind, stop it!"

"Oh please, I've got to, ten seconds - OW!"

I have just embedded my thumb and forefinger in the dough of his fleshy bum and given him an empurpling pinch.

"Now pull up your trousers," I instruct, suddenly all headmistress-y. "Perhaps another time, not now. We're near Raven's Towers and it would do neither of us any good to emerge from the car all dishevelled."

"Darned women..." he growls under his breath. But I hear him, the filthy fat scrote, as Germaine might say.

*

How depressed I am as I march out of the lift after the tumble in the car. Not so much depressed - depression after all is an illness that's accompanied by appetite loss and the like; and I must not exaggerate my mood. But certainly I feel low because I know in my heart that Roger is simply not clever enough to do something to flush Max out of Brightworth.

The hologram cock fiasco was just psychic confirmation.

I was never quite certain what I expected Roger to do about the Max Thing, the Max problem, but whatever it was, Roger ain't my modus operandi. I think "ain't" should become one of my Now-words after years as the buzzword of illiterates.

Every business lunch covers its cost in its post-mortem - in my experience. So I now consider. How dare Roger say or imply to my face that Max is nuts! I'm Max's wife after all. How dare Roger tell me of how Max recruited him! What do I care about corporate body-searches at the Plaza – God knows what Ivana will do to the place now she's running it. More to the point, how can Roger be so certain that I am not a party to a Max conspiracy to unsettle Roger?

The issue is not whether I am such a party, but that Roger appears to have ruled it out in his calculations.

This is not a wise omission. It is not theoretically wise - leaving aside the facts. Hypothetical wisdom is a significant guide to nous. Much of life is pre-ordained in mental rehearsals. Anyone condemned to work with other people knows this without saying.

Roger has failed to allow for the possibility that I maybe as treacherous as any of one of the others - including himself - at Raven's Towers. Whatever the outcome of this saga I will insist Roger be removed on the grounds of political ineptitude.

In any case, he failed to tell me what I had told Lee to tell him, of Max's whereabouts. How untrustworthy is that! Had he told me he knew of Brightworth Pier I would now be his friend. His career is effectively over.

It is now left to me to find a solution to the Max Thing. I will have to be decisive. I will have to act fast. I will have to devise a plan which physically forces Max off that fucking pier and back to Raven's Towers.

But what am I to do? Why is it always I who has to find the answers.

I'm in a terrible mood now as I ingress the corridor which will funnel me to my office. I notice that hardly anyone is back from lunch and it's 3.32pm! I have half a mind to take back the bottles of champagne Lee has distributed on my instruction.

Fortunately I know how to resist every daft or loony impulse deriving from tipsiness.

Germaine!

We almost bump into each other as I pass her office space. She looks quite awful: crazy black mane alive at the mains. I throw my head forward with slighting contempt - as near to giving notice of a non-verbal sacking as is possible within the petty restrictions of employment law.

If she doesn't get the message I will roast her slowly on a spit. I'll have the plumbers - the Raven's Towers' utility task force, as Max calls them - disconnect her phone to start with. Then I'll ignore her memos, re-commission writers, query expenses - all the usual tricks.

*

In my office a pleasant surprise awaits My reflexologist Anna is waiting for me.

"You're late!" she barks at me.

"Darling," I say, "....". No, it's hopeless; I can't lie to Anna. "Darling I forgot all about you."

Anna's had a hard life what with one thing and another and she takes my confession with the pinch of salt she always declines as a vigilant nutritionist.

"Your secretary has been most charming, Vicki. I suppose you've been eating something from the microwave."

"Darling, I nearly ate a roasted ortolan drowned in Armagnac but thought better of it. Poor tweetybirds."

"Shocking!"

Anna's so thin it's a wonder she doubles as a nutritionist. She looks like a malnutritionist. Her hair is lifeless and dark, her face pale and grim, her cuticles all over the place - but then she is a reflexologist.

"Take your shoes and tights off," she orders.

I lie on my office blue Howard 11 sofa where a few of my disloyal staff were seated before lunch.

With not so much as an apology she drives her rivet-hard thumbs into my soles in the task of stimulating a high percentage of the 72,000 nerve endings in my feet which are connected to various parts of the rest of me, apparently.

"It's painful because of the build-up of uric crystals, and do stop squirming," she says. "Oh, I can feel them now," she relishes. "It's like popping bubble-wrap!"

"Oh please Anna, I can't bear it. It's so painful."

But she is deaf to my ows and arghs.

"If you took the nutritional supplements I give you and lived your life sensibly and actually slept once in a while - are you listening Vicki? - these sessions would be a joy. But no, you want to suffer, so suffer you will!"

And with that she drives her thumbs deeper into the pads of my big toe with a navvy's spite. How I howl. The Baskervilles have heard nothing yet.

"Oh Anna, Anna - I love it!"

Thank goodness for Anna. Someone to take control of me for a while. Umberto, Franca, Madame Smith, even Max in his time – they're all there to give me a rest from me.

"Your thyroid reflex is a disgrace," shouts Anna. She sniffs when she is in torment so that I imagine many of her patients must wonder about their personal hygiene.

"You have so many crystalline deposits of uric acid and excess calcium beneath your skin - Vicki! Pay attention – it's no wonder it's agony. Let's face facts, Vicki. You're no spring chicken anymore."

Dear Anna. She is one of the few individuals granted licence to speak frankly. Umberto may flatter me, and Madame Smith may yet tell me what I want to hear, but Anna can tell me to my face - or feet, in this instance - that I am no spring chicken (or ortolan chick for that matter). Somebody must be free to tell me the truth. Not even a modern mind can know it all. All I know is, when I succumb to discomfort the results are longer-lasting.

"Ouch, oh! No Anna, you've gone too far."

My big toe is not mine any more but in Anna's custody.

Then she tells me that the nerve endings in the big toes correspond to brain function. Remove the uric crystals from the big toes and somehow my brain will perform better.

And, it's funny, but the moment Anna says this I do feel my head clearing.

The mental windows are flung open, the stale air is dispersed and fresh thoughts fly in.

I play with the thought that Max and Roger are acting in concert, all part of a plot to get at me; anything is possible after Max's terrible words to me before he left. But no, I sensibly dismiss that suspicion.

One thing is for sure: any theory I formulate to explain Max's conduct will be wrong by virtue of its being thought. Max cannot be "read" in any normal way. That much I know after forty years of marriage.

Anna finishes her work by rubbing and talcing her hands in a towel. I lie back on the sofa, almost cooing.

My feet throb with joyous freedom.

My feet feel as if I have gambolled over beach pebbles. Ah, beach pebbles, beaches - Brightworth.

Anna's work draws my mind to the coast and to Max's Brightworth Pier in particular.

Out of this foot-throb a distant, shimmering mirage, a devilish thought, limbo-dances into view, into my mind.

The more I think of Max's beach the more I see it as enemy territory ripe for invasion.

If I cannot think of a way of getting Max back to Raven's Towers, then I shall unleash Raven's Towers on Brightworth. A full-scale artillery launch with *Glossy International*'s elite marine corps.

Sent pronto!

I think of Glenda and Timothy, my twin tortures of this morning

(Germaine is another matter). I shall punish them for upsetting me by sending them to Brightworth and they in turn will somehow be my unwitting instruments of punishment of Max as he attempts to snooze his way out of my life in his poxy pier chalet.

It's all too perfect! I have never felt more excited. All I have to do is think up some pretext to send the two of them down to the south coast. Some editorial pretext.

"I've done what I can for you," says Anna, smothering her hands in more talc. Her words have broken me from my seaside plotting.

"Which is always your best, darling," I purr. "Lee, be a sweetheart and show Anna out and then book me brunch for the day after tomorrow at the Hors d'Oeuvrerie at the World Trade Center. There's a duck. I've suddenly got a taste for their spring rolls. Can you explain that Anna?"

She tut-tuts. "No nutritional value. None whatsoever."

>><<

CHAPTER NINE

Video No. 8: "Germaine" >>>

Something odd is happening. The phantom taste of Big Apple spring rolls has barely left my tongue, and I've just put the next video on; and I now sense I am in Germaine's head - the way I was in Max's head before (and in my own, but astrally – you know what I mean).

I have just seen myself - Vicki - pass Germaine by in the corridor from lunch: this is all around 3.30pm.

"Fucking pissed old cow," she (Germaine) whispers to herself at the sight of me (earthly Vicki), as I (earthly Vicki) sneer at her (Germaine) more nastily than I (earthly Vicki) intended. I (astral Vicki) won't over-explain lest confusion breaks out.

I hear Germaine's terrible thoughts, and can think my own, but cannot control or switch off either. Is this not the true experience of hell?

From her allocated office space, Germaine strides to one of the express lifts, presses the button for the top floor, and up we go. Whoosh!

At the top she then presses for the first floor - and down we plummet 1600 feet per minute – Max once gave me the figure.

My God! Belly tickles!

The belly-thrill of falling.

I feel sexy - Germaine feels sexy - we all know how she likes to screw on high places: I'm even picking up her crude speech.

I feel such a longing between my legs, all because I'm falling, falling. It's like accelerating up bridges and hills for that delirious past-the-brow descent; a va va voom in my womb - death by tickling - ecstasy in otherwise life's last throe; what a way to go.

The lift soars again like a NASA rocket from the ground and I throw my head back to float in the dizzy vacuum of blood-drain before consciousness may sweep me back to earth. I am an astronaut breaking out of earth's orbit. Breaking out of Vicki Cochrane's orbit.

Vicki Cochrane fascist cunt.

The lift offers a simulation of the pleasure-death experience, Germaine's last fling at Raven's Towers. Typically, she's playing it safe. She is the feral child in the jungle who has escaped the lions – by joining safari package holiday-makers.

She is the outsider to the intimate villainy of the group.

She exits the lift at *Glossy International* to collect her things. She's thinking: "No point hanging around here waiting for the bitch to strike. She passed me by and ignored me in the corridor. She was drunk.

Sozzled."

Germaine gazes at the panel of *Glossy* cover pictures on a wall, a showcase of the pastiches of the pastiches of yesteryear. Of bold new looks and pouty-pouty, hat tricks and shiny hair. Lying mirrors for womanly readers, model dreams for self-reproach.

"Stop smiling you stupid bitches," Germaine screams. She tears at them with her nails. Not one is left stuck on the wall. "Goodbye styles to die for, goodbye white teeth. Ugly."

Fragments of cheek, eye and teeth litter the carpet. She's panting and giggling. "They're all out to lunch. They'll have something to talk about when they return."

She picks up the bottle of champagne left her from me and, in a violent lunge, throws it into a computer screen - "Here's looking at you, kid." Glass and liquid blur together in a waste of hissing bubbles.

She wants to sing and drive and fuck some old scrote on a pier. "Yeah, that's what I'll do. I'll go see old Max at Brightworth. Nothing to lose. I'll tell him all about his slag wife and his slag company."

>><<

I've broken out of Germaine. I'm in my white waiting room. She's deranged. So! She wasn't having an affair with Max at this moment. I sensed no intimacy with him in her. I was wrong. How bizarre that she would wish to go to Brightworth. Just like that, on a whim. I think she plans to seduce Max.

OK, so: if I hadn't told Lee to tell Roger about Max and if I hadn't told Freddie Smith to film my staff and Germaine in particular, Germaine wouldn't have run away to the thirteenth floor just in time to overhear Lee and Roger gossiping and thereby learn of Max's whereabouts.

I get it, it's all my fault!
Blame me!
Quick, **Video No.9: "Germaine & Glenda & Timothy & Leona Humperdink"** *>>*

CHAPTER TEN

"Are we *quite* ready?" It's me talking to Lee in my office. I've called her in for dictation. My reflexologist Anna has this minute left just as Timothy delivered the bottle of Elizabeth Taylor's Passion for Madame Smith. He held it as far from his nose as arm length permitted, as if entrusted with a stinking baby's nappy, in a melodramatic if explicable attempt at distancing from celebrity merchandise. "Miss Taylor's latest production," he said primly, placing the lavender and gold art deco packaging on my desk. I noted his self-restraint. He'll need it for what's to come.

"Lee!"

I hope the sharp edge in my voice will act as a scratch and alleviate Lee's back-itch. I presume it's a back-itch. She has been surreptitiously rubbing her back against the side of her chair for a good twenty seconds and not paying exclusive attention to me.

Then I change my mind. "Do you know Lee, I fancy a hot chocolate."

"With choccy-chip biscuits?" she asks, smiling.

She knows me so well.

"I think, after all, Lee, I won't dictate memos to Glenda and Timothy but write them myself. There's something more imperative about long-hand I always think. I think I'll use green ink."

Lee giggles.

"No, my red pen," I say. "I'm in a red mood."

"Dear Tim - no." I pick up the phone. "Sorry Lee. I've changed my mind again. Will you tell Glenda and Timothy I want to see them immediately. Tell them to come together. It's urgent."

I remove my rings and pour a blob of moisturiser onto my hands. They slide in and out of each other, in lubricated matrimony, a whiff of peach, summery, blossom, skylarks. Against any normal practice I have decided that I, personally, will make the travel arrangements for Glenda and Timothy.

First class British Rail to Brightworth.

Well, they may as well enjoy the trip. I want as few people as possible to know of this project. On this occasion I don't want Max tipped off by Lee that *Glossy International* is about to re-launch Brightworth!

I want him to suffer and then come running back.

"Ah, darlings," I say at the sight of them in the doorway. "Come in. Close the door."

Normally I wouldn't have Glenda and Timothy in at the same

time, except conference-time, because of their conflicting essences. Lavender and pine needle normally tear me apart together.

But today is exceptional, and so I must be exceptional. I am emboldened by a wonderful idea. And inspired by Anna's footwork; even Umberto's chignon is rallying at long last. And there's Madame Smith later.

I am invincible.

I say, "Now I want to know whether we are any closer to resolving our 'house' idea. I trust we have been talking to each other."

Timothy pulls at one of his wing collars. I do wish he would properly wash his shirts once in a while. And have his clothes ever felt the smooth edge of an iron? "We think we have the perfect solution, Vicki," he says pompously. "But allow me not to trespass on Glenda's territory."

Glenda smiles sweetly and starts as a sweetener: "Thank you for the champagne Vicki. It was a lovely thought."

"Don't think of it darling."

"Well, what we thought," she says squirming in her poncho, glancing at Timothy, "is a...doll's house."

"A *doll's* house?"

"We thought," interjects Timothy, "that we would make-up a doll's house, its hinged façade opened ajar so that one can see within, all the rooms - juxtaposing girlhood and the demands of womanhood and the Now-ness of the house concept within the ironic framework of the doll's house."

I give them the briefest of my dark lilacs. Best to soften them up for what is to come. "No! I will not have a doll's house in *Glossy International*. The very idea! Where would we get a suitable doll's house? Frankly darlings I'm disappointed. You are both award-winning stylists yet the simple task of conceptualising the house theme is beyond you. And don't look like that Timothy. A doll's house!"

"I thought it was quite witty," says Glenda, quivering perceptibly. Then in a bold rush at me she says, "May I say it was you who suggested the doll's house. In your memo before lunch."

I am furious at her audacity and memory. "That was then and this is now. I don't expect one of my throw-away suggestions to be thrown back in my face, Glenda. A doll's house! There's too much postmodernism about. Too much wittiness! What I want is some straight-talking." I soften my temper: "And, darlings, I have the perfect solution."

Both sets of eyes widen in a reflex of impertinence. True, I rarely have ideas - why originate when you pay a staff to do so? - but thanks to my reflexologist....

Lee enters with my hot drink. "Do you want anything?" I ask Glenda and Timothy. Both shake their heads in unison. They don't want to prolong their agony.

I continue: "I have this wonderful idea which I think very neatly unites your departments on this controversial 'house' idea - under a new project! For heaven's sake, Timothy, stop pulling at your hair. It's a nervous condition. What's it called now, trick or treat or something...?"

"Trichotillomania," he says to me in a premeditatedly slow unfurling of each syllable, as if English is not my first language, which in fact it isn't.

"Yes! You really should see a therapist, Timothy. Now this idea of mine. I am going to start a new series in the magazine. It will be called Eyesores."

"Eye what?" asks Glenda.

"Sores," barks Timothy.

"Eyesores! Eyesores!" I shout. "Do listen Glenda. Your problem is you never really listen. That's why you live in a permanent state of surprise because you don't follow what's going on around you."

Then I address them both firmly: "You two will work together on the Eyesores project. There will be foreign travel. This will be a high profile, controversial assault on...eyesores. The eyesores of the world. Glenda, name me an eyesore."

She drops her lower lip. "I don't know what you mean Vicki. What sort of eyesores are you thinking of?"

"Perfectly and utterly hopeless," I say banging my desk with the flat of my hand. "Let's get Benny in and ask him about eyesores."

At this point Glenda actually starts to get to her feet.

"Sit down you fool," I shout. "Now you're making me cross. Timothy! An eyesore. Name one."

He places a forefinger to his mouth in mock-thought and then crosses his eyes. "Why Vicki," he says, all nelly and mince, "Raven's Towers."

I decide to laugh. Wit is all about timing and Timothy has timing. "There, jest you may," I say generously, "but it is quite conceivable that some people would think Raven's Towers an eyesore. By eyesores, Glenda, I mean famous edifices, famous buildings, which could do with a major retouching job. We will publish before and after pictures. And I don't mean retouching pictures in the art department. This is field work. I mean *Glossy International* will beautify the actual structures according to our stringent aesthetics."

"Oh Vicki," cries Glenda, "Will this involve heights?"

"Don't be so ridiculous." I am brutal. "Do you think we could afford the premium on insuring you? You can stay earthbound while Timothy does the climbing! Now let's think of some examples. We could beautify a pyramid for instance, I'm sure the Egyptian Tourist Board would welcome the publicity, and I have a particular loathing for the Eiffel Tower - put a good coat on it, that's what I say. It looks so cold loitering about in the centre of Paris."

"How would we put a coat on the Eiffel Tower?" asks Glenda.

"Ask one more stupid question like that Glenda and I'll have you and your Benny thrown out! You know I'm capable of anything. The Eiffel Tower's coat is your problem. It should suffice that I think up these ideas."

"What I should like to do with the Trump Tower," says Timothy, absorbed in some plan of private vengeance, catching my drift as he always does.

"That's it," I say. "The Trump Tower is one of the worst eyesores of the western world. All that black stone and smoked glass. White-wash it! And Buckingham Palace could do with a good sand-blasting. It's filthy."

Timothy is all vervy and animated now. I've won him over. "Buckingham Palace, let's do it Vicki. Those dull Hanoverians could do with a sprucing-up."

"Buckingham Palace certainly is in my mind, Timothy. But first, darlings, for the eyesore treatment, the first in the series, I want something a lot more challenging. And the thing I have in mind is perhaps not one either of you would have guessed at. It is the Brightworth Pier."

Both sets of eyes glance off me into two of the four top corners of my office. "Is she mad?" they are thinking.

"What exactly is the Brightworth Pier, Vicki? Does it fulfil your criteria of famous edifice?" Timothy has deepened his voice in mockery.

"Now don't be like that Timothy," I say lightly. "The Brightworth Pier is a valuable contributor to the nation's coffers in terms of tourism, fishing etc. And readers expect something down-to-earth from time to time to make them feel cosy and secure. Admittedly the town of Brightworth is not exactly Versailles. It's really a very big hospice which sells ice cream and boasts a famous Romany clairvoyante. But the reader letters I have had complaining about the Brightworth Pier eyesore! Indeed I freely confess that it was the Brightworth Pier which sired the Eyesores idea. The Brightworth Pier is a metaphor for Britain, a rusty appendix locked in the past, barnacled, weedy and rotten. *Glossy International* proposes to change all that. We will give it a good Thatcherite make-over, something grand-spanking, so that when we are done, it resembles something that wants to be taken seriously and be privatised."

"Ahem," begins Glenda. She is the only person I know who ahems. "But what has this to do with the 'house' idea, Vicki?"

That's a good question. I had forgotten about that.

"I was coming to that Glenda, if you don't mind me catching my breath. Since it is I who must do everyone else's job these days! For the Brightworth Pier, think of something, er, housy. Take some domestic, um, something, and put it on the pier. Yes, that's it. Somehow the finished result must say something about the British house. I want a satirical element. We beautify but we mock the thing beautified. A little. We mustn't be too clever. Most of all, think of spectacle; think of an image which will capture the nation's imagination. I have made contact with the mayoress of Brightworth, someone called Elsie something or other, and I am arranging your travel and accommodation. Old Elsie is more than happy to open her arms to some considerable above-the-line - or is it below? - promotion of Brightworth. Timothy, make sure she agrees that Brightworth Council shoulders some of the costs - all if possible – we're doing them the favour.

"You have only this afternoon to make arrangements and book photographers. Shake that pier up. Hire workmen. Wake it up with hammers, drills, anything. Blow it up if necessary. Just do it! You go early tomorrow morning, sharp. Make the pier feminine if you wish. Just make sure it looks like nothing we've seen before. Go mad. I have taped this conversation just in case I have to fire you and you try to sue me for unfair dismissal. This is a water-tight order. I suggest you both apply for jobs elsewhere if you don't feel up to delivering the goods. And talk to no-one here about it! This project is hush-hush!"

*

I doodle a valentine heart at the bottom of a memo. I hear a voice - "Vicki."

I look up. It's Roger and his head, seemingly caught in the vice of door and frame.

"Darling. Quite recovered from l'ortolan, we hope."

"A wonderful lunch." His fat face is a swathe of wide smile. He shuts the door. "Thought I'd let you know private dick is on parade," he whispers.

"Private dick darling?"

"The detective agency. They should find Max."

As I thought, Roger is an idiot. Does he seriously imagine that we are not both involved in a charade? This is another demerit against Roger for his failure to arrive at a useful strategy via fateful intuition. Thank God I have Glenda and Timothy on the Max case.

"Oh, yes," I say heavily. "Where will it start? Max quite likes Snowdonia for walking trips. Perhaps he's stuck in some air-conditioned yurt on the side of Moel Hebog – there, I have a head for place names."

"That's interesting. We'll start there then." He cocks his head over my desk. "Mm, red ink. Sign of madness, they say."

"That's green. Letters in green ink are always written by the demented. Or the demented always select green. By the way, we are going to have to terminate Germaine. Lee tells me she went berserk in her office and caused much damage. A computer was completely destroyed with a champagne bottle."

"Why would she do that?"

"Drunk? Or she can't cope with any kind of pressure. Max's absence has compelled me to be more exacting than usual. Standards must not slip just because the man at the top goes AWOL. This is what happens when one irresponsibly derogates. Look at this, I can't use it."

"What is it?"

"A piece Germaine commissioned on adult magazines. Hopeless."

It is in fact Unity May's October copy on supper-party soups.

"Do you read adult magazines Roger?" I raise a choccy-chip biscuit to my mouth. I twinkle.

"I have the odd browse - funny question."

"Men wank over them - don't they darling?"

"Er..."

I bite into the biscuit. "Do you wank Roger?" Crumbs pitter-patter onto Unity's Pumpkin Soup in a Pumpkin recipe.

"I don't have to!" he explodes with a laugh.

Indeed not. It's rumoured half the brats in the Raven's Towers' crèche are his, and their mothers well hoisted up the career ladder. But then the corporate stud servicing a staff seraglio is not a new thing.

"By the way," says Roger, "I have just had a look at the GlossRam fashion show on one of those virtual reality helmets."

"What!" I am furious. "Why have I not been invited to see it? Naturally I am only the editor."

"I'll take you up there now if you like - have you ten minutes?"

I'm on my feet before he has finished. "We'll have to be quick," I say. "What's the time? - five past five. I must leave early today."

We make for the studio on the twenty-eighth floor.

As we stand in the lift I notice that what I took to be Roger's erection bulge in the Notre Dame is nothing more than a starched fold in his trousers, lending the effect of all-day priapism. I giggle. He asks why I giggle. I say it's nothing.

In the studio I feel a little nervous as we put on the 3-D virtual reality helmets - thank goodness my hair is slicked back: Umberto's prescience.

The moment the headgear is on I am transplanted to a perfect world of dayglo and angularity. Here I know nothing can go wrong because everything is programmed. No sneezes in the audience, no shadows under models' eyes, no chest-blushing or bustling photographers.

A world of perfected Nows.

3-D cartoon models swagger up and down the runway at natural speed with all the high-stepping, horse-like affectation. How much better Versace's black and white chiffon shirt looks in this world.

By moving the joystick about, or whatever it is called, I'm on the runway one moment, examining the clothes; the next, in an audience of affectionate caricatures of our international society guests who will be at the Jaipur premiere - a little joke of ours to encourage the darlings.

There's Ivana, looking so much younger than she ever did; and do I spot Lady Ina? With her boas?

At last one is liberated from the unpunctuality of the collections and sitting about waiting and having to tolerate personal space transgressions. This will take the power away from the over-empowered couture designers - who do they think they are?

In another programme we escape the restrictive runway, and relocate the clothes outdoors minus the models - a Ralph Lauren tuxedo wrap dress is seen riding a virtual reality horse and a Lagerfeld leather ankle boots climbing a virtual reality ladder: I insisted we show what the clothes look like in different disembodied situations.

A Lagerfeld on a ladder looks so different from a Lagerfeld on the runway. Clothes really do have a life of their own.

The *pièce de résistance* is a runway show starring those society queen, or rather their VR caricatures - in their favourite designers! I am confident that none of them will suffer a crisis of personal deficiency as they spectate at idealised versions of themselves; such is the thoroughness of plastic surgery and psychoanalysis these days. Everyone here stands straight and tall, no bent bones or misaimed lipstick bleeding up philtrum fine lines; everyone aged 35-looking. If only one could live in this vivid place all the time - so clean, so designed.

No, that's silly. Where would Fate find a place? We'd die of boredom.

I can see that.

And I do begin to develop a headache - perhaps because of the bright vividness. I take off the helmet. Roger has already taken off his, and I catch his eyes dart up from a furtive feasting on my legs.

"Stunning," he says.

"Thank you, Roger. It is better than I could have hoped. I didn't realise how simple it all is."

"An inspirational idea, this virtual reality fashion show. You're a genius."

"If only Max were here to see it. I did grow so bored of seeing actual models on the runways - they earn so much, and many of them think they are more important than the clothes. And there is no such thing as the perfect body. This VR machine solves the problem. At least the models in the machine won't be going out with pop stars and having catfights over damned actors.

"Fashion is a church of sorts and it suffers if it collides with what some people call real-life. Even when I was young I thought that models were the fundamental flaw in haute couture - there was always this danger they would manifest signs of life up there on the runway, or off it, and in the process occlude the point of fashion, which is that it is a dream. I was furious when Jerry took off with Mick. Now, when one sees her, one only thinks of him, not the clothes. This machine is a wonder, a miracle!"

"So making models unemployed is your inspiration!" Roger says, chuckling, jesting, in the wrong sort of way.

"That, and Princess Leona Humperdink," I chuckle.

"Did she give you the idea?"

Roger's stupidity amazes me.

"Indirectly," I jest.

Perhaps I'm too optimistic in supposing that the acting chief executive of Raven's Towers would or would not know whether Princess Leona Humperdink is high society's little joke on the world.

"You do realise," I add, improvising, "that Leona is only a ventriloquist puppet."

Suddenly Roger is nodding his head with some ferocity. Did he really think Leona an actual person? His over-nodding suggests he hasn't a clue. The sap.

"Surely you know that Leona is operated by that silly alternative comedian P.B. Jones," I say matter-of-factly. "Mr Jones was discovered on some talent show on cable TV - you must know this! - *Vanity Fair* did the story the other month - yes, Jones came on stage with this rather clever satirical parody of a New Yorker social queen. He - or rather she -

was a wow, as they say. Quite the phenomenon. Leona's a three foot hand-puppet: she has the silky blonde hair softly waved, the sharp chiselled features and Michael Jackson nose, the skeletal shoulders - slightly bowed - and the dress by Valentino. And Jones' arm up her bottom!"

Roger roars at that. He's at Raven's Towers and knows nothing of his subject-matter. He's having visions of Miss Piggy already. Where's the quality control?

"Jones does the social queen voice brilliantly - all rush and squeal," I ramble on. "You can't see his lips move. In fact he does it so well that the real-life social queens started inviting him and Leona to their charity soirées for a giggle - to show off how hip and broad-minded they are. Indeed these days not to play along with Leona amounts to a faux pas. I always say the sincerest form of flattery is taking the piss - something those alternatives know a thing or two about.

"And before you knew it Leona could be seen at La Côte Basque moaning along with rich men's wives and vacationing with them in Aspen. Of course there are rules. You only talk to Leona, not Jones. God forbid you should talk to Jones! That would show you don't understand alternative comedy, or society for that matter. It is odd. She really is sort of evolving into a society gal in her own right. Leona gets all the society gossip. People confide in this doll. Fashion is a total fascism, Roger - you don't question it till it has moved out."

I put down the VR helmet on the studio console, dizzy with my bullshit. "But that's fashion," I say resignedly, shrugging my shoulders. "Leona's day will come when she stales." Am I staling? I suddenly wonder to myself. "But for now Leona owns the moment and she will be at our fashion show - minus Imelda, I pray!"

Dear Roger. He is shaking his buffalo head, grinning to himself - he looks so much younger when he smiles like that, lop-sided.

Finally he levels with me and says in an all-too-brief moment of mental clarity, "You're having me on, Vicki."

I give him one of my wordless Mona Lisa smiles and say, "Maybe I am, Roger. Maybe I'm not."

>><<

CHAPTER ELEVEN

Video No.10: >>>

What a farce. While I'm wasting time talking to Roger, having dispatched Timothy and Glenda to Brightworth, Germaine has secretly made her own way to the pier and Max.

I am now standing near the tollgate of the Brightworth Pier whose clock atop the amusement arcade reads 5.01pm.

A small mercy is that I am not in Germaine in this sequence. I stand unseen beside her – oh....

She's off. As she boards the pier my ears ring with a typhoon of wolf whistles directed at her, the mating cry of the local fishermen who are loitering on the rusty iron landings below.

This typhoon touches off an alarmed slopping of thermos flask Typhoo tea along a row of occupied deckchairs. "Bloody gulls," croaks a sexless crone, tartan rug pulled up over legs, damp with spilt tea. "Must be foreign."

Germaine looks awful, truly cadaverous, in the late sunlight; so dead. The fishermen must be necrophiles. Or maybe they are not used to seeing a single white - and I mean white - female on what they think is their territory.

With a degree of grace I would not have expected of her, she strolls up the pier unperturbed by all the pre-rape banter and other sundry bonding rituals of the unreconstructed male trash. These days we are appalled that in Victorian times kids were sent up chimneys. Two hundred years from now, people will shake their heads in disbelief that once upon a time men were allowed to exhibit their maleness in a one-sex group scenario. In public.

It always leads to sexual assault. Or war. Usually both.

I maybe perverse but I feel a little pride in Germaine as she advances south. I notice a slight waddle in her gait which is sure to evolve into a waggle as she gets older and discovers the joy of eating.

Effectively sacked she maybe but she still represents, in a manner of speaking, *Glossy International*; and it is only to be expected that the magazine's exposure - through its personnel - to what is termed ordinary life (that is, the tiresome organic expression of repetitive mindless living) should result in explosive mayhem.

The *Glossy International* concoction is well sealed by the eco-system of Raven's Towers. And like certain volatile gasses and liquids, like fashion itself, it is not designed to be exposed to normal, breathable air. In this context Germaine is transformed from editorial pariah to (well, not ambassador, as there is no tact in her)… let's say, to a microcosm, yes, editorial microcosm in the gross macrocosm of the Brightworth Pier.

People in rainbow straw boaters and flowery hats are skipping and larking up and down the pier.

"Penny for your thoughts, love. Come on pick a ball. Penny for your thoughts," says an over-rouged woman with a stick-on black tooth and a bad Cockney accent. She has thrust a huge basketful of plastic balls - presumably containing the "thoughts" - under Germaine's nose.

"Come on then, love, it's all in a good cause. Penny for your thoughts."

"Fuck off," says Germaine.

This may sound harsh but one has to be firm in these situations.

"No need for that young lady."

I can hear a band's great booming and clashing caterwaul on the west side, not far from Madame Smith's Psychic Pagoda - closed this early evening.

The words on the drum announce: The Brightworth Edwardian Society.

"Come on me luvverlies," bellows a man in a blue-stripe jacket.

Then the band seems to expire in a death rattle of cymbal sibilance and trombone hoot. A woman with a yellow tulip rooted in her scalp takes centre stage. The band starts up again:

"My old man says follow the…" What's the word? Van? Band?

Suddenly, the troglodytes sniffling under their tartan rugs over their Typhoo tea in the deckchairs, shake to life. A new ancient choir of quavery voice grates the ear. *"And don't shillyshally on the way."*

The dentured codgers are crooning at least three notes behind the tulip. Band and choir compete with the gulls and the tulip feels left out so she stops. The tartaned coach party don't notice. The old needle is stuck in place, scratching out a dirge down memory lane – which is odd because the Edwardian Society's output must pre-date even this lot's formative years. But the band plays on, hijacked by the tartans.

This is the world of Max. A *Carry On* nightmare. And he's looking for change!

Germaine strides past the amusement arcade. More mad noises, shrieks, alarms, sirens - World War 2 is being re-fought for 50p. Or could it be World War 3? 4?

Little bastard kids in baggy trousers and overhanging lime tops pound about, setting up a perma-vibe on the deck which tingles the feet. I can feel it myself and think of Anna, my reflexologist.

Against this hellish din the sea is but a visual backdrop, noiseless and alive. The glitter, the surf. A spitfire scream - or a gull - or a decrepit pensioner spilling her tea. This is Brightworth.

We pass a small emporium of personal services: graphology, printed T-shirts, burger takeaways. That time Max brought me here six months ago I was depressed for weeks after, not just by what he said to me but by the fact of Brightworth.

By the horror-jollies.

That's Brightworth. Horror-jollies and everyone's given up. I can't remember whether I invented the "horror-jollies" or read it somewhere. The depression returns. I have the horror- jollies - that terrible melancholy that any civilised human being must experience in any enforced fun farm - at a holiday camp, a fairground, on a pier.

Followed by an overwhelming urge to blow everything up and start again.

The glass and wood-panelled central windbreak, which partitions the pier down much of its length, gives up and gives way to a bulbous growth near the end. This is the Mississippi steamship called the Southern Pavilion. Max is somewhere on the top deck but Germaine can't know that yet.

She peeps through clear slits in the lower deck main entrance door's frosted glass. I peep through other clear slits. Another challenging sight.

Beyond a short hallway and another set of doors we see seated people arranged in two-by-two rows, just talking, and all smoking. There are six lines of these rows. In the main lower deck hall. Coiled fairy lights trim its ceiling perimeter.

Germaine walks in.

In the hallway, a man in blue blazer with gold buttons, sits at a desk and rests his cigarette in the groove of a glass ashtray. His right forefinger nail is yellow.

"Good afternoon, young lady. Are you here for Fag Right?"

She stares at him with that albino parrot fish face of hers. I wish Germaine would answer promptly. She tends to the statuesque pose when she's unsure: a great white block waiting for the pigeon crap.

"What's Fag Right?" she says after a ten second gestation. "This the local gay group or something?"

The blazer chokes on that. Thick tar erupts into his trachea; and the very thought that Germaine may have to give him the kiss-of-life turns my stomach. His mouth makes a great O, his eye-whites blow out, his tongue arches and then the terrible crunching sound, as if his bones are yielding to some demonic pressure that must account also for the gurgling seizure in his chest just prior to a heaving blow-out, presumably caused by expulsive blasts of his thoracic diaphragm.

After he has completed a disgusting, anaconda-like swallowing action, he says between gasps, "No, young lady. We are Fag Right. A pressure group campaigning to liberate smokers in public places."

"Got a fag then?"

I don't know why Germaine has adopted this way of talking. It must be the influence of the Edwardian Society. She pulls out a tiny white untipped log offered her from the carton and lights up. "Ta".

Germaine approaches the inner hallway doors for more observation of the Fag Right membership.

"Cool," she says. "So why are they all sitting like that, in rows?"

"It's our God-given right; it's therapy," rasps the blazer. "It simulates the experience of sitting in a train or coach. This country is going to the dogs if decent, law-abiding taxpayers can't have a smoke in a public place any more. So we come here to smoke without shame. Want to join? Free membership, but to join you have to tell the group of some shameful experience you have had at the hands of the anti-fag police in a public place. I was thrown off a train at Crawley, at midnight, because I wouldn't extinguish...."

"Thanks, but I'm just here on holiday, y'know. I hear people live here, on the pier?"

"Do they? I didn't know that."

"So you don't know anyone who lives here?"

"I think you have the wrong pier young lady."

Germaine lets her left leg go limp in a dismissive, all-too-familiar stance. "Quit the 'young lady' bollocks, fag breath."

*

I've not put on a new video. I heard the words "fag breath" and suddenly I'm in this newsagent's. In a flash. Like in *Star Trek*.

I'm back in my earthly self again. The shop's clock says 5.35pm – I've just left Raven's Towers and Roger and the virtual reality helmets, and I've popped in here to get some sweets - I have a taste for Murray Mints.

Yet I'm thinking: "Big hands. What a waste." Yes, this seems familiar.

I cannot bear to see a man's powerful, sexy, big hands tinkering about in a shop till. I'm admiring the shop assistant's big hands.

Fate made big hands for manly things. Digging up roads and gripping saws and carrying me to my boudoir. I hate to see big hands wasted on holding pens or opening envelopes or fussing over cutlery. What a waste of big hands.

I feel big hands about my waist, down in me. Big hands probing Vicki Cochrane. Give me a big hand any day.

"Your change, madam," says Big Hands, the shop assistant.

As I make my way out, I am blocked by an elderly woman pushing on the door clearly marked pull.

I can sympathise with senility. Age-induced gaga-ness should evoke our compassion before care homes are turned into euthanasia drop-off points. What I won't abide is sad little paws splotched with brown currants and purple channelling – as exhibited by this sympathy-seeking wretch struggling with the simple physics of a door. What's she fucking been doing all her life? (Astral me apologises for sounding like Germaine.)

"Come on you silly bugger," I say loudly in my head.

I take control of the door during a lapse in her concentration and force enough pace on the swing to make her feel that life is so much faster these days; so rushed. The door narrowly misses the white head of self-pity.

"Cull them," I hiss.

I walk briskly to my car. Now I am in a foul temper. Mad rage rehearses itself for the Final Solution of the Old. Is there anything more contemptible than some time-worn cyclist who clicks along the high street in first gear perpetuity, grid-locking a whole city?

There's no excuse for being old – that is to say, for adopting a vulnerable, raddled and hopeless persona (both physical and psychological) simply because a certain age threshold has been reached. *Glossy* must run a provocative piece on the necessity of age apartheid, to ensure that the young are not overrun by the old, and the old not run over by the young. That approach will ensure balance.

These are my thoughts as I step into the Daimler. Not even Elizabeth Taylor's Passion package on the back seat can distract me from the issue of decrepitude.

How can one live to seventy and not know of the daylight moon? My mother never knew of the daylight moon till I pointed it out.

Oh, I am in a bad mood! And not just because of the old age reminder in the newsagent's.

I remember that my mood collapsed twenty minutes ago when I returned from the virtual reality fashion preview with Roger to be told by Lee that Madame Smith couldn't make L'Escargot - I was to meet her later at Blakes for my consultation.

Perhaps I'm over-sensitive but I grew gloomy. I imagined the awful auguries which prompted Madame Smith to change her plans.

In the car I pour a drink, a scotch, neat. We're inching along Oxford Street. I'm on my way home. I've alerted Franca to the probability that I shall be having a bath, before I see Madame Smith.

The car phone rings:

"Ciao, *mio tesoro*!" screams a voice.

"*Chi è?*"

"Leona!"

"Leona!"

"Darling."

"Leona. Darling!"

"*Mia cara*!"

"Leona!"

"I've tried everywhere. You're avoiding me! You hate me!"

"Leona! Darling. Don't say it!"

"Some sexy man called Roger gave me your car phone number."

"Roger Masefield? Sexy?"

"Yes."

"Scandals. I have no more secrets. He knows you?"

"Oh no. He sounded very nervous, honeybunch. Why would I want to know someone called Roger? I got tired of your PA and went to the top - or nearly the top, to get you! I hope you don't mind but I have to talk to you."

"I'm sorry, Leona. It's been a buggery of a day. Simply the worst in living memory."

"Oh, no. It's London of course. It's not the right season to be in London. You should be somewhere warm. But you working girls!"

"I'm a slave to my life Leona. An automaton. My life is not mine any longer. Max is not well."

"I heard, darling. Is it serious?"

"You've heard? What have you heard?"

"Well, nothing. I've heard nothing, darling. I was waiting for you to tell me."

"I think he's lost in Snowdonia – it's the sort of thing he would do."

"Snowdonia! Perhaps he's been abducted! Come on a shopping trip, Vicki. I've collected a group of us from LaGuardia to comfort Imelda during these difficult times. What is this virtual reality fashion show, darling? We're all intrigued. We'll start at Kuala Lumpur, fly to Beijing, onto Paris for some mustard and thence to Delhi's Dariba Kalan before we fly on to Jaipur and your exciting show!"

"This is too much. You shopping and me stuck in Oxford Street.

It's karmic! Didn't you speak to Imelda? She can't attend GlossRam with all the scandal. It would damage…."

"I've done nothing *but* in the last few days. But you know Imelda. Headstrong to the end. She was so upset. She said the least we could do is show a little support for her after what the Philippines gave us through the Seventies and Eighties. She has a point."

"We can't have Manila stirred up during GlossRam, darling. She's no longer the iron butterfly - and her bad luck may attach to us. The press will say birds of a feather!"

"You don't want to argue with Imelda while she's singing *My Way* five miles up. Nancy's astrologer says it's all going to be all right for Imelda. Frank says he'll take her on as one of his backing singers if all goes really bad."

"Leona! Bad girl."

"It's The Tan she really worries about. I mean, it's true love. And he's done so well out of Imelda. She gave him $6 million to buy her a house in the States."

"No! How's Nancy?"

"Oh, the same. Mommie Dearest! Frank is not the fave babe at the moment."

"You can never be too careful, Leona."

"And Michael Jackson. Liz told me he was at the White House last week. Told me about Madonna nude. You know who he looks like these days? Sophia Loren. An uncanny likeness. I mean, tack. That's the trouble with showbiz. It's all tack."

"And La Belle?"

"*Trop* St Tropez! Now when are we getting your Manhood of the Century nomination?"

"Leona! I can't. I'd never get the plaster cock through customs."

"GlossRam will fail without the pre-show revels. And you've wriggled out of telling me what a virtual reality fashion show is darling. And it will be I who carries the cocks, darling. Nominees so far are Errol, Marlon, Mick, Ari, Rudi (for the kinkies), Porfirio - I need a name darling for the mould. It all takes time. Why don't you nominate Charlie?"

"I never went to bed with Charlie. Too old even for me!"

"Vicki! This is not confession time. It's size queen time. He was a ten-incher! The girls are having a riot."

"Charlie, Leona. I give up."

"Love you to pieces. See you in Jaipur. We may go there early!"

"Love to all the girls."

"Ciao."

"Ciao."

I switch off the phone.

What's the world come to when it's *de rigueur* to chit-chat about superstar cocks? Yes, even I have to ask. Poor Roger doesn't know the half of it.

That's fashion for you, the magic of fashion. Some people wear a puff-ball skirt. I discuss megastar cock size. At least Leona gives good phone.

I am perturbed that Roger gave her my number so freely. What if she had been a terrorist? I must reprimand him.

I sip more scotch. My general mood is unimproved. It's being stuck in this traffic jam. I need to talk to Max. It is precisely in moments like this that I need Max - to moderate me, channel me; and it gives him a sense of control over me. It's not all one way. He gets as much as he receives. I'm so tempted to call Max - but I must not. He would be able to tell in my voice that I am up to something. He's very good at reading voices.

I am already having second thoughts about the wisdom of sending Glenda and Timothy down to Brightworth. It's a cruel thing to do to Max though he has been cruel to me. No, it has to be done. The brutal truth is if Max abandons Raven's Towers I shall be abandoned. That's the bottom line, as Roger might put it.

I'll decide when I shall be abandoned.

I gaze out at the world; at real-life. The shit-rinks called pavements make a hopscotch player of everyone. A Martian would think the human kind a type of kangaroo, as I watch everyone skipping this way and that to avoid piles of dog mess.

And then there are those loose pavement slabs waiting to throw up submerged pools of rainwater by the lightest of weights and drench one's feet. That happened to me the other month and I caught a chill, ruining a lovely pair of slippers by Robert Clergerie.

Now I rarely wander beyond the hailing distance of my car.

Outside my office, my car, the plane - any of the scented cabins I much prefer - I am vulnerable. Things happen. I think of Leona again. The ultimate creature of fashion. In a sense she's just one more mockery to add to the other mockeries at the international collections.

Thank God for homosexuals.

They seasonally goad women who thank them by changing their wardrobe. That's the way it is and it feels right. It is the great paradox that men (who prefer men) should design clothes for women (who don't eat) worn by women (who eat and prefer men, usually). Does anyone prefer women, apart from the primal Rogers whose fashion sense starts and ends at Marks & Spencer?

Oh, my head! The jarring vibrato from a passing motorcycle! How I pray it ends in the skid and clatter of death.

I snatch at the phone.

"Franca! Start pouring my bath, slowly. Use the Dead Sea salt, half a block. I must take to the waters."

"*Si*, Mrs Cochrane."

I switch off the phone.

Can my chauffeur help me? "Stephen, say something. Say anything."

I want my mood changed.

"Er, I don't know."

I clasp Elizabeth Taylor's Passion.

I shudder at an earlier impulse to throw the lavender and gold package under the wheels of an articulated lorry. Chypre and cheerful it maybe, but it is now my talisman. Making a gift of it to a Romany astrologer will forestall bad luck.

I pray Madame Smith will guide me, tell me something I don't know already. Perhaps she will approve of my Timothy/Glenda initiative - if I tell her about it. I am certain I cannot proceed without Madame Smith's blessing and insight.

And I much admire Miss Taylor's work on behalf of Aids sufferers, and she is the mega-Now of the century; an honorary post.

Perhaps some of her incredible karma will seep into me via Madame Smith's gratitude.

I think of my bath and feel a bit cheered

>><<

CHAPTER TWELVE

Video No.11: "Germaine & Max & Madame Smith & Vicki" >>>

I am standing behind the tousled raven of Germaine. Her hair. On the Brightworth Pier. More precisely, we are on the top deck of the Southern Pavilion, port side, if I know anything about naval terms.

It's twilight now. I no longer hear the Edwardian Society din. A few kids are still pounding about on the lower deck. Fishermen have collected their rod and tackle and gone home to inflict misery by their very incidence; by the simple fact of their existence. Men are heavy and cumbersome and not really designed for the smallness of the modern home or nuanced intricacies of family dynamics.

Their egos and hands are too big for the sheer micro-scale of relationships and twinkly TVs, push buttons and all the little kisses that make life bearable and take the aitch out of whine.

Germaine is not on the wrong pier as that awful cancer case from Fag Right suggested. She has found her way, as perhaps she was destined to do.

Germaine knocks on an old wooden door darkened by an ancient portico scribbled with porno love graffiti – ancient Pompeians would feel at home here. How many Brightworthians have been conceived in a frantic knee-trembler on this spot?

Sounds of wood scraping on wood within. The door opens.

There at last I see Max. Or at least his silhouette. I wish I could switch off the hard light from the anglepoise lamp within. My unseen person moves closer for inspection.

He looks like a cleric Heathcliff grown old with that curious white scarf wrapped around his neck.

"Hi. Sorry to disturb you," says Germaine.

Max takes a step forward. He must wonder whether Dracula's mistress has come for her supper. How will she seduce him?

"Is it Germaine, Germaine....?"

"Harper."

"Yes, Germaine Harper. What are you doing here?"

The sea air has done nothing for Max. The fleshy hoods over his eyes have grown heavier. The two curved riverbeds running either side of his mouth from the cheek - deeper.

"Yes, I'm Germaine," she says awkwardly, redundantly. "You must be wondering what I'm doing here."

Max says nothing, waiting for something to happen. Behind him a tallboy is rubbing up against a dumb waiter. Even inanimates flirt.

She says, "I thought I'd pop by."

"Just *pop by*? I see. Who told you I'm here?"

"No-one. But I overheard Vicki's PA Lee tell Roger Masefield while he was fucking her on the thirteenth floor. Sorry, I mean making love. I was just passing by there, too."

Tell it as it is, Germaine! The ducking stool would have soon been consigned to the rubbish tip if mediaeval witchcraft had depended on her courage. Strange how Germaine's voice has submissively gone up an octave. Timothy was quite right to call her just another power-crazed con.

"I see," says Max, unfazed by her deluge. "So who sent you and who else knows I'm here?"

"No one sent me. I've left the magazine for good and I thought I'd come down to the seaside to recover. I don't know why I'm here. One minute I was at Raven's Towers. Next I was doing a ton down the M23."

"Why have you left the magazine?" he asks.

"Because I think Vicki is a load of crap. She's bad for my career. I know she's your wife, but you asked."

"And you think I might do better for your career?"

"Don't know. I came here on impulse. I didn't plan it. I wanted to see what would happen. I've nothing more to lose."

"Has Vicki sent you? Or Masefield?"

"No. No-one knows I'm here. Except you." She tries her luck: "Shall I go now?"

I know my Max! How ensorcelled he is by this surprise. He who always prays for the unexpected. If pre-cum had legs….

He takes another step forward. His reading lamp light loses custody of him to the glow of an early moon in the eastern sky.

He says in a low monotone, "I don't think you should go until you explain why you're here. It is of vital importance that I know. You could put an entire project in jeopardy by your being here. You don't realise what you have done."

He's just play-acting, the fake.

"Sorry about that. I'll be off now then."

"I can't stop you but I should prefer it if you stayed with me now - until the project is finalised - a few more days."

She curls one side of her upper lip in an impromptu impersonation of Cliff Richard impersonating Elvis Presley: "A few more days?"

He's encouraging her! And don't think I didn't notice his failure to defend me against her insult.

"There's plenty of room here," he says. "At least come in for a while so that I can be convinced of your story. You look tired. I have food and drink and the view of the sea is lovely at this time of day."

"K."

*

I am in my bath.

All this chopping and changing!

One minute with Germaine and Max. Next in my tub. This is all happening simultaneously, I suppose. As it did on April 27 at around 6pm.

Ah, yes. I am full of excitement at the prospect of seeing Madame Smith at Blakes. Yes, Fate finally released me from Oxford Street. I notice Dead Sea salt leaves a vile tidemark on the bath when mixed with soap. It reminds me of the coast and Brightworth, a refuge tip, a sea-compost of our trash; a filthy shoreline fringe in need of total sterilisation!

"Franca! Franca!" I have to get out.

She takes my arm and helps me out of the bath. "Scrub the bath later, darling," I say, dripping. "And throw away the rest of the Dead Sea salt. I feel more dirty now. I feel like seaweed."

"*Si*, Mrs Cochrane."

I dress quickly. Madame Smith awaits.

Elizabeth Taylor's Passion buoyed my mood to my bath. And Blakes idea of style buoyed me in the car to... Blakes.

Yet my heart sinks at the sight of Madame Smith.

It is one thing to parody the swinging Sixties. Even I have been known to wear long black eyelashes as a giggle-trope. But it is another to be living the Sixties as if bodies are still doing the twist to Chubby Checker.

I lose my grip on Madame Smith's teased beehive heap, I bump unceremoniously down her tight black top, I hurtle past her black mini-skirt and I thud at the foot of her black stiletto heels.

What is it about these tellers of the future that keeps them rooted in the past? What does Madame Smith think when she reads *Glossy International*? - oh, I remember; she said she didn't read my magazine.

I suppose humility is the admission that one can never know the answer to everything.

"Darling," I say, anxious to resuscitate a positive outlook on life . "You remembered to wear black – thank you. What a pleasure to meet you again - off that pier! Do you like your room here?"

"S'right, Mrs Cochrane." She looks like a crucifix in the doorway.

"No, Vicki, please."

"Vicki."

I unbutton my orange wrap-over cape, head tilted up slightly. Actually I am observing Madame Smith in the mirror above the mantel.

Suddenly it strikes me as entirely proper that an astrologer whose family line stretches back well before Christ should be dressed in a past-reference mode.

After all, the art of divination does belong to another age. But like the crocodile it has survived pre-history and subsequent purges to lurk in the modern world.

If Madame Smith were now adorned in a merely fashionable dog-tooth check coat, opaque tights or suede ankle boots - all these would put into question the timeless integrity of her trade.

This is a significant moment for me.

Because at this moment my earthly self becomes aware of an important exception to my usual fashion rule. Quite simply, I realise, as I drape my cape over the hotel sofa, that notions of fashion cannot be applied to a person whose trade makes a nonsense of time's arbitrary divisions - past, present, future - with her horoscopes and clairvoyance.

What a relief to be freed temporarily from my own fashion strictures. It is as if I have found a sanctuary in a church where the ordinances of the worldly world do not apply.

It is like putting my head in Umberto's wash-basin and knowing nothing matters - at that moment. I am in Umberto's hands.

Right now I can be myself before God - or at least Madame Smith - and confess all. And not be rumbled.

My mind begins to create again. What is Madame Smith's essence? What flavour or smell does she evoke to explain her effect on me? There's her timelessness, yet also a fragrance of the past...something rooted, salubrious. Yes, I have it! She is an ancient Fenland recipe...yes, an old Norfolk punch.

I remember: I felt this the first time we met in her Psychic Pagoda on the pier six months before. It's just I hadn't found a name for her brand.

She is a potent deconcoction of herbal things - picked, I'm sure, during the right phase of the Moon. And spices. All pounded by hand in a pestle and mortar and steeped - yes, steeped (Glenda's word) - in natural underground waters.

At last Madame Smith has been bottled in my head.

I hand her the gift of Elizabeth Taylor's Passion.

"Ta very much. What's it like then?"

I swish my mental net to catch the right word. "Allusive."

"Yer wha'?"

"Oh. I mean, er, suggestive."

"A turn-on you mean?" I notice a pair of sunglasses long forgotten in her hair.

"Well...sort of."

Madame Smith's heady herbal brew, the Fenland recipe, is beginning to take effect on me. I do not know whether Norfolk punch is an opiate in real life, but I feel it ought to be.

I am bathing in her lake of expansive peace despite her eye bags, her curious pallor - boozer's paste I call it - and her jet hair: surely the result of an ink pot accident.

I see Madame Smith take out her horoscopes. But I am drunk.

Drunk on Madame Smith's punch.

She is a draught of all-season goodness to be sipped by those lucky few who entrust themselves to the secret science of prophesy. I am warmed by its proximity and comforted by its tone of certainty. It is not so much the "future" which interests me as the here-and-now and its quality. She is guiding me through moments. If she can just guide me through these moments, then the next lot may not be so bad. That's hope.

In another way, consulting Madame Smith is like deciding to see one's doctor or dentist. The decision itself, in many cases, is sufficient to lift the pain.

Making decisions: that's the cure - or part of it. When, in the morning, I have to choose between wearing scent X and scent Y, making the decision resolves the problem, not the scent itself. I can't quite work that out but I sense the truth.

Madame Smith may grapple with the solar system and beyond to understand Vicki Cochrane, but it is Madame Smith's essence, distilled through generations, which is her true value to me.

She is my new tipple to go with my lovely cape behind me whose gentle cashmere caresses my neck, restoring all my missing parts.

I watch Madame Smith close her folder. Good heavens! Is the consultation over already? I look at the reproduction Queen Anne clock on the mantel - Madame Smith has been unwrapping the future for the last half hour and I've not listened to one word, inebriated as I was on her Norfolk punch.

What a lost opportunity (again!)!

*

I don't wish to try your patience but I am partially inside Max. It's not quite like before when I entered his being and discovered he went through a homosexual phase in his youth. I say "phase", but who knows with Max. This time I am physically separate from him, but our heads are in some kind of connection; yet I can still think and observe independently....

Truly this wicked astral exercise spares me nothing. A lab rat's suffering at the hands of a sadistic vivisector is nothing compared to this.

I hear words. And more words. Germaine's words. I never knew she was so talkative, the creep. She's babbling on but he's not taking much in. His mind is full of the sea, concentrated on the pier's creaks in the pitch and swell below. He wonders when the pier will be swept away - as he wondered as a youth fifty years ago. Past and present united by a single question, a simple fear.

Noises - all distinguishable in Max's head.

We are standing in Max's chalet on the Southern Pavilion. I look about. I am astonished. It is as if he has set up his own alternative office on the pier. There's the fax machine he mentioned to me, a personal computer, a telex, files, phones - and a videophone. What is he up to?

I thought he said he was here to get away. To rethink his wretched life and dump me.

All those words jumbling up in Max's head. Max is standing. He still has that ludicrous white scarf about his neck, concealing his wattle. Maybe that's what it is for. I have made him self-conscious. He's put on a pair of half-moon specs since he dragged Germaine in. He rarely wears them - hardly needs them because he has contacts - but I think they help him to think. I've noticed this.

I concede he has a rod-straight back - he always did have a good posture. I can only make sense of some of his thoughts. Most remain hidden by the sheer bulk of his life. Imagine trying to unravel a lifetime of brain.

Germaine's effervescing with words. Listening to her is like...bathing one's face in the fizzy spray of fresh champagne: Moët mist for the shock of the tingly cold. One of Max's more irritating diversions at tiresome receptions.

He is visualising little word bubbles swelling from nowhere on some mental interior of Germaine and then popping up through her red-gashed gob. He hears the hiss in her voice and feels the pressure to let it all out before she explodes. The shame if Germaine Harper were to blow up on the Brightworth Pier!

Max is improvising a tune on Germaine's rhythmic pauses, on her rushed hushed tones and switches of accent. He tastes her disappointment.

Yet what a delightfully fresh tingle she is on the tongue.

That's a good start. Roger Masefield would never have come to the New York Plaza had he not been disappointed in his job. Max is thinking this. Roger was delightfully fresh on the tongue, too; once.

At last he has had enough of Germaine's noise. He holds up his right hand for silence. He is silent himself. How eerie. Then in an odd move he sits at his desk, slips a sheaf of paper into a manual typewriter - quicker than the computer; but ageing - taps taps fore-fingered lickety-split, then pulls out the newly minted document.

"Sign here," says Max, pointing at a dotted line. "Next to the cross."

"Wha' - ?" says Germaine. She reads the document; eyeballs actually zipping side-to-side like a cartoon. Then: "My resignation? Haven't you listened to anything I have been saying?"

"Yes. Just sign."

"Why should I? In any case I've already left. I'll probably be seeing a lawyer for constructive dismissal, harassment and bullying. And what about my pay-off?"

"No pay-off. Sign."

"Absolutely not. I am not signing away my rights."

"Sign it as a mark of trust in me."

"Trust? What are you on about?"

"Raven's Towers is a house of many mansions," he says. "There are many good other jobs I could offer you. If you resign I'll re-employ you. Trust me. You could work closely with me, for instance. You don't have to work with Vicki if you wish not. Think of that. And how do I know that you will not report to others that I am here? To Vicki. Roger. Or perhaps another company."

"Well, I'm a mercenary. Who's the highest bidder?"

"Probably me. At least I am your best bet. Sign."

Germaine crosses her arms: "I don't trust you. Nothing I know about you would induce me to trust you."

"You're finished anyhow as things stand," says Max. "Sign it and risk everything for an interesting, unknown future. Just trust me. Everything begins with trust."

"Screw it!"

Max smiles – not the happiest of sights. Some faces are not suited to express pleasure or charm. He picks up the document and screws it into a ball, and says gently, "Good".

A typical kinky Max ruse!

She makes a menacing approach. "That was easy," she growls.

Her red lips are drawn back over her teeth: not attractive. "Why did you ask me to sign that? You didn't want me to sign."

Max takes plucks off his glasses and rubs the lenses on his jacket sleeve - I wish he wouldn't. "Why sign away your rights even if you have already walked out? You're perfectly correct. Only a fool could have been inveigled into that."

"A little game. God...."

"We chief executives must be allowed a little fun. Had you signed I would have led you out of this room and waved you off. And no pay-off. Think how close you came to that. Don't you shiver at the thought?"

"I wasn't even close. If I left now I'd go straight to the newspapers."

"Oh! There are ways of shutting them up."

Germaine roosts herself in the pink wicker Lloyd Loom and crosses her legs. It's a gesture whose parentage is defiance and curiosity. She breathes heavily, belying her cool. "Haven't you anything better to do than play God?" she asks boldly.

"I am not interested in silly father-fixated females. It's very important to weed them out. They're the blight of international business at this time in the transition of the female to economic *and moral* independence. They are a huge nuisance. Had you signed that document you would be saying you thought we had some sort of special understanding requiring my protection of you - which we don't. I am pleased to see you're not looking for someone to take responsibility for you."

"I aim to please. It's certainly true I'm not screwing Roger Masefield," Germaine says gratuitously, leering.

Max says nothing to that: as well as he might not!

"Drink?" he offers.

Germaine nods. "I'll have some of that over there." She's gazing at a quarter-empty bottle of Black Bowmore, "distilled 1964", a single malt whisky. Expensive!

He spins the top off with a flick - another irritation - and pours. "So you witnessed Mr Masefield's congress with Lee on the thirteenth floor."

"You knew about it before I told you?"

"There's not much I don't know about Raven's Towers."

"You've bugs everywhere?"

How amazingly familiar is Germaine's tone: no respect for Max; or anyone.

"Not everywhere. That would be too expensive. You would have to employ armies of secretaries to transcribe the tapes and retired security police to analyse the film. Resources are better invested in talented staff - here."

He hands her the glass. She sips the dark toffee-coloured liquid. And coughs.

"It's a good malt," he says. "Let it rest in the mouth till the tongue feels almost numb, then swallow. Won't burn your throat then. No need to repeat."

"How did you know about Roger and Lee?"

Max replaces his specs. "Should I tell you secrets? Can Germaine Harper deal with reality?" he says, as if thinking aloud. "Well, you won't be returning to *Glossy*. I anticipate you remaining with me. And in any case, personnel will be altered. Lee, as you know, works for Vicki. But Lee reports everything to me. For instance, Lee had to ask me first if she could tell Roger I was here on Vicki's instructions. Vicki actually knows this. I guess Vicki told Lee to tell Roger as a warning shot to me. Warning me to return to Raven's Towers. I allowed Vicki to do that."

"Why?" asks Germaine, forehead furrowed. I think she thinks she's stumbled into a creaking Agatha Christie novel.

"Why not? It's interesting to see what will happen next. The story's not over yet. Whom will you report to?"

Germaine bangs her glass down on a side-table. "Look, I'm here for me. I don't know why I'm here. I just decided."

"You sound a bit like me," says Max. "'Let's do it. And see what happens'. That's my motto."

"Yeah! I could leave right now."

"Oh, that old one. The equivalent of 'chicken'. True, you could leave."

"But I'll finish my drink first. Good advice."

"It's a fine malt. Pity to waste. Now Vicki took a calculated risk. That's good. She's gambled that Roger may do something silly - like leak the news of my whereabouts to the press and thereby force me out of Brightworth. Which is what she wants. She wants me snug as a bug in my Raven's Towers gulag. But if I know Vicki she's probably worked out by now that Roger is not a risk-taker. He has already thought to get the board onside against me but bottled out. It's very difficult to unseat a Founding Father whose seat is still warm, and Roger has little courage. Roger's mistake is that he never thinks laterally. I don't expect him to do anything significant in my absence."

"Is this a time and motion study or something? All this control, and all this office hardware here." Germaine scans the room with the return of her curled upper lip. Pure theatre.

"It reminds me of home."

"You're a control freak."

Max shakes his head slowly. "Believe it or not but in my dealings with Raven's Towers I leave a lot to chance. Vicki and I are alike in this respect. We control, but we allow for the unforeseeable, which means letting go once in a while. For the sake of it. Sometimes Vicki forgets the importance of letting go, to see what happens. I allow things to happen in their way. I keep an eye on things."

"And on Vicki?"

"I don't particularise."

"She's your wife!"

"Not in this context. She is just another very talented person who works for Raven's Towers. An extremely talented person - "

"Sounds like true romance."

Max smiles. Or rather his lips thin out a bit. "Vicki has a huge capacity to surprise – that's attractive. So what else to tell?" Max is almost skittish; a very rare exhibition in a near-stranger's presence.

Germaine pipes up. "Yeah, the post-boy - who gets blow-jobs from a redhead? I saw that too on the thirteenth floor."

"Oh, you saw that as well. You have been busy. There's a place for you at Raven's Towers. You mean, young Matt. He answers to me. As for the redhead - she answers to Roger the Dodger. I permitted Matt to tell her to tell Roger of the chaos today at *Glossy International*. Well, what's the harm?"

Germaine's making faces into space to convey disapproval - the con. Then she says: "What are you going to do about Vicki? She's gone crazy."

Now Max pulls a face (or rather, pouts) - to lighten her insolence: "Vicki is not crazy at all. Certainly no more so than usual. She has dealt with you properly in my view. You had no business not cooperating with Freddie Smith and the GlossRam preview film - yes, I know all about that from my various sources. And you were very insulting to her in conference this morning. And it was silly of you to play games with your colleagues. Ordinarily I would say you are not suited to corporate life. But then you did an odd thing. You came to Brightworth. A masterstroke. An illustration of the benefits of doing something surprising."

She grabs her drink on the table and rests back in a sulk. Defeated.

He continues: "Of course, I am not as clever as I may sound. Raven's Towers is like a garden with a life of its own, with its own subterranean life, no matter how much tending. After all, I didn't know you'd witnessed the activities on the thirteenth floor. Some surprises are very unpleasant, and there's the occasional blight. The garden lives by itself. And out of this living place a wild creature turns up on the Brightworth Pier one evening wanting to be tamed. By the way, what do you know of Her Royal Highness The Princess Leona Humperdink?"

"Christ!" Germaine is choking up booze. "Warn me next time you mention her. What do you want to know?"

"What is she?"

"Some silly cunt with too much money. They make them at a sausage factory in New York. She one of your spies, too?"

The lip-stretch once again. "Just an idle enquiry. Shall I tell you what I am certain of though?"

"Go on then."

"That your tape recorder is on. Am I right? No don't move. We'll bet. You mustn't be given the chance to switch it off. If it's off, I'll order you to leave. You'll be at liberty to talk to the tabloids but you won't have the tape. If it is on, I'll give you an editorship - so long as you give me the tape."

"You're on." She takes out the machine from her bag. The tell-tale red light is on.

"There! Perfect! Well done," says Max. "Were you planning to sell the tape to the tabloids? You'd make lots of money. In fact you can keep the tape. A gesture of good faith. If I don't honour my promise of an editorship you can sell the tape. How's that?"

"Suits me."

He turns to face the huge bow-window which dominates the room and opens up the Channel. Its arc twins the horizon's. And the hideous net curtains protect Captain Nemo on the bridge from prying strollers' eyes. He is lost for the moment in the dusky grey of the sea, and once again his mind swirls with strange images, mouths, bodies....

"What the hell are you doing here anyway?" Germaine asks at long last, her tongue even looser now with alcohol.

"I was born in Brightworth and now I'm waiting to see what happens," he replies. "That is the only answer you're going to get. I will also add that I plan to set up a new green magazine for coastal readerships - you could say I'm researching its potential by being here. It's appalling what is happening to seaside environments...."

"Sounds fascinating," says Germaine, barely awake.

"I'm so glad you think so – that's the editorship I have in mind for you."

"What?"

"No discussion, Germaine. Take it or leave it. You'd be perfect. I don't want some ecology drip with hennaed hair and a whippet in tow running such a venture. I want an instinctive capitalist with a market-driven awareness as editor who sees and seeks the money potential in a green revolution. You look the part. Much cash and opportunism have not been spared in making you look so achingly definitive of this moment. That's why Vicki took you on, I guess. You look as if you want cutting-edge power, to participate in the money market. And you've got a big mouth. Be honest."

Germaine backs away from the challenge. Wise girl. I see his point. Instead she says, "So what do I do now? You said you wanted me stay here for a while."

"Yes, I don't want you out of my sight. You look as if you could do with some fresh air. I think you will stay with me out of curiosity and because you know it's a wise career move. You can familiarise yourself with your new editorial challenge in my little hometown. I shall sleep in my bedroom in the back and I have a sleeping bag you can lay out here. I hope you don't snore or breathe deeply - otherwise I'll put you in one of the B 'n' Bs on the coast. You won't like that at all. Landladies! Now. if you're quick you'll catch one of the 8-to-8s for toiletries and all your womanly needs. And by the way, to avoid misunderstanding, I don't desire you sexually - and avoid chattering to the clairvoyante on the pier, Madame Smith. She's another one of Vicki's agents."

"Wha'?"

"Don't ask me how I know. Oh, but of course, she's not here on the pier tonight. She's up in London with Vicki. I wonder what will happen next."

*

I was wrong! He doesn't fancy her. But those pictures I saw of them together. I give up!

*

"Pleased with your reading then?" asks Madame Smith.

"Oh, yes," I stumble. We're back at Blakes, "It's amazing what you pick up in your horoscopes."

"Not just horoscopes - clairvoyance too. It's like bugging people." She cackles. "Bugging their auras. Know about auras? Yeah, I hadn't thought of that till I just said it! Fancy a drink before you go?"

She has at least one social grace. "Yes, a little scotch with ice, thank you," I reply. I'm quickly thinking of ways to get her to reprise what I just missed – I'm so annoyed with myself.

She fills a cut crystal tumbler to the rim. But that's pleasing. I actually wanted a big drink and Fate has answered my need through Madame Smith's rustic unworldliness. I have been saved yet another difficult decision.

"Auras, you mentioned auras, Madame Smith."

"Yeah, we've all got auras. Lovely colours they have - seen the photos."

"Pictures have been taken of our auras?"

"Amazing what they can do."

I am also busily trying to wash out of my head the Fenland recipe of Madame Smith's Norfolk punch essence. The best means to that end is to get a grip on the moment. So I concentrate hard on Madame Smith, on imagining a reconstruction of her body which stands before the small fridge:

First I would make a low horizontal incision in Madame Smith's bikini region to draw back her surprising pot belly obtruding from her sparrow frame. A carbon dioxide laser sandblast would murder the crow's feet while a chainsaw could work on those knobbly knees and ankles. Silicone implants and transferred fat would fill out hips, thighs and calves. And a vacuum pump would suck out what little aspirated fat there is into a calibrated container to help pull up her bosom flaps.

No.

It's hopeless. No well-meaning body sculptor could improve Madame Smith. She must be left in her imperfect state. She who stands out of time should not look entirely right, as a corporeal reminder of her singularity.

"S'funny," says Madame Smith.

"Yes, Madame Smith?"

"Well you and your husband, like: I always think someone like you, you know, an editor of a fashion magazine, you know, would have all the answers - to problems."

"Oh. Well, we don't have agony aunts or anything like that on *Glossy International*."

"All those articles on relationships."

"We are not *Cosmo* - though, yes, I see what you mean."

"Yeah."

"But, well, our articles are not intended to have a prescriptive value."

"...." I see Madame Smith is lost.

"*Glossy International* is not about telling people what's good for them. Not where relationships are concerned."

"Oh yeah." She pauses with I would describe as a conniving expression on her face; eyelids at half-mast.. Then: "Know what I did this morning? After I talked to you and your hubby and before I came up here? I buried my husband's shirts in the garden."

"Madame Smith! Why?"

"Had it coming didn't he. He always moans about me being out of the house when really he wants to go on the razzle without me, y'know an excuse, like – to pop down to the local yacht club for a booze-up. Not that there are any yachts. Shouldn't think any of them have been in a rowing boat let alone a yacht. Last night he threw this Vesta chicken curry I'd bunged in the microwave - threw it out the window. So I thought, right! I waited for his lordship to leave the house and when he's gone, I got out the shovel and buried his shirts." Madame Smith squawks. "That'll teach him. That's the sort of stuff people want to read."

I am stunned. I sip. I dream.

"Still with me Vicki?"

I am dreaming of those shirts that Madame Smith has buried. I imagine them sprouting up as shirt blooms. An Eden of shirts on a lattice panel.

"Mrs Cochrane!"

"Madame Smith. I'm sorry. I was miles away. A habit of mine. You buried your husband's shirts. Well, it's one way to deal with husbands, I suppose."

"Excuse me for saying it but it's a funny thing for a husband to go live on a pier. Sure he hasn't got something on the side? It's difficult to tell from his chart."

"I suppose your husband doesn't wear Hawes & Curtis shirts, Madame Smith?"

She gives me a very peculiar look. Can you blame her?

"What's that then?"

"No, it doesn't matter - you asked if my husband was seeing someone else. The truth is I don't know. I would say No. My husband has never gone with other women. It would have been simpler had he. Much simpler."

"I'd castrate my John if I caught him in bed with some tart."

"You're quite a militant activist, Madame Smith. It never occurs to me to do things like that."

"You never buried Mr Cochrane's shirts in the garden then?" She squawks again.

"Not...quite. I'm not sure burying Max's clothes would quite work. He has a huge wardrobe. I would have to hire a gang of grave-diggers."

I can hardly tell her that I am about to do something far more ambitious and bury the Brightworth Pier.

"How did you meet him?" asks Madame Smith.

"Meet him? Max? Goodness." Yes, it's only right that an ancient Fenland recipe would want to know of the past. I hold the glass to my chin. "I stalked him."

"Yer wha'?"

"Stalked him."

"You leapt on him?"

"No, no. I am not a leaper, Madame Smith. I stealthily crept up on him."

Should I tell her? I hate to discuss my private life. Well, she is an astrologer.

"We met in Italy. You probably know I am Italian by birth."

"No accent."

"That's very sweet of you. My maiden name is Vittoria Valentinuzzi."

"Oh, like the Queen."

"Sorry?"

"Queen Victoria."

"Yes. *Vitt*oria. No 'c'. We worked for the same publishing company; actually he was on secondment from an English company. He was very attractive to women. Still is, in some ways. I personally had not really noticed him and...oh dear, this is going to sound very odd."

"Go on then!"

"Well, in those days, in Italy, I had a problem with transport. I couldn't abide the train journeys. And then walking from the station to the office. It was a lot of things. The air. The smells. I am...hyper-sensitive to these things."

"Can't stand garlic breath myself."

"Really?. Well, there you are. We all have our sensitivities. So, because I couldn't afford to go to work by taxi each day, I developed an odd habit - you know, I've never told anyone this, apart from Max...."

"Yeah...." Madame Smith gulps her drink. Ice cubes bobble.

"This habit...I developed this habit of walking behind men who wore lotion or certain types of aftershave or scent. On the train I would select a man on the basis of his scent and follow him as far I could on my walk to work...just so I could inhale his scent. It was...like being in a scented bubble for a short while. A scent bubble. It was a defence against the city stench. To be caught in the wake of a masculine fragrance! Of course it all depended the way the wind was blowing. But usually it was safe to follow behind, down-wind, as it were.

"And that's how I met Max. One day a woodlands cologne hit me as I walked in the street. I danced on its pine top note and spun on the juniper, sandalwood and hint of fougère...of dear, Madame Smith...it was Max. He told me later that he had noticed me do this on a number of occasions, observing me in shop windows or shielding his glasses to make a spy mirror. He could hear me sniffing, little sniffs, barely audible. But Max notices things like that. He has an ear for noises. A bat's ears. Somehow he had worked out my little secret.

"I was so astonished that any man should work out my strange little habit - and not laugh - he never laughed - that I had to have him. He was mine then on. He later told me that he was so astonished by my little habit that he decided there was something about me he had to have. It was a fateful - as things turned out - collision."

Madame Smith places her glass on the table with deliberate care. The expression on her face is something to be seen.

I have said too much, talked too long, and exhausted Madame Smith with my eccentricities. Of this I am quite certain. I am too foreign a flavour for Madame Smith.

"Well, that beats me," she says finally of my love story. "Y'know, if you don't mind me saying, Vicki, but you don't want to be too clever. Men only understand direct action - take it from me. If you want that husband of yours back, you go down to that pier and drag him back. That'd surprise him. That's what I'd do."

I find her words utterly thrilling. "Would you do that, Madame Smith? Really? I have thought about doing that."

Yes, in fact Glenda and Timothy will do it for me - oh, I'm aching to tell Madame Smith; but I must not; even she cannot be trusted. No one can be trusted.

"Get down to Brightworth and drag that bastard back on his arse!"

Madame Smith looks at me in amazement. I can't believe I've just said that. It must be Madame Smith's powerful essence getting to me. She took possession of my voice box and tongue for a moment there.

"Now you're talking, girl!" she says. "None of this stuff about smells and how he's the only man who understands you. You have to fight – it's in your chart."

At last Madame Smith has said something that makes sense to me; something I have actually listened to; something with which I wholeheartedly agree - in my own terms, of course. Without realising it she has given her blessing to the Glenda/Timothy offensive.

I kiss Madame Smith on both cheeks before I leave – something only Leona Humperdink experiences in my social circle.

Only later do I remember Madame Smith has failed to give me the Romany weather forecast she promised on the phone earlier.

Oh well, nothing lost.

Glenda and Timothy.

Hope renewed.

Into battle - against Brightworth, for Max!

>><<

PART THREE

CURTAINS

CHAPTER THIRTEEN

Video No.12: "The next day, April 28, 12pm" >>>

I am seated in a first class train carriage. I can tell because there's off-white linen where heads go. There's Timothy. There's Glenda. On their way to Brightworth. Glenda has been rocked by the cattle truck to a paraplegic nod-like sleepiness - her head loose at the neck, and stuffed in the nose judging by the snore.

Timothy has decided to revenge his dispatch to Brightworth with a ludicrous, shameful suit. He wears a Moschino short-sleeved matador jacket in black and gold tops with a matching gold fan on a long chain attached to his lapel. I suppose this is the toreador who will bait and butcher the thick bull of English provincialism.

Worse are the double hoop gilt earrings and figure-hugging black tights. He is quite obviously not wearing any undergarments - not even some sort of jock-strap.

I would have fired him on the spot had I known.

Timothy takes out a cashmere cream sweater with a lurid sycamore-leaf pattern.

I remember that.

The mayoress of Brightworth, Elsie whatever, had asked me on the phone for a considerable discount on the sweater - part of a special offer in the latest issue of *Glossy International*. In return she gave me her word that she would not mention Max's presence on the pier - God knows what Max has paid her already to keep quiet.

Timothy smirks and then folds and places the top back in its cellophane wrapping.

Glenda wakes with a rousing snort as the train slows in its approach to Brightworth station.

"I do hope you had lovely dreams Glenda."

"Oh be quiet. It's bad enough coming here. What are we going to do with this pier?"

"We could have discussed it. But you chose to take a catnap instead."

"You haven't a clue. Like me."

"Where do we meet this mink-lined cunt Elsie Bush?"

"Don't use that word. It's offensive to women."

"Cunt, cunt, cunt."

"You're so childish Timothy!"

The train pulls into Brightworth Station to squeals of ungreased iron. Timothy opens the carriage door and watches Glenda stagger out after him, almost plunging into the gap between step and platform, with all her bags.

Glenda was only made for offices and soft padded places.

I am astonished at the posse of local journalists waiting outside the station. The mayoress said *Glossy International*'s interest in Brightworth would arouse much parish controversy. She's made sure of that.

"Out of my way ladies and gentlemen," declaims Timothy to an applause of flashlight. "Let not the indigenous cottagers of Brightworth escape your worthy pillory."

A freckly young ginger-headed reporter, with what I suspect is a promising sharp ear for discordance (often leading to atheism), pushes forward. "*Brightworth Evening Argus*. Can I quote you on that, Mr Timms?"

"We are very happy to be in Brightworth," interposes Glenda, thank God. "Please make way for us. And we hope to introduce your lovely pier to the best of *Glossy International*. It will be a fun thing."

"Just what exactly is that scrap of old rolling stock doing to my case," bawls Timothy at an elderly porter, throwing aside a female hack and cutting a swathe through a herd of inexpressive cheap day returns.

Glenda continues: "Brightworth is at the heart - Timothy!"

With a rude shove Timothy has parted elderly porter and case, the latter which he now throws with a reckless back-swing into the boot of a cab.

"Yer fuckin' great poof," snarls the British Rail brute, a tidal wave of spittle frothing over his choppers beyond the vow of Pearl Drops.

Timothy stretches tall. "Get off with you, you insanitary clog-pored...." He is stopped by his own alarming pirouette, spiralling to the ground, unconscious. Fresh air has gone to his head.

The coastal paparazzi rush forward, stoop and flash at the corpse of haut monde.

"Make way, make way!" Glenda bends over Timothy and slaps his face. He's groggy but alive, overcome presumably by Brightworth.

*

"Where am I?" gurgles Timothy, sounding heterosexual. He is rolling this way and that on the waterbed of Glenda's bosom.

"You are in a Brightworth taxi and your name is Timothy," says Glenda matter-of-factly.

The driver glances at them in his rear-view mirror.

She adds, "You have just made a total fool of yourself and we are heading for the Promenade Inn before our excursion to the Brightworth Pier. Remember?"

Timothy moans. I crouch down close to examine him. He looks up at Glenda. What he sees is a crimped aureole of honeyed chiffon lit by a beatific smile. He must think he's in heaven at last. The Madonna herself has slid down the astral tunnel to welcome him personally.

Glenda says, "Mrs Elsie Bush maybe there to welcome us. But she may have been offended by your instruction to her to keep well away. If this gets back to Vicki...."

"Mrs Elsie Bush?"

"The mayoress of Brightworth, Timothy."

"Ugh!"

Suddenly the taxi screeches, bucks and we are all thrown into a heap.

"*Pardonnez-moi, señor!*" shouts Timothy, raised from the dead and rising like the rest of us from the floor. (Even in my astral state I was thrown, sympathetically.)

We look behind us. A crumpled Brightworthian lies sprawled and lifeless on the road, first victim of *Glossy International*'s cyclonic arrival. "They'll never learn," mutters the driver to himself, stepping out of the car. "Hedgehogs the lot of them."

He strolls unconcernedly over to the small crowd shuffling in a circle around our roadkill.

"Now we'll have to walk," says Timothy.

"Rest your head here," says Glenda, "and relax."

*

After the two of them have booked into their hotel, a bearded council official called Mr Latham (in a waist-length green gabardine anorak: hood [back] with fake fur trim) enters their lives and suggests they "take a butcher's" at the pier while the tide is out.

They and I wander into a wet desert and its name is the Brightworth sands.

Crabs sidle between rocks, fearful perhaps of *Glossy International*. More appalling however is the sight of Timothy who is Carmen Miranda in absurd black wellies, earrings flashing. He hops from one sand islet to another in a grey expanse broken only by fast rivulets running south from the shingle - before tide repetition.

I gaze up at the pier.

There! I saw the net curtain twitch, in Max's chalet. That's

Germaine's hairstyle. So she has stayed the night. I wonder if Max and she did end up sleeping together. Improbable. Judging by her jerky head movements I should say she has spotted Glenda and Timothy. I don't see Max.

Timothy halts and takes in the pier as if attempting to come to terms with the preposterous. He does not see Germaine's bobbing head on the Southern Pavilion top deck.

Divested of its briny culottes, the pier stands naked and cold, barnacled legs soaring up into an eerie undercarriage of rusty girders and rotting joists. Somewhere in this netherworld aloft, trickling water foretells death and resting pigeons already coo an elegy.

Timothy shivers in the breeze. "This won't do at all."

"Sorry?" responds Mr Latham.

Glenda is biting strands of her hair because the pier has put the bit between her teeth. "No wonder Vicki said this was a challenge," she says.

"The Brightworth Pier will simply have to go, Mr Latham," says Timothy, waving his gold Moschino fan dismissively at it.

"Go, Mr Timms?"

"Go I said. This is a monster. A carbuncle!" He strobes the edifice for the encapsulating metaphor. "A whore!"

"What my colleague is trying to say," fake-smiling Glenda says quickly, slipping her arm into Mr Latham's, "is that this pier is a marvellous example of its kind and we're going to make it fit for a spread in *Glossy International*."

"Fit for scrap!"

Mr Latham says, "Mr Timms, the Brightworth Pier is a major tourist amenity, a venue for all sorts of family entertainments."

"I hardly think this paint-chipped mangle of Edwardian filigree, hanging with rotten weed that reminds me of woodcuts of Vlad's impaled victims outside Brasov, can be of any possible interest to anyone except vendors of soft-focus picture postcards," says Timothy, his eyes shut. "Still," he opens them, "I suppose we could go on deck and ogle at that perfectly hideous lookalike steamship growing like a boil on this fetid hulk."

*

"Amazing the number of cripples that are still about, Mr Latham," says Timothy, stepping over a human bundle with a bandaged foot and neck near the amusement arcade.

The bundle is curled into a ball, concealing its head. But I recognise that double chin...or wattle....

"What with electro-crystal therapy, micro-neurological surgery, and bionics, there really is no excuse for...this...this…" - Timothy jabs the bundle with his boot - "...this leprotic display of bodily dysfunction. It's all emotional really, a cry for help. It all starts in the womb. We all labour under pre-natal unhappy memories. And mothers these days are simply not foetus-friendly...."

I observe carefully the "bundle". As I suspected, it's Max. His barely disguised wattle is the giveaway. How humiliating that the chief executive officer of Raven's Towers is reduced to this kind of role-playing, like some jailbird on the run. What on earth is he doing here like this? And what has he done to his foot? It's all freshly bandaged.

I hear wolf whistles rise up from the southern end of the pier. A familiar sound. Last heard when I followed Germaine here and a gang of fishermen subjected her to their group- bonding pre-rape banter.

The object of their lust today is Timothy who's making a spectacle of himself west-side of the Southern Pavilion.

Brightworth's prime sirloin have established eye contact with Timothy who is fanning himself akimbo just above the iron landing used for fishing, as if he were modelling pouched underwear. He shouts at them - "You're all homosocial, homosocial, yes dear, homosocial, yes, you, the one with the Fire Island moustache, know what homosocial is?"

Evidently none is familiar with the term and all think he's saying something else; and they start heckling my beauty editor who now turns to a worried-looking Mr Latham. "I am completely amazed by this spectacle, Mr Latham," he bellows, audible I think to a few of the primitives below. "One should have thought that an establishment such as the Brightworth Pier would have barred these homosocial redundancies. Never have I witnessed such a display of homosociality in all my life- at least not since the school playground. In my pages I shall advise decent mothers to give a wide berth to this bagnio of cod-buggery."

The fishermen can't have a clue what Timothy is on about - even I don't catch all the nuances – and certainly Mr Latham is none the wiser - but I suppose the rabble know an insult when they hear it, and begin as one to surge forward in a violent mood. I am certain they are inflamed not just by Timothy himself but also by the conspiratorial, catalytic rage they sense in each other, a kinetic collective rage which binds them and has its own momentum – perhaps rooted in evolutionary survival strategies of horned bovines. All revolutions and gang rapes start this way. I am certain of it.

"Break his fuckin' legs."

"Kill the bastard."

"Fuckin' nancy boy. Throw the iron overboard...."

Both Timothy and Glenda run for the safety of the Southern Pavilion itself. But Mr Latham intervenes, clank-shutting the exit gate.

"Life-bans for you all if this doesn't stop here," he roars at El Toro.

After a few grunts they turn to cattle again and go about their preparations for sea-grazing.

That was close.

*

Glenda, Timothy and Mr Latham are strolling and chatting east-side of the Southern Pavilion when I see Max sneak by unspotted by the earthlies. With extraordinary speed and agility he limps up the outer west-side staircase towards his chalet. He has already a taste of *Glossy International*'s boot; and I'm curious about that bandaged foot.

I follow him.

Max rushes into his chalet and before I get to the door he slams it shut in my face. So I float through it - clever! First time I've done that.

There's Germaine, feverishly exhaling ciggie smoke. I see blankets arranged on the floor. That's a relief.

"Where have you been?" demands Germaine. "Bloody Glenda and Timothy are here. Is this another game of yours? What's wrong with your foot?"

Max is crimson with exhaustion . "I have just come from the hospital. A bloody taxi ran me down."

My God! No! It was him we ran over. Not some Brightworthian. We could have killed him.

"Are you badly hurt?" asks Germaine neutrally, clearly unconcerned.

"No, but it aches. Nothing serious. This is Vicki's work. She has sent Glenda and Timothy down for some mischief. I can't understand why Lee didn't warn me - I must phone her. Vicki must have hidden this from Lee."

Quite right. Poor Max is jabbering. What joy it is to see.

Max says, "He actually kicked me."

"Who?"

"That Timothy creature. Just now. With his boot. Called me leprotic."

"He *saw* you?"

"Of course not. I rolled myself in a ball – he thought I was a

169

tramp."

"Sack him. He takes bribes from the cosmetics houses. Glenda told me. He's bad for Raven's Towers."

"Shush! Get your head down," whispers Max, forefinger on lips. They both crouch against the arced wall below the bay window.

Just outside are Glenda, Timothy and Mr Latham, staring blindly into the chalet's interior with cupped hands.

"Why net curtains on a pier?" we hear Timothy asking. "What are you hiding in there, Mr Latham?"

"We have occasional residents, Mr Timms."

"Net curtains, Glenda. Mm. Yes. Could net curtains be the way to beautify Brightworth Pier?"

"I don't follow Timothy."

"Aren't net curtains quintessentially suburban? Net curtains enable us to embark on those crucial eye journeys which brick walls and decency would otherwise forbid us. Good for snooping, in other words. Net curtains. The vital 'house' accessory."

"Yes!" says Glenda. "But how could we use them to redecorate the pier?"

"I have it! We will dress the pier up in net curtains. Think of the effect in the breeze! It will be like a huge apparition! A ghost of its former self! A suburban thing to transform a pier into something quite mystical, something the opposite of suburban. A style paradox! We must order acres of net curtains. Get the labourers. Vicki will love net curtains. We mock suburbia and prettify the pier. An inspiration."

"Sometimes Timothy you're really worth it. Brilliant!" cries Glenda, ecstatic, relieved.

"Why thank you fair lady," says Timothy, bowing to her.

"What the hell are they talking about, Max?" whispers Germaine. "My leg's dead."

"I think I know what's going on. This is Vicki's revenge. I did not anticipate this."

His lips thin into the defeated smile that has rarely seen light of day in a life of anticipated, wearying success.

How odd. He does seem pleased.

*

Hours later Timothy is talking to a very old-looking woman who's the spitting image of Miss Marple as played by Margaret Rutherford in the movies.

Both are propped on stools at the bar of the Promenade Inn

"lounge". She's eighty if she's a day, her face a glaciated terrain of bumps and slips, with wild careering gorges.

"*Amanuate*, dear mayoress," he says.

"I don't think I know that word Mr Timms," she quavers. "And Club World is my second home."

"No doubt, madam. *Amanuate* is an Atlantean word for the salutation "Good evening". So, good evening Mrs Bush."

"Atlantean?" she queries. "I don't think I've seen the brochure."

"Yet to be printed, sadly," says Timothy, picking at the salted peanuts. "I am speaking of the lost continent of Atlantis which sank beneath the waves thousands of years ago - long before the Pharaoh Tut was but a bandage. Atlantis remains safely wrapped until the Age of Aquarius, the New Age, dawns properly."

"Heavens!"

"And when that happens, Mrs Bush, Atlantis will rise again. It will stretch from Iceland in the north to the Falklands in the south. Think how many lives could have been saved if Atlantis had risen just as Mrs Thatcher's Task Force entered the icy seas of the South Atlantic."

Mrs Bush sips her g 'n' t and wipes a patch of glass of its sweat. The lounge is a sconces-and-scones rest room, red plush, overlooking the Brightworth Pier. Every minute or so one hears things being dropped. Bottles. People.

Mrs Bush puts her hand on Timothy's. "But where will all the water go when, er, this Atlantis rises up?"

"Atlanteans are not interested in trifles such as water displacement. The water will trickle where e'er. My own private view is that the swamping of parts of Canada, Alaska, the Poles, Brecqhou and Northern Ireland would be no great loss."

"Goodness!"

"I was an Atlantean - and am - and we Atlanteans are being returned to this terrible world for the New Age - to re-infuse it with beauty and spirituality. That's why I work for *Glossy International*. I was told by a regression medium that I was once the Keeper of the Records of the High Temple of Atlantis. It was my task to look up a seeker's Akashic Record - do you know what that is Mrs Bush? The Akashic Record? From the Sanskrit word *akasha*, meaning ether. It is the record of our lives that is kept in heaven, of our past lives and present life. It is our cosmic national insurance record, that we look over when we die. So my task was to look up a seeker's record and tell them what life had in store for him or her. A little peep into the heavenly plan. In fact I have a distinct recollection that we have met Mrs Bush. Imagine it. Fifty thousand years ago you sought your Akashic Record and now we sit at the bar of a Brightworth hotel. What felony did we commit to deserve such a fate? I bet I knew a thing or two about you Mrs Bush!"

I have not heard of this Akashic Record. Perhaps that's what I am doing - looking over mine.

The mayoress' face corrugates in a wide smile to Timothy's cheeky insinuation. "Now, now, Mr Timms."

"As the Keeper today I would tell you why your soul is burdened with the responsibilities of high office. Unfortunately I cannot gain access to your Akashic Record any more on account of all the electromagnetic pollution in the air. But we have a destiny. And doubtless you are fulfilling yours."

What's Timothy up to? The creep.

Mrs Bush's arm bangles peal with joy as she raises a hand to her crown. Her walnut paw then appears to ricochet off a membrane of stiffened blonde tresses. "You know all this from this...akashit...akardic....how do you pronounce it?"

"A - as in amour - kay - shick. Akashic."

"Akashic Records?"

Timothy places an arm on her shoulders in a bold intimacy - one does wonder about him. "Did you know the world is infested with Lemurians - not like the Atlanteans. The race of the Lemurians came just after the dinosaurs. They're instinctual and animalistic, and there are a lot of them about still - sportsmen, fishermen, young Tories, all criminals and terrorists and the ugly. My whole life is dedicated to covering their tracks. The Atlantean race followed the Lemurians in the evolutionary process and we are still trying to phase out the Lemurians but they are resistant and it's touch-and-go whether they will be expunged from the planet. Their survival trick is the finding of simple, horrible pleasures. They find satisfaction in inventive little things - like threading a worm on a hook, joining activity clubs, tapping a ball, kite gliding, et cetera.

"You are an Atlantean Mrs Bush. You have a sensitive, intelligent face. It is because of us and what we put into the world that filth, moral and actual, does not entirely overwhelm our planet, hobbling alone cankered and kinked as it does."

"I'm an Atlantean? Goodness. I thought I was British."

"We're talking about your spiritual nationality now. Did you not feel out of place at school? That life had set you apart for purposes not easily explained to your peer group as they skipped in the playground and played tag or whatever it is that ordinary children do to fill the vast void they later call their happiest days?"

"Well, children never wanted to sit next to me in class."

"There, Mrs Bush. The classic sign."

Mrs Bush slides off her stool with surprising ease and onto her feet. "You've explained much, Mr Timms. Now as a fellow Atlantean would you do me a favour? If we left this lounge right now and stood under the awning outside, would you be gracious enough to grant an old woman's wish and allow a photographer to take our picture for the local paper? Not for any political purpose of course."

Timothy holds her hand. "Only because we are Atlanteans - though there is the small matter of the net curtains to sort out."

"Yes," she says, suddenly brisk. "Mr Latham mentioned the net curtains. Apparently you want over a mile of net curtains - what on earth....?"

"Madam, I have already ordered lovely Italian polyester with a pink stripe - silk would be too fly-away. Labourers are hired. Photographers booked. My editor has given her blessing. We play tomorrow. It is my view and that of my assistant Glenda York that Brightworth Council should bear in part the financial cost of this promotion. The resultant publicity of beautifying your pier will stir the world. I needn't mention to you Raven's Towers' pan-global syndication agency which would ensure that everyone got to hear of Brightworth. Think how much it would cost Brightworth's Poll Tax-payers if you chose to advertise Brightworth globally. We are saving you millions of pounds. And naturally the government will applaud your enterprise, and you never know: with all the foreign visitors who come in the wake of our tremendous project you may even be able to reduce the burden of Poll Tax. Might not an invitation to Buckingham Palace be expected for the bestowal of an honour? This is the marriage of *Glossy International* and Brightworth: a multi-national monster in bed with British heritage. Of course, you will have your left-wing critics."

Mrs Bush laughs and places her free hand on his which traps her other. "Yes, yes," she says, conceding his blatant guile with chirrups. "You go make a silk - or polyester - purse out of a sow's ear if you can Mr Timms."

"Now what have I here?" Timothy reaches down to a plastic bag resting against his stool. "I've brought you your sycamore-leaf sweater. A gift from me to you."

The devil!

"Mr Timms!" she cries, cellophane crackling its welcome. "But I agreed a discount with your editor, a most delightful woman. I must pay something."

"She is indeed delightful – and before I left London for Brightworth she said to me, and I quote: 'Let's take the cash out of the cashmere for our new friend by the sea.'"

How easily he lies!

"Now where's that David Bailey of yours, Mrs Bush?"

"Follow me!"

*

After the pictures Timothy kisses Mrs Bush's hand adieu.

"A pleasure Mrs Bush. And now I intend to promenade the Brightworth coast. I take it I shall not be mugged or otherwise molested."

"We don't have that sort of thing down here, Mr Timms. Crime is the friend of anonymity - and here, everyone knows everyone."

Timothy looks about on his journey. A passion-fruit peach washes the western sky, and a pock-marked old hag in the sky has already thrown down her shimmering, laddered stockings upon the sea: an invitation to romance.

I smell that awful brackish pong which characterises these places and that reminds me of a question Timothy asks when he wishes to irritate me: Who exactly takes any notice of the fashion and beauty dicta in *Glossy International*?

I wondered myself as I surveyed the signs of premature ageing and ill-health in the seaside patrons of the Promenade Inn. So many mismatched clothes and colours stretched over stressed-looking skin stretched over bent bones and pot bellies.

Do they not know that humble hydrospheres, one hundred times smaller than wrinkle-delaying liposomes, can replace lost radiance in seconds? Has the message not yet hit home that the Sun, once the source of all life, is now also a photo-ageing furnace? Why do they not know that the slightest responses in our skin to changes in conditions involves an array of micro-chemical signals running throughout our intercellular tissue and that proteoglycan is a key component in this process of intercellular communication? Thank God for Helena Rubinstein and her discoveries.

I always talk shop when I'm bored. Filth and decay: perhaps the world is full of these so-called Lemurians. Brightworth is Lemuria. Raven's Towers is Atlantis. Oh! A creature has manifested itself on Timothy's way – a spectre of La Luna perhaps.

"Hi. Mr Timms?"

Timothy turns and then down-gazes. "Y-a-a-a-a-a-a-h-s."

"Do you remember me? I was the reporter at the station - from the *Brightworth Evening Argus*."

"Oh, really."

"Are you better now?"

"Thank you for your enquiry. I presume you've brought grapes."

It's the ginger-haired reporter - could be a cub. Looks no more than twenty. Height: five-eightish. Arms crossed with hands hugging his rib-cage. Will be stocky. Voice modulated by an imbalance of what Timothy calls preponderant homosocial company (too much footie, maybe). Trousers baggy.

"Yes, I seem to recall now your little...impertinence."

"My name's Gary."

"Oh dear. Well, let's rechristen you immediately. Good evening, *Gareth*. There! In one stroke I've removed the impediment to career progress in the grown-up world. Doors stuck fast now open up to you, Gareth. Leave a tip at the door."

"Actually, I was wondering if....I mean...."

"Y-a-a-a-a-a-a-h-s."

"If you could spare me some time to talk about magazines."

"*Whether* I could spare you the time, not if. *Whether* is my preference. And why would the infant prodigy such as yourself - I say, your left sideburn is slightly longer than the right - want to be talking about magazines? I presume we're not talking about granny's soaraway *The Lady*?"

Gareth drops his head and chuckles. I can see Timothy is heading for trouble. He likes nothing more than the laddish. He should be wary of stripling career climbers. So many a mature lady novelist has been flattered by the sensitivity of a young male hack who rewards her generous disclosures with ridicule and betrayal in a merciless, sharply-observed write-up.

"And why should I want to help this young man once called Gary? What have you to offer that is not already to be found in abundance in a whole raft of copycat glossies - each hack a star for a season before the bear garden of Fleet Street beckons; and his or her voice grows hoarse from all that shouting across wine bars. And invariably he or she develops cancer at fifty-two and dictates a ghastly diary about it, pretending that he or she has kept it all his or her life. Is that what you want to know Gary? Gareth."

Gareth looks about furtively - there is no answer to Timothy's epic question. Somehow I don't think he wants to discuss magazines. Then hesitantly he says: "What's that you said about the cottagers of Brightworth?"

"Cottagers, Gareth? Did I mention cottagers? Is it that you wish me to spell the word? Or give you the guided tour?"

"There's an empty beach hut over there," he says quickly, no longer hesitant at all, pointing north.

"Indeed...." Timothy tickles Gareth's chin. "Is it true what they say about redheads, Gareth?"

"We'd better go to the hut - people might see us."

The two walk rapidly to the shack which has been clearly vandalised. This gives the lie to the mayoress' claim of Brightworth's immunity to the blight of crime. In the dimness they step over broken timber, rusty cans - something clatters underfoot.

Timothy gets on bended knee and unzips the cub. "Mm, it *is* true what they say about redheads." Timothy lowers his head....

Just then I spot the outline of someone in the hut's entrance followed by flashlight, freezing Timothy in X-rated horror.

For a moment spots play before my eyes. A damned photographer - from the *Brightworth Evening Argus* I'll be bound.

A classic stitch-up! By whom?

*

April 29, 10am >>>

"What the....?"

Brightworth Pier shudders to incessant hammer blows.

"Germaine!"

"Max, look."

I am in Max's head again and he's in his blue pyjamas and Germaine has spent a second chaste night with him. Was I wrong about them! Outside are workmen carrying huge log-rolls of white fabric. Others are doubling the hems of gauze around thick rope before fastening to the deck with giant nails.

Timothy's net curtains.

"What the fuck are they doing?" screams Germaine.

Max, with a slight limp, approaches the window. "These must be the curtains Timothy was talking about yesterday. They are dressing up the pier."

"How can anyone fucking dress a pier?"

Timothy comes into view outside the chalet, looking wan. "Mitts off the fabric," he bawls to a galley slave. "You are engaged in the making of art, not digging up the M25!"

Shielded by the chalet's net curtains, Max takes a close look at Timothy, only four feet or so away. He's thinking: what a lunatic; like Vicki. Deaf and blind but to his inner voices and visions. Driven.

So Max does think I am a lunatic.

"We must leave now Germaine," he says.

"That's what I've been saying for two days now."

"We'll just go ashore. We can't see anything here."

Germaine persists: "We should leave Brightworth. The town is probably crawling with Raven's Towers' staff."

"They've hired a charabanc you mean," he says drily. "Come on, get dressed. There's a little café over the road from the pier which can be our spy hole."

They exit east side (Max unimpeded by the result of his recent collision) almost bumping into Glenda who is stupidly absorbed in finger-following the tide timetable.

All the length and breadth of the pier, men in overalls are around us, bearing carpet-lengths of curtain and hammering them into the deck edges: a pier turned to labour camp. Exactly what I intended. To shake Max with the power of *Glossy International* and remind him he cannot disown it. But did he ever intend to disown it?

Still, *Glossy International* does not waste time. It annexes speedily. Nothing is too soon or too much. It sets aside priority and humbles bureaucracy. We would never thrive on ordinary rules.

We hear Madame Smith complaining angrily to the tollgate master - "What about me trade then?"

*

"Good morning Mr Timms. An incredible sight," says Mrs Bush who is wearing a cockleshell-patterned headscarf. The tide is receding with face-forward waves, like a royal flunkey.

"Good morning Mrs Bush."

They stand on the esplanade facing the work camp. Shoppers normally done by eleven, and who would now be routinely preparing for the lunchtime TV soaps, are delighted to be kept in town by the prospect of a civic spectacle.

"Well, you don't waste time do you Mr Timms?"

"We do not have time to waste Mrs Bush. The pier will be unveiled this afternoon, around five." Poor Timothy. He is subdued.

"I wasn't thinking of the pier, Mr Timms. I was thinking about the episode on your constitutional walk last night - in the beach hut."

Timothy turns furiously to face the mayoress, her sapphire eyes ablaze in a matt cake.

"What do you know about that?" he shouts.

"A certain picture has fallen into my hands. In short, if your magazine is prepared to bankroll the entire operation of redecorating the Brightworth Pier you will hear no more about this picture."

"You filthy blackmailer! You sent that little...."

"Now, now, Mr Timms. Atlanteans should watch their language. Are we agreed?"

"And what will you do with the picture?"

"It will be destroyed once your magazine has paid all costs. In these days of Poll Tax and unemployment I couldn't possibly countenance the expenditure you propose. Now, how are we to proceed?"

*

Dead on five Brightworth Pier is reborn.

Up and down its entire length a fabulous white waterfall of Italian polyester erupts from the deck railings, heaved over with a tremendous roar from the workmen.

The fabric unfurls in majestic surges to the wet sands floor; veiling at last the pier's varicose beams and girders.

At once the pier dances and twirls in its new shimmering frock, and an amazed crowd on the beach cry "Bravo!" A gentle breeze proves to be the perfect choreographer. Mrs Bush and her cronies salute Brightworth's entry into international tourism with champagne pops on a south-facing Promenade Inn balcony.

I see Timothy and Glenda on the sands, one east side, one west side, race towards the rippling seas, ahead of a militia of photographers, deployed here and there to catch or create the full beauty of the pier's transformation.

I am so happy, happy, happy to see this - the most wonderful thing I have witnessed astrally. I could never have imagined anything so stunning. Of course I saw photographs and film afterwards; but nothing compared to this living moment.

I am astonished to see Freddie Smith directing his own film. What is he doing here?

The pier's dress billows and falls and fills again in the style of Monroe's hot vent skirt classic, nature herself helping to turn the spectacle into a waltz.

I love my Timothy. I almost love Max for (unwittingly) leading us to this point. But most of all I love this new pier.

*

Max and Germaine are observing the pier's transmogrification from a seaside café. There they are, in window seats. Verbal noise emission is high within the establishment quite simply because *Glossy International* has delivered a trigger for conversational liveliness. The inside withers without the outside (I'll give greater thought to this aperçu on another occasion: glibness is always a risk).

But back to the couple of my interest. It's as if they're at a drive-in movie starring Brightworth Pier. The name has a new ring to it. I could imagine a handsome actor called Brightworth Pier, or Pier(s) Brightworth. I watch Max intently and I know his thoughts.

"What an insult," Germaine says, extinguishing cigarette in her coffee cup.

"Must you do that?" snaps Max. "That disgusting hissing sound."

"Sor-ry," says Germaine, not sorry.

Max has a thing about cigarettes fizzling out in coffee dregs.

"Well," she says, almost triumphant herself, "Vicki's well and truly screwed you."

"Screwed me?"

"It's a personal insult - look at that sight. Brightworth Pier will be never the same again when they see the pics round the world. An insult to you."

"Why an insult?" he asks, stupidly.

"It's obvious. Vicki's undermining your manhood by dressing you up in a dress! The pier's part of your history, isn't it?"

She's just made that up; a good point nonetheless.

Max says ponderously, "I am not Brightworth Pier. I know what Vicki is up to."

Germaine persists: "She knows what the pier means to you. She's publicly mocking you."

"Not exactly. She didn't think up the net curtain idea herself - we both heard Timothy dream it up yesterday, on the spot. Vicki would have only thought of the workmen making a din on the pier and upsetting my peace. She wouldn't have thought it through. She's not into details - thank God. She lets things happen. Ingenious."

Germaine gives him what I think is called an old-fashioned look."You're very cool about it." I see she has no lipstick – naked for her!. "It's almost as if you admire Vicki for humiliating you."

"I am not humiliated, Germaine; but I am very surprised. I want to relish this moment - look at the way the curtains are moving - amazing! I don't want to talk for a moment."

In the silence between them I am drawn unwillingly deeper into his mind. What a mess it is.

I see the sex-mouth float by, a sea wave collapse, a harpoon gun.

Now, in his head, Max is on a barge of gold set adrift in sea of net curtain, trusting to perilous currents and a wing and a prayer.

My new pier has given him a metaphor for his own life, I think. The gambler, the pier-gambler in his sea of net curtain. Minds are very odd. This is not what I - Vicki - wanted to hear or see in Max's head! I wanted the Titanic.

He is thinking of Timothy - a glint of earring, a wave of ponytail - he thinks Timothy is me revived, a mad person, a genius, a classic type.

He remembers reading of angels. The book said angels have no intellect, no brain as such, and therefore no freewill. Ordinary people have freewill and their purpose is to muddle through life, making good through trial and error. But an angel fulfils the idea of Creation. It does not analyse. Angels are spirit automata programmed to lift mankind. To make actual all that life promises.

He thinks the angelic undead like me and Timothy galvanise us all to do wonderful things, to splash colour on the world and dab intoxicating fragrances behind global earlobes.

He had better not be thinking about replacing me with Timothy.

Does he think me a mere idiot angel? What is this baloney?

Max ends his private reverie and says to Germaine, "Let's take a walk along the pelmet when the people are gone."

"Pelmet?"

"The pier deck, in this instance. Let's look down upon the sails and journey like Antony and Cleopatra."

"Jeez, Max!"

*

A relief to break away from Max. I am back with sane (ie literalist) people at the Promenade Inn.

Mrs Elsie Bush is saying to Timothy: "Congratulations, Mr Timms! A fabulous show. Brightworth is reborn."

Her face is all champagne blush, her eyes now muted as winter's Venus in smog. She fills more glasses. Men with nose and ear hair protrusions are displaying dental gaps through the medium of belly laughter. We are in a hotel room.

The pier in its ball gown dances still.

"Thank you Mrs Bush. May we speak in the – where's free? Ah yes, the bathroom?"

"The bathroom. If we must."

The two withdraw and Timothy locks the door.

"Is that really necessary Mr Timms? Have we decided what we

are to do with the photograph I have of you?"

I glance at the loo and spot something perfectly ghastly posing on its cistern: a transvestite Action Man toilet roll doll dressed up in a hand-knitted dress and hat finished with pearls, ribbon and rose detail. This really is...oh, Timothy is talking....

"Indeed we have Mrs Bush. Now allow me to understand fully what you are saying. If I arrange for *Glossy International* to pay for everything that we have witnessed today, thereby ensuring your re-election as mayoress of Brightworth, you agree to destroy a certain picture and negative in your possession which depicts me in a homosexual encounter with a grubby local hack whom you hired for the purpose of blackmail. Otherwise you will publish this same picture to my humiliation and downfall."

Mrs Bush has a wry smile which she deploys now: "You have a way with words Mr Timms. You wouldn't have a tape recorder on you, would you?"

Timothy brings out his wry smile - "My dear, the low-grade activities of the town council stop at its noticeboard. Would you like to search me?"

"Yes, I would."

The sight of the mayoress of Brightworth filling out Timothy's pockets and pulling up his shirt to reveal his hursuit tum is something which reconciles me to my entire astral trip.

Finally she mutters, "One can never be too careful. Now Mr Timms, enough of this nonsense. This picture will be circulated in Raven's Towers and sent to the *News of the World* if you do not cooperate. I'll give you one minute - and unlock that door!"

Timothy shouts out - "Did you hear that Glenda?"

The shower curtain is pulled back and – well, there's a surprise - dear Glenda emerges.

"I heard everything Timothy. It's all taped."

"Oh!" Mrs Bush stamps her foot.

"You should be ashamed of yourself Mrs Bush," scolds Glenda. "Blackmail is a criminal offence. If you publish that picture we will take this tape to the police and your career will be over."

Mrs Bush sighs (I quite admire her speedy pragmatism), "You win."

"And we shall expect Brightworth Council to pay our hotel bills," adds Timothy.

Well done both of them!

*

In another hotel room Timothy buries his face in Glenda's bosom, picks her up by the waist and spins her about. "What a heavy moo you are."

Then he loses his balance and together they fall – almost into the reproduction Regency fireplace.

"Oh my bottom hurts," says Glenda, hamming.

"Let Timmy rub it better."

"You're such a naughty boy picking up reporters." She's drunk.

"Well I picked you up instead." He's nearly drunk, on all fours.

"You really upset me the other day. Calling me a drudge. You don't deserve saving from moral ruin."

"Did I call you a drudge?" he says puckering his lips. "A foul calumny. May he who calls you a drudge die slowly."

"Let's order more champagne!" shouts Glenda.

"And anything else vaguely expensive. That'll teach that old Elsie cunt."

Alarmingly, and without warning, Glenda legs Timothy over onto his back as he tries to get up and sits on him, straddling his belly: a horsewoman gone mad.

"Glenda!" says Timothy not at all cross; curious, "what are you up to?"

"I love hairy tummies," she says, pushing her hands up his shirt. "I noticed when Old Elsie was feeling you up. Germaine thinks you've a crush on me - I think it's time you enjoyed the love of a good woman."

And she bounces up and down on him: a Jilly Cooper invention, possessed on a maddened steed.

"Oh, oh, oh - Glenda stop it, I'll burst, oh."

She unbuttons his shirt. "What a hairy top you've got," she says with a smiling dimwit expression on her face. Then she rubs her hands all over him.

"Not my nipples - oh."

"Your E-spot!"

"My G-spot! No Glenda, no!"

She ripples all her fingers over both his whiskered tits at once.

He moans. He twists. He wouldn't stop her for the world.

"Stop it Glenda!"

She stops. In silence she lowers her top half on him, muffling his face with a pillow of breasts. Another moan. From below. Silence. A noise. Then he lifts her up, gasping. "Are you trying to suffocate me?"

She bends down again. This time she allows her bosom just to tease his face.

"I love your stubble, Timothy, it's all prickly on my...." She shakes herself gently, and I notice a new awakened interest in Timothy, transfixed as he is by the wobbling.

I don't know whether to leave the room. I hate anything that wobbles – even in my astral state. No, I'll stay. I can't believe this other side of Glenda, the milkmaid in her, making hay with the farm boy. Or the other side of Timothy for that matter.

"Well, well, Timothy, I can feel a lap bump."

"No, don't Glenda...."

She throws her hands behind her, pulls down his tights and grabs hold of his, his.... In one muscular feat she tears off her pants and gingerly reverses herself onto him. It's such an incongruous sight as to warrant an interspecies rating. She moves back and forth frantically, screamingly, a Rubens woman riding a Lowry man; and all the while he fixes his gaze on her breasts, holding them now in his hands.

There's the clue. I know my Timothy. I crouch on the carpet to get his eye view. As I thought. Her bosom is the spitting image of a labourer's bottom cleavage - minus the fluff, as he would say. Poor Glenda. Miscast in someone else's movie.

The two jerk and collapse, serially.

"Oh Timothy," she sighs.

*

I am outside, away from the coupling.

The sea is swelling with confidence once again, shifting and reclaiming, after the pier's Cinderella party piece.

Already the tide tugs at the giant frock. An accomplice updraught fills the pier's skirt, lifts and pulls, and strips away an entire section of the net curtain, tearing it up into the air, up and up, and for a moment it hovers over the amusement arcade in an eddy before it dances the seven veils towards the town centre, dipping and soaring, twirling like a Cossack, twirling over Brightworth High Street, a virulent wraith come to haunt, alarming passengers on a bus top deck towards whom it makes its descent in an uncertain conga-line, but at the last second changing its mind and netting instead a fine catch of Brightworthian councillors staggering out of the Promenade Inn, making bed sheet ghosts of them all.

*

"Now I suppose you're pregnant," says Timothy petulantly,

mopping his member.

"I suppose I am. It's time I had a child."

"Me too. I always want to blow my nose after coition."

"Pass me a Kleenex while you're there, sweetheart."

>><<

It's not over till it's over, as Americans say. And I'm not over.

I know I am still alive – in the sense you'll understand.

I sense that my bodily body is about to live again between those two groynes at Brightworth and that any minute now my life essence shall return to it.

Something tugs at me at a great distance. I am not long for this place; this no-place tribute to white. In that distance I hear a dog bark, the sea roll....

I just pray I'm not crippled or scarred. But then it's either that or watching those two love birds Timothy and Glenda.

I can cope with disability.

Throughout this chronicle I secretly hoped that we would not get this far in my story. No matter what I've said previously, I kept my fingers crossed that I'd be spared the Brightworth Pier curtains spectacle whose biggest victim, aside from me, was the GlossRam fashion show. I know I've led you to believe that the show would happen, but it didn't - I feel no shame in pre-empting the matter.

If I play Video No.13 all will be explained I'm sure - 13! A typically unlucky number for me - but I warn you now: I had my reasons, or thought I had at the time to do whatever I did: what little good it did me!

Video No.13 features my "death". Well, I know I have cheated death - so I shall play it just to irritate any of my enemies reading this - for the dramatic irony. For the reverse schadenfreude.

I'm tempted not to play it...shall I?...in it goes....

>>>

CHAPTER FOURTEEN

It's April 30, the day after the pier show, and I'm in my office at Raven's Towers. I know this because I have the morning papers open on my desk. I am experiencing the usual symptoms of shock: instant gut drop and cold sweat and dry-mouth which can result in halitosis if you're not careful.

No-one has had the courage to warn me. I thought Lee looked furtive. Franca had been quiet. No one has had the courage to warn me of the inside page headlines.

Samples:

"It's curtains for the pier!"

"Frock on the rocks!"

"What a fine catch!"

I predict that the exclamation mark will be the vogue punctuation mark of the Nineties and beyond!

"Lee!" I scream. "Come in here!"

Her face is shiny - a sign of stress.

"What do you know about this pier business?" I ask her.

She's baffled, her eyes are swivelling.

"Nothing, Vicki – I...."

"Did you alert the press to what Timothy and Glenda were up to in Brightworth?"

"N- no: I didn't even know they were there till I read the papers."

Suddenly earthly me thinks Lee maybe telling the truth. I had not involved her in Timothy and Glenda's travel arrangements precisely to catch Max unawares.

I never intended this public spectacle. But then what did I expect? That the pond life of Brightworth Council would not tip off the newspapers of what *Glossy International* planned for its town?

That must be what happened - that Elsie whatshername, the mayoress, told the papers. To promote her tiny empire.

"Oh God, Lee, what a mess! I never intended this."

"What? Vicki."

"*This*!" I shout, waving my glinting hands over the newsprint and pictures of Brightworth Pier waltzing in its dress. "Timothy said on the phone he was going to do something with net curtains, and I only wanted to upset Max a little bit - now we are all humiliated. I'm finished."

Lee steps forward uncertain whether to touch me for comfort. She knows I'm not a touchy-feely person as a rule, but I could do with a hug right now.

"But, Vicki, everyone is saying the pier is an inspirational idea."

"Are they? Where?"

"There. Look, read it."

I read a style report in the *Guardian*. Apparently *Glossy International* has taken "postmodernism to its logical conclusion" and "deconstructed celebrity in order to alchemically reconstruct kitsch and other dead things." Sounds like crap to me - yes, I freely use Germaine's word - but, well....

"What you don't understand Lee - look, sit down for a moment. What you don't understand is that Max and I have been having our differences of opinion lately. I only sent Timothy and Glenda down to Brightworth so that they could upset his day - a bit. I thought a few bangs on the deck would shake him up in his chalet - and Max hates noise. I thought he'd run back here. I never intended that our marital and professional difficulties should be paraded in the public prints like this. I feel like some tart who's sold her kiss 'n' tell story to a tabloid. I feel I've betrayed Max, *Glossy*, everyone, with my stupidity."

Lee leans over and holds my hand - a bold move. "Vicki, there's no mention of marital difficulties in the reports. No one would think that the pier has anything to do with you and Mr Cochrane. There are just photos and fashion articles."

"But Max knows why I did it. He knows the subtext. I've gone too far. Timothy's gone too far. You don't know what that scummy town means to Max. And that bloody pier. It's his past, his memories. I've stamped all over his fucking nostalgia - I hate nostalgia - nostalgia is rehearsal for death. Fuck nostalgia!"

I'm going on a bit and being indiscreet with Lee because I know she will report back to Max. She will tell him of my sorrow, vehemence and tears - that should repair the damage. Call it a tactical retreat.

Lee rises gently to her feet - her tights must be silk because I don't hear that static sound that sets my teeth on edge (God, I'm as bad as Max)....

I look up at her – I see there's something else wrong. She's hoping I will read her hesitant body language and then ask her what's the matter.

"What's up Lee? There's something else isn't there? What is it?"

There is something else wrong. She's not a hesitant person as a rule. She's umming and erring, and throwing her silky blonde hair about the way shampoo models do in TV ads. Silly bitches.

"Lee, stop doing that. Just tell me."

"There's something you should see in the internal post. It arrived anonymously - I was going to wait until later."

"Show me now!"

My earthly gut plumbs deeper depths of anticipated despair. Lee returns to the office with a large buff envelope.

"They're photographs, Vicki."

She hands me a few.

"Who's that?" I ask, scanning them.

"Max."

"I mean, who's with him?"

"I - uh – er...."

"My God. It's Germaine! What - what's she doing there? Oh!"

It's Germaine, arm-in-arm with Max. On the Brightworth Pier on the day of the frocking - yesterday!

"Oh, Lee! Oh - he's having an affair with Germaine - oh God, no."

What did I say about dramatic irony?

Lee tries to soothe me - "It may not be what it seems."

"No, Lee, it all makes sense now. He left me to conduct his sordid affair with that tramp. No wonder she was so rude to me the other day in conference. She knew she'd be replacing me soon. She set out to make me get rid of her so she could force Max to choose."

"That doesn't sound like Mr Cochrane."

I glare at Lee. "What do you know? I bet you knew about Germaine, didn't you. I know how you spy on me. I know how you go running back to Max. You deliberately withheld this information from me while I made a complete fool of myself."

"No, I didn't."

"Don't bleat lies to me. You have failed me. You have betrayed me. How dare you spy on me."

"But Mr Cochrane said you knew...."

"What? Do you seriously think I would acquiesce in my own betrayal? And what about that bloody Romany, Madame Smith? Why didn't she tell me about Germaine? You've all failed me!"

God, I feel so hurt. I replay Max's words to me - that he wanted change in his life - he wanted me to change - nothing lasts - he used my kind of language to excuse his misconduct: his treacheries are multiple and layered: a history of intimate dialogue thrown in my face, and all because of some third-rate nothing called Germaine.

"Who took these pictures Lee? Who took them?"

"I know nothing, Vicki. I honestly know nothing. If I did I'd tell you."

"I bet fucking Roger has something to do with this - what did he say to you?"

"Nothing. Believe me."

I throw the photographs away from me. And in one sweep of my arm I clear my desk of the newspapers and all else which tumble to the floor. The only thing that remains on the shiny black ash - cheap crap wood! - is a colour photograph of Princess Leona Humperdink that I tore out of *Vanity Fair* a few weeks ago.

I move to sweep that away, too, but then I stop.

Something stops me.

I look at Leona again.

It's strange how grief sharpens the mind. Even in the midst of the wildest trauma I notice small things. I have noticed something very big.

"Lee, sit down. Be quiet. I may be about to hallucinate. I'm not sure...."

"What's wrong, Vicki? Would you like a coffee?"

"No. Be quiet. Jesus! Oh no...."

"What?"

"QUIET! I'm realising something."

It's Leona's hairstyle.

It has the usual lacquered waves, the architected complexity, it's the right kind of blonde - honeyed, shiny, silky - but most of all it's very big.

"Lee, cancel GlossRam - it can't go ahead, oh no...."

"We can't, Vicki - some of our guests are already at the Rambagh."

"Cancel it! We've overlooked something."

"What?" she asks inanely, spinning the picture round her right side up.

"The size of Leona's hair! Can't you see? How will we get the virtual reality helmet onto her head? How will we get those helmets onto any of our guests' heads? They have to put those helmets onto see the show."

I'm praying that Lee will correct me, reassure me, point out an immediate solution. Instead she sucks her hand to her mouth and pops her eyes - "Oh my God."

Those three words of hers sum it all up. Her horror adds dimension, reality, to mine. Now I know we're in very deep shit – Germaine's vocabulary is infecting me. Lee's face haunts me.

No-one, certainly not those fools in my fashion department, have thought about the limitations of the VR helmet. Each of our society gal guests will have spent upwards of $5000 to turn her thin grey locks into a blonde lacquered soufflé - just for the GlossRam high profile event.

None of the helmets Roger has shown me could possibly fit your average high society head, inflated to twice its normal proportion, in pursuit of the bigger, glossier mane.

They couldn't possibly be asked to reduce the size of their hairstyles. The smaller head just looks poorer, and simply doesn't work for the society pages - ask any paparazzo - which demand freaky-chic for those crucial drop-ins.

I always suspected that Nancy Reagan had a cranial extension.

"This is Max's fault!" I scream. "If he hadn't deserted me I would have foreseen this problem. I would have given more thought to GlossRam. Oh, Lee! You know what pressure I've been under these last three days. I never fuck-up as a rule."

I take deep breaths.

Max.

Germaine.

Big hairstyles.

No GlossRam.

"Lee, pass me that fruit knife."

I'm looking at the serrated blade embedded in the courtesy fresh apples and pears on the coffee table in my office.

"Why?"

"Don't ask questions. Just get it here," I shout.

She leaps up and passes me the knife.

I grab it, and in a wide arc over my head, I bring it down - madly I know - on Leona's picture, slashing it and scoring the black ash in the act, tearing off fragments of photographed hair and throwing them into the air like confetti, making flying hairstyles.

"Vicki, what are you doing?"

"I'm tearing up Leona, tearing up her hairstyle. And then I'm going to see to Max."

"Vicki – I'll get you that coffee…."

"No! Call Stephen. I'm going home. I'm taking the day off. I'm taking the rest of my life off. Cancel India, GlossRam, it can't go ahead."

She has the good sense to call Stephen and before I know it I'm in one of the company Daimlers being driven home to Belgravia.

Flying hairstyles. I remember them well. Now.

*

"Mrs Cochrane – you're home!"

Franca looks alarmed. My return at this time of day is

unprecedented. I don't think she's ever seen me in natural light, the natural light of mid-morning. I am not sure I've seen the house in natural light (perhaps I exaggerate) - I see dust motes in sun beams; everything seems tarnished. Daylight is so brutal to surfaces.

For some reason I still have the fruit knife in my hand. Perhaps that's the real reason why Franca looks alarmed.

"Don't you ever clean this place Franca?" I scream.

"I was just about to signora."

"Were you indeed."

I phone Roger.

"Hey! Fatso. Did you send me those pictures of Max and Germaine?"

"Wha'?"

"Don't wha' me, you fat bastard."

"Are you well Vicki?" asks Fatso.

"I know you're screwing my secretary and you thought you could screw me. Well I have news for you - you're fired!"

I hear one nasal exhalation of mirth.

"You're in no position to fire anyone, Vicki. In fact I have this moment dictated out a recommendation of your suspension from Raven's Towers. I am faxing a copy to you and to Max - I know he's in Brightworth, by the way - I am suspending you over GlossRam. Lee has just told me about the helmets. We stand to lose hundreds of thousands of pounds because of your negligence. and perhaps countless millions in lost goodwill and advertising – and lost marketing. You're not well Vicki."

"Just fax the recommendation over – enjoy it!"

I hang-up.

"Franca, I'm going out."

I get to my own car (I have no idea of its model – the way the door clunked met with expectation) and throw the fruit knife on the passenger seat.

In the rear-view mirror I see a face pink and bare. I wiped most of my make-up off on the journey back from Raven's Towers – I still see Stephen's astonished expression in his rear-view mirror even now.

Sad. I shall never have the chance to suck Stephen's chin. That lovely shaven beard grain. Virility. How poignant that sounds in my head.

Roger has freed me. I am no longer answerable to Raven's Towers - to anyone. So I can just fly south and do what has to be done.

I have something to do. Then I may be absolutely free. Like that black bird my dream Red Indian (or Native American, as I prefer) talked about in my head the other day. I'm the black bird, the freed raven, preparing to croak bad news in the ear of Max Cochrane. I shall pluck him up and take him to a Bloody Tower of my making and stick him on a gibbet and feast on his corpse.

Brightworth here I come. Max, prepare yourself.

I like my new naked face, though the dark lilac eye shadow remains. And I like the top-heavy menace. I don't think I've ever looked more youthful, not since it first occurred to me that I'd lost my youth and the serious maquillage era commenced. My mind is recreating; re-positioning me in a new role. It may not be celebrated; it may not endear me to those inclined to worship status and glamour. But I'll feel better. Happier.

I have wasted too much time analysing Max, examining his every thought and action these last forty years, like a Roman augur over a lamb's entrails.

Over our intimacy of intolerance.

*

Two hours later I am parking my car in a Brightworth coastal road. Flocks of seagulls are making a melodrama above me. I grab the fruit knife and put it in my bag.

I am not quite sure what I plan to do. I cannot rule out murder because it still figures optionally in a range of pre-meditated revenge fantasies evoked by the thought of Max.

It's strange. I don't remember driving here. I did everything on automatic - signalling, turning; the lot. We are all robots at heart. Even our subtlest, most human moments, are formats. Each one of us just adds the personal recollection (some worthy of autobiography – most not) to the template. This is what I'm thinking in Brightworth.

Right now I am the aggrieved wife, spurned for a younger woman: I watch my own drama in a common drama; and with one simple twiddle of the inner dial I could be laughing into the seaweed and licking crab shells. Tragedy is a hoot!

As I step onto the Brightworth Pier I recall my late father's words – something about life being but a short passing. Well, it is in retrospect. He was an alcoholic so he had reason to cover his tracks. Addiction makes whores. But still, his words were potent. They stuck in the ancient limbic thingy-part of the brain that governs emotions – I read about it once. I have applied my father's words to everything and everyone in my professional career, but never to myself. Not until now.

Those words, so terrible to me for so long – yes, a father's curse!

- comfort me, reassure me, for the very first time. Only in my ruin is he of any use. (Though actually I've not done too badly up to this point. That's the trouble with both DIY psychoanalysis and tragedy. They cherry-pick for misery's sake. Take Prince Hamlet, for example. He was privileged, wealthy and feted, notwithstanding the unfortunate turn of events in Denmark. Today, he'd make the eligible bachelors' list in a society magazine - was he unmarried? I can't remember. You can't judge a life by just how it ends. Even in lunacy or "lunacy" I can debate with myself.)

*

    I do not forget my manners. "Good afternoon," I say to the pier's tollgate master propped up in his booth – Punch to a deserted Judy. His response is to hold my gaze a little longer than the last time I visited the pier. I interpret this as foreplay. I give him £4.50 more than required; inviting him to keep the change from the five pound note placed on the scratched steel counter. I don't think he has washed his hands lately. The corners of his mouth drop a little in acknowledgement of my unintended generosity. I interpret this as passionate consummation of our brief acquaintanceship. Beggars of love can't be choosers.
    Ah, but there's the deck. I forgot about that minefield….
    I walk with tentative care because I am wearing high heels. The gaps between the boards are designed to rob me of my dignity (such as it is) should I ignore them. I could slip off my shoes – but I am not ready to go barefoot. In name (at least) I am still editor-in-chief of *Glossy International* and all its foreign editions. This is no time to go native.
    Just as I pass Madame Smith's Psychic Pagoda I feel this sudden, enormous rush of air against me and a terrible roar; flash light, heat.
    I am flying, soaring - I glimpse the beach below.
    And then I am dead.

*

    And then I am not.

>><<

CHAPTER FIFTEEN

I am alive. Just. My consciousness – or life essence - has returned to my bodily body on Brightworth Beach, between those two groynes. The freezing cold, the pain. The white death room of light has yielded to the black void of life on earth.

The sea hisses close, then drags itself away in a sizzle of stone, as if the whole world were an ocean of Coca-Cola.

I feel something wet and jellied on my legs but I cannot move. Each pebble is biting into me and doing its bit to refrigerate me.

I smell the salt and the shit - I cannot open my lips.

My first thought is that I am alive. I have outdone my astral tapes, so to speak.

My second: Am I damaged?

A dog barks over me and then I feel a hot comforting trickle. Someone says something and the dog yelps.

I know I am safe now.

CHAPTER SIXTEEN

"You're alive."

That's Max's voice. He is close to me, physically proximate.

I open my eyes. I am in a white place. At first I see Max in a haze standing over me. I do not ask: Where am I? I guess I'm in hospital so there's no need for the bedside orientation exchange.

The astral film is no more but I know it runs on someplace. I feel its eye.

My first words are: "I dreamt I was reborn, Max."

My mouth is dry, salty, dusty.

I say: "I felt wet walls pressing in on me, wanting to squeeze me away. And I wept because I knew it was time to leave. I was a fish in fluid, I was certain I would not be able to breathe outside. I was so afraid."

"It's the antiseptic," he says quickly.

"The antiseptic?"

"A memory of your own birth, Vicki. You smell the antiseptic and you think of the moment you were born. You've never been in a hospital since then. You're alive, by a miracle."

"No. You don't have to interpret it for me Max. This was not a dream. I really was in another place. A screen. Tapes of my life. I was in water - what happened?"

"There was an explosion. On the pier - yesterday."

"I'm thirsty."

I hear Max open the door and call a nurse. I feel a glass at my lips and I sip. I smell tap water; hint of fluoride and something else...what is it? How I miss buttery Evian, from the snow on the peaks of the Northern Alps... "Well done Mrs Cochrane," she says. "You're in Brightworth Hospital."

"Am I damaged? Am I scarred." My eyes are shut again.

"Not permanently. There are many cuts and bruises but they will heal. Your left ankle is broken and we will have to X-ray your back as a precaution. But nothing too serious. You'll live!"

I drift into another place. In my head.

*

Sometime later I wake up. Sometime later I hear Max say, "May I stay with her?"

"Just five more minutes Mr Cochrane." I hear the door close.

Max sits at my bed.

"How are you feeling?" he asks, gently.

"I ache all over. I feel very alert suddenly."

"Good. What were you doing on the pier Vicki?"

He sounds anguished. I have never heard anguish in his voice before - except maybe that time I wanted to end the marriage - I don't think I've mentioned that. I had left him just after our marriage and I told him we could not live together. I couldn't tolerate his noise intolerances. Maybe I did mention it.

I reopen my eyes. They begin to focus. The drip suspended over me, a plastic vein of fluid running in or out of me, reminds me of a roller coaster. I imagine corpuscles going "Whee!"

And I am Frankenstein, the monster.

The second hand of a wall clock ticks and shudders. Max looks up at it. I sense his irritation. He like his clocks quiet.

"I came to kill you Max. The fruit knife must be somewhere. What happened?"

"Kill me?"

"For the best Max. You're no more use to me. You have become a complete nuisance."

"I see. The newspapers are full of the net curtaining of the pier and the explosion and you in hospital. There are reporters all over the place asking questions…."

"Max, what happened? Why are you alive?"

"I wasn't on the pier. I was at Raven's Towers."

"Raven's Towers?"

"Lee called and told me about GlossRam and the photographs - she did mention a fruit knife now I think of it; and then I saw that idiotic fax from Roger recommending your suspension - I was planning to return yesterday anyway - we must have passed each other."

"How funny. You returned to Raven's Towers. Well, well."

"Yes."

I breathe quietly for half a minute or so. Then:

"Max, give me a kiss."

"A what?"

"A kiss, Max. I'm your wife."

He hesitates. Then he begins to lower himself like an old crane cranked up after forty years of disuse.

At about the midpoint of his journey towards me, he suddenly jumps from away howling, a hand on mouth; his eyes petrified in puzzlement and hurt – an organic moment. "You mad bitch! Why did you do that?"

I have just landed a punch on his puckered lips. It took some planning. First, earlier, I had the nurse remove the remainder of my nails – my acrylic nails; some lost already, inevitably. Second, before Max's visit, I pulled the blankets free at the edges to permit maximum liberty of movement. Third, Max had to be enticed to come close – hence the request for a kiss. Fully prepared, I offer you the behind-the-scenes director's cut of what has just occurred: I clenched my concealed right fist and then, from under the bedding, threw up my arm towards his face when it came into range with puckered lips: all he saw was an eruption of blankets heading towards him; and then biff! Only I could turn bed linen into a boxing glove! This cushioning of the assault was designed to ensure no real injury – to my delicate hand as opposed to his lips.

"That's for everything!" I spit out.

*

Later:

"I dreamt I was in heaven, Max, looking over my last days on earth. On these astral video tapes. They were numbered in order. I saw you. I know about Germaine. I understand about the photographs - a misunderstanding. At first, or at the end - depending on whether we're talking astrally or earthly - I thought you were lovers. I saw how she sneaked down to Brightworth and finagled her way into that chalet of yours. I heard you say you did not desire her sexually - you were enthralled that she had surprised you at all by turning up unexpectedly like that. She put a fresh tingle on your tongue. Had I not been so nasty to her she wouldn't have come to you in the first place. But, as ever, I created the conditions for your surprise. Inadvertently. By the way, *we* ran you over in Brightworth - Glenda, Timothy and I – well, astral I. Then I saw you rolled up on the pier when Timothy kicked you and I saw you rush up to your chalet when no one was looking – mind over matter with that injured foot of yours! I bugged every living moment of your life, Max. Everyone betrayed you. Even your own psyche. I know of your sex-mouth, Max, of what you did all those years ago with the fishermen and everybody. Was it just a phase? I always did wonder about you. I know everything about you. There's a microphone, a transmitter and a receiver in every one of our cells connected to everyone else's cells and all these cells together form a cosmic bugging computer which has no data laws against cross-referencing. There's no such thing as privacy where I have just come from, Max. Every experience is there for the snooping. Isn't that the ultimate bliss?"

I am talking to a small video camera fixed with microphone. Max is safely in another room. He arranged the installation of a videophone link-up in the hospital after my "violent attack" on his puckered lips.

It's like being back at home. I see him on the screen.

This is better. He looks better. The TV dots airbrush his wrinkles away and deflate his eye-hoods.

Somehow I prefer him on the television. I don't have to hold his gaze. I'm freer this way. He'll have to get that wattle seen to. It adds ten years to his face. Stretch back all that turkey flesh and he could rediscover his youth without the nonsense of returning to Brightworth.

He is not usually a demonstrative man. But even he cannot disguise his astonishment at what I have just told him, about the cosmic spying racket.

"My God," he says eventually; appropriately. "How did you do it? I had the pier checked out for bugs. What kind of surveillance company did you hire? We must get them for Raven's Towers."

"That surveillance company is all around us, Max."

I have decided to add a cryptic oo-ee-oo touch to my expression to deepen the genuine mystery of my experience. People who think they've just seen a ghost or UFO, and are surrounded by doubters, will know what I mean.

"I watched your every move. I was in your head, in your soul. I know you so well now that I could pass as Max Cochrane myself."

"Was it Madame Smith spying on me? I know you hired her."

"How could Madame Smith have learned of that sex-mouth of yours, of how you used to give blow-jobs to all those fishermen when you were in your teens? How disgusting, Max! It's just as well sex doesn't matter between us anymore. I know of your private fantasies about the staff - how you lick them like a pastille in your dreams until they lose their flavour and you spit them out!"

"Quiet!" he shouts. "You're hallucinating again. I don't know what you're talking about. And *not* on the videophone."

His hands are sandwiching his face, crumpling up the folds of his wattle. I hear his breathing....

"Max, you're breathing. Would you please not breathe so close to the microphone."

He is silent. He does not react to my attempted provocation. He is thinking and calculating.

"A near-death experience," he concludes. "I have read of these things. It was in *Reader's Digest* once - how some people died temporarily and thought they had woken up in a supernatural place. Floating over their bodies. How interesting."

I explode. "Don't try to explain this away! I don't care what you read in *Reader's Digest*. You bastard! You're to blame for everything."

He appears relieved by my explosion. The eye-hoods flatten even more. It takes us back to familiar territory. "I did what I felt had to be done."

"And what was that?"

"To see what would happen."

"Rubbish."

I switch off with the remote.

*

My second - or is it the third? - day in the private wing of Brightworth Hospital. The back X-ray is done and there is nothing but perfectly postured vertebrae.

The nurse has told me that I lay on the beach for five minutes before I was discovered. Five minutes! I was unconscious for ten hours in this hospital. It seemed like years in that astral place. Was I dreaming after all?

I have dared to apply a little manufactured colour to my face. But for a graze above my left eyebrow and some bruising my face is untouched - a mercy.

My pillows are built up. I can eat soup (flavoured water in every other respect) - what a way to lose weight.

I prepare for transmission. I switch on the videophone at the arranged time. Yesterday I ordered Max to shave when he comes again and to wear a suit. Just because we're out of London doesn't mean we have to look like Brightworth refuseniks. He promised to tell me what had happened. What was happening.

"Is Raven's Towers still alive?"

Max is alarmed by my question. "Of course."

"This is the longest I have been off-duty," I say looking into the black dead lens of the camera. "It's like truancy. In my absence I feel everything will collapse. I cannot believe the thing will run without me."

"Yes, it's an addiction."

"No. It's my life. I would not have it any other way."

"That's why I left for Brightworth."

"What are you talking about? You're a workaholic like me. No, not a workaholic; you're a jobaholic."

"What's the difference?"

"A jobaholic has to be on the job, at the place of work. There are so many jobaholics who do not work. They sit in their offices fifteen hours a day because it is preferable to home. They sit there gossiping, plotting, doing anything but work. You're a jobaholic, Max. I am a workaholic. You had too much time to wonder about things. You're not involved in the creative birth-work of Raven's Towers. And that leaves you idle to wonder what you're supposed to do all day. It leaves you wanting new surprises! Who blew up the pier?"

"Madame Smith's gas heater."

I want to faint in my bed. But losing consciousness while prone lacks drama.

"What? What are you talking about? You blew me up! Or bloody Roger! Someone blew me up."

"It was a freak accident, Vicki. No one blew you up. Madame Smith forgot to switch off the gas heater in her Psychic Pagoda when she went off for lunch. For some reason it just blew up at the moment you passed by. It was a billion-to-one happening. Quite a most remarkable coincidence."

"And I suppose you've worked out the odds on your calculator! That's another big surprise for you then."

"The police think that the gas heater ignition mechanism may have been damaged by the vibration from all that hammering on the pier - to put up those net curtains. I didn't realise how fragile gas heaters are. Apparently...."

"Max," I interrupt. "Not in one billion years will the mechanism of gas heater ignition systems be of as much interest to me as clearly they are to you, as your half-dead wife lies crippled in a hospital bed."

"But what were you doing on the pier, anyway?" he asks.

"I'm not sure myself. I was certain you were running off with Germaine - I saw those pictures of you and her...."

"I know. Lee explained. She phoned the moment you left Raven's Towers. I would have called but I thought it best to talk to you face-to-face – not on the pier but back at the offices.

"How considerate."

"I know who took the pictures of me and Germaine."

"Freddie Smith?"

"Oh, you know." Max is deflated. He'd hope to trade some goodwill from me for his revelation.

I say, "I saw Freddie in Brightworth - on the astral tapes. Did he confess all?"

Max is mouthing wordlessly, or catching his breath. He wants to dispute the existence of these astral tapes, but is confounded by the baffling accuracy of my reports.

Finally he says, "When I got back to Raven's Towers I called in Freddie Smith - I'd spotted him myself in Brightworth when the net curtains were dropped from the pier. He soon admitted Roger had hired him. Roger had planned to send the pictures to the press anonymously. He hoped the negative publicity would see the end of me at Raven's Towers. He changed his plans when he saw Germaine with me - an unexpected bonus for him - and he sent the pictures to you knowing you'd go crazy and most likely do something against me. Roger must have been unhappy to take such risks. But he wasn't clever enough."

"How did Roger know in advance of Timothy and Glenda's presence in Brightworth?"

"Elsie Bush tipped him off. He's all webs and no spider."

Well, naturally. I fall back against pillows (actually, I just push my head deeper into the pillow). I could have scripted it myself.

"Did Lee know Germaine was with you in Brightworth?" I ask.

"No."

That's a relief.

I ask, "Do the police wonder what the chief executive of Raven's Towers was doing in Brightworth on the pier?"

"The press are having a little fun at my expense about that. Mrs Bush has kindly explained I was holidaying on the pier."

"You bribed her to get that chalet, didn't you?"

"How did you know that?"

"I guessed. Who else could have arranged for you to stay on that ridiculous pier."

"And I suppose you bribed her to agree to the curtaining of the pier. I think we should both get our money back."

"Yes. She tried to blackmail Timothy over some photographs, and he and Glenda stitched her up by the medium of a shower curtain...."

"Timothy told you this?"

"No. I saw it all on the astral tapes."

Max shuffles about awkwardly. He changes the subject: "I know you nearly had sex with Roger Masefield in the Daimler. I didn't need astral tapes to learn of that!"

"You had the Daimler bugged?"

"His chauffeur reported it. He was my bug."

I sigh.

I explain: "I had an awful experience with Roger in the Notre Dame - I actually imagined his erect penis in my lap growing out of me, and I wanted to see...."

"Perhaps we'd better not talk about it on this link-up," Max says sensibly. "It's just as well I know you, isn't it?"

"Get rid of Roger."

"He's gone already. Paid off. After seeing Freddie Smith I called Roger in and ordered him to resign."

"At last some good news. He was hopeless. He couldn't think laterally. He couldn't beat us, could he?"

"No, he couldn't," Max says shaking his head.

"If a thirty eight-year-old can't beat a couple of fossils like us he has no business being with us, has he?"

"That is correct."

"What do you mean you've paid him off?"

"Half a million (sterling) plus pension contributions and other things to go quietly."

"What a waste of money. Still...."

"I think Raven's Towers has had enough publicity lately."

"Yes. Your fault. None of this need have happened had you been straight with me from the start. All these games of yours...."

Max interrupts, "You intend to return to *Glossy International*?"

I am enraged. Furiously I throw an ancient empty Soviet table-glass at the TV console which on contact explodes in a muffled *phut*, glass singing on the floor.

I scream at the steaming wreckage - "Don't even think I won't, you bastard. I know why you went to that pier you cocksucker!"

I think he may have heard me through the walls.

*

Third (or fourth) day in hospital. Soon I shall be released. Knowing that Max wants me back at *Glossy* - he wouldn't have asked otherwise - means I can wallow here in freedom. This wallowing can only be relished if you know the expiry date. A universal truth.

The police called earlier. They told me of Madame Smith's gas heater but asked me *en passant* if I suspected anyone of wanting to murder me. A long list flashed up on my silent indictment sheet but it pays not to surrender to idle paranoia. In Roger's case I made an exception and allowed his name to trip off my tongue, as if a consequence of acid reflux. I discounted Max on grounds of advancing senility.

"I suppose it gave you pleasure to say that," Max sniffs, after I tell him.

He's in the room again, in person. There hasn't been time to replace the video monitor.

"Well," I say, "it's the truth, isn't it? Part of the truth. Senility. Fear of it. That's why you absconded here."

"There's no one reason why I left the company and came to Brightworth."

"You were cruel Max, to say what you said to me about *Glossy International*, about its wastefulness. What a hypocrite you are. On the astral tapes I heard you say to Germaine that you wanted a hip capitalist to run your new green magazine - yes, I know all about that. She called Leona a silly cunt with too much money - you were cruel to Germaine to lead her to think she can edit this new magazine of yours."

"How....?" He means to ask me how do I know this. He knows the answer. Then he says: "She will edit it."

"What?"

"As launch editor anyway. It's worth a try."

"Is Germaine one of your angels, Max?"

Poor man. He cannot keep up with the results of my surveillance. He has no more secrets.

In a sudden change of mood, thinking of all the suffering I have endured, I say: "How I wish you had gone up in the explosion, you bastard!"

He is impassive, secure in his perception. Some might say he is stubborn. This is infuriating in its own right.

He says, "I had to know the company was strong enough to survive me - I won't live forever. I'm 64. Seeing that abandoned copy of *Glossy International* on the Brightworth beach that day we came here did affect me - you were right when you said that. Men of my age have heart attacks. And I missed Brightworth - when we visited here that time, six months ago, I felt a longing to spend more time in my hometown. There were many blurred reasons that came together on that visit...I thought: Why should I, with all my money, and at my age - why shouldn't I have another chance to be near my memories? And life was dull."

"I see. So you wanted a change in your life yet you wanted nothing really changed. If you wanted change, Max, why test the situation? Why not just walk away?"

"Everything has to be simple for you, Vicki; everything neatly explained...."

"Bullshit! You were bored. You wanted new surprises; you wanted me to prove something...."

"Yes, I can't deny that."

"You admit it!"

"I wanted you to remind us that we both can still run the company - that we are the best people for the job. Anything less and we must go. Then we look to change our lives. I had to make you feel things might be coming to an end to see how desperately you would fight - to see if you were as hungry for the fight as I still am. I had to trust my instinct that you would do something to restore my faith in us."

"And it fell to the net curtains to restore your faith," I say sarcastically. "I was with you in that seaside cafe with Germaine, when you looked out at the pier and wondered how anyone else could have made it look so beautiful - so astonishingly different. That's when you realised we were still in business - on the cutting-edge! Who else could have worked such a style miracle on that rusty memory of yours - I mean, the pier!"

Max is shaking his head slowly, not in denial, but in bewilderment. He knows I speak the truth.

I continue: "And you were prepared to risk dumping your own wife. You're barely able to admit it to yourself yet, but you will Max, you will. All I am to you is a professional thrill, someone who keeps you going."

"And what am I to you, Vicki?"

Oh, that was clever. Clever Max.

"Max, I'm going to give you another surprise now."

In a lightning move I throw my right arm in a wide arc across the bed and hit him flush on the head with a metal food tray I had hidden under the sheets. Max falls to the floor holding himself in shock.

He didn't see it coming.

A nurse, alarmed by the tray's deafening pang, rushes into the room and asks me what happened.

"Get him out of here. This bastard tried to kill me and I defended myself. He thought he could take away my life - GET HIM OUT."

*

I switch on the new videophone.

"It's best if we talk this way. Like at home," says Max on the screen.

"You were rubbing your cuff with a finger nail, Max. That's why I hit you with the tray."

"I don't know what you are talking about. You were making the noise with your foot."

"Ah! So! The plaster round my ankle was chafing the sheets and you couldn't stand the noise, could you? You mentioned the origin of the sound first - so you heard the noise first! So, the neurotic madman that you are, you started imitating the noise with your finger on your cuff - admit it!"

"You must be suffering concussion Vicki. It was you who made the noise and you who attacked me. It's as if we are just married again."

"It's your old trick of trying to make me self-conscious of making any noise - drawing my attention to the noise by imitation. Why don't you go lock yourself up in a padded cell! There's no noise there."

"I have déjà vu, Vicki. We've had this conversation a million times. You make the noise. I make a noise. You connect the two. You are the one who has the hallucinations. You're the one who is obsessed with smells, with essences. I am the one who reads from the dream book and makes you sane again. You are the one who assaults me."

"You're the one who's obsessed, bastard. You're the one who sucks people off with his mouth, who licks his staff and then runs off to seaside piers. You're the sickest man I ever met. Have I a surprise coming for you!"

Without fanfare, Max knows how to re-engage my constructive attention. He utters the magic words, "The future."

"We are going to have to get rid of some staff," he adds.

"That's the first sensible thing you've said since we married. Starting with that Germaine."

"No. I want her to start-up the ecology magazine. We'll see what happens after that."

"Sack Timothy!"

"No, he's too talented. Don't forget the curtains, Vicki. 'Curtains' is our new word for rebirth. You need some competition. You won't last forever."

"Nor will you, pillow-eyes! You can't sack anyone. Hopeless."

"We will sack all the interconnecting people - the postboys, secretaries, assistant publishers and the like who have been our eyes and ears. We will find new eyes and ears."

"Yes. New eyes and ears. I used that phrase of Madame Smith."

"Do you want to sue her for negligence - because of the gas heater?"

"No. I am superstitious. She served her purpose. She is an ancient Fenland drink who may yet relax me again - I want to sack everybody at Raven's Towers. All the staff essences are tainted by the recent outrages. There should be a great sluicing. It's going to be hard to carry on with the same lot. We need a new staff. *Glossy International* shall start again. To recover from the tremendous assault perpetrated by its own father."

"You can't sack everybody at once," says Max. "I have already resisted a board demand for your suspension because of the GlossRam fiasco."

"That was your fault. Did I ever cock-up in the past?"

"No. I want you to try to be sensible Vicki. We shall move slowly, and gradually change the staff - it will take time - two years, three years...."

"Yes, you're right...and, Max, who ought to edit *Glossy International*? You thought to replace me with Timothy didn't you?"

He looks stunned. I'm guessing. Guesswork is a good substitute for espionage.

"Only in passing. In Raven's Towers we have to be more than man and wife. Raven's Towers is more than our marriage."

"Ha!"

CHAPTER SEVENTEEN

I take in the sight of Raven's Towers gleaming in the early sun and sigh (but see below about another kind of sigh), yes, sigh, at the peacock blue tracery on a flat ocean of emerald.

As I've said before, this is how I (still) prefer my oceans, saltless and dry.

But for the limp you wouldn't think that I had been blown-up by a clairvoyante's gas heater: language has this awful habit of truncating experience into absurdity when really everything happened for a reason.

The emerald green makes me think of absinthe and absinthe reminds me of Timothy: *fin de siècle* (well, it is 1988), addictive, faintly illegal - and best sipped behind closed doors.

I shall continue to keep my eye on him because he has caught Max's eye. In Timothy's future lies my sequel. And, by the way, I've not forgotten his remark about poppies, plastic or otherwise.

I have thought long and hard about my astral experience. I conclude that my mind did indeed pass to another place - perhaps within a deeper recess of its timeless self where we dream - and somehow tapped all recorded transmittable information.

Max tells me that nothing simply ends as nothing. Light disperses into infinity and our bodies turn to humus.

Everything becomes something else, nothing ends, only changes. He concludes that in that case no experience, word or gesture is lost in the cosmos - and it was just typical that I should have discovered the ultimate bugging device.

If all this experience is stored someplace, then logic says it can be accessed. Hopes Max.

But where's the storage plant? Not even *Reader's Digest* can answer that one. Max is thinking about it, and this new interest should exercise him for a while and keep him out of my way for a good time yet.

His current theory is that the "supernatural" influence of Madame Smith catalysed my imagination beyond normal boundaries, enabling me to unearth, *inter alia*, long-lost secrets in Max's psyche, secrets he says he cannot recall, and in general denies (vehemently) having. So intrigued is he by Madame Smith that I have learnt of a certain hush-hush meeting between them – there is talk of a "populist" paranormal magazine in the works with Madame Smith as its multi-media figure-head psychic and astrologer. My guess (remember what I said about guesswork) is that he hopes to chance upon an untold key in her person to explain my temporary omniscience. Madame Smith will prove to be a long-lasting Fenland pastille on his tongue, I foresee.

So what has been the purpose of my astral experience? I have no idea. It certainly disturbs me how pointless much of human conduct is - to think of all the energy expended in espionage, alone! I see that Max and I are more dependent on each other than perhaps I might have once admitted: but this was not a discovery to me, only a dusting away of doubt.

I know my weaknesses. My incessant need to control, my failure to achieve control, my use of people, my awful egotism. I'm sure I've said already that the modern human being is educated on his or her defects of character.

We spend so much of our time in a self-critical quasi-fantasy, and wondering why other people are doing this or that, dreaming of something better, planning other people's lives, being somewhere other than in ourselves. Novelists, especially, encourage these distractions – good prose rendering is the laundering of a vile tendency.

However, it's not enough to have these things pointed out to us, is it? It's so much simpler to live with a vice than with a virtue. Isn't it?

No starring role for me in a biblical parable! I have no moral to impart. The Prodigal Son in my tale will run off again after his return - and so he should. We have to keep things moving, changing. And thereby change nothing. The price of wisdom is death – or its living equivalent: the longueurs of *being out of it*. One of the obvious symptoms of this dread condition is the quoting of wise sayings followed by a sigh. If ever I write a novel (can you imagine?), I shall call it *Sigh*. It will be about the human song of disenchantment, redundancy or despair; of what-might-have-been and what-was; of falling for the lies of dreamers or simply falling by the wayside. I strongly recommend that you ensure against ever *being out of it*.

In an empty space, everyone can hear you sigh.

If you adore the dream - the wonderful scents, the curve of a bottom, the touch of (puckered) lips, the endless speculation, the sudden nova of a voguish Now, the anguished intrigue, the sheer ghastly fascination of being among others who are only variations of ourselves - why opt for something else?

I recalled my father's words as I drove to Brightworth - that life is nothing but a passing; or whatever. For the first time then - perhaps the only time - I applied them to me.

I accepted for an instant that I would not last. That one day Vicki Cochrane would end up as bric-a-brac. But actually, I knew this all along. I was just dreaming-up a moral in case there was an accounting.

Wise is the word.

Never mind.
It will soon pass.

***

END NOTE

Hilary Gialerakis

Blue Angel, the front cover painting, is the work of the late modernist artist Hilary Gialerakis (1923-2003), reproduced by kind permission of her daughter Antonia Gialerakis.

Hilary's art exhibitions in the Fifties, Sixties and Seventies enjoyed critical acclaim. In 2008, Antonia curated the first major retrospective exhibition at the OSO Centre in Barnes Green, London.

Cubist in essence, many of Gialerakis' geometric paintings emphasise the two-dimensionality of the canvas with figures seemingly carved from wood. And a great many of her drawings are Surrealist or Dadaist in style. Striking use of colour vivify dream-like, haunting or sometimes disturbing worlds – perhaps a partial expression of her tumultuous life, described by Antonia as "Sylvia Plath-like".

In 2012, Quartet brought out *An Unquiet Spirit: The Memoirs and Diaries of the Artist Hilary Gialerakis*, edited by Antonia. Born in Poole, Dorset, Hilary studied in London at the Chelsea Art School and Central and St Martin's Schools of Art. She later settled in South Africa. A couple of her paintings conceal repaired bullet holes, the result of misaimed shots from Hilary's gun during emotional tempests.

To see more of Hilary's work, photographed by Roger Smith, visit his exhibition of her paintings and drawings at Flickr.com.

Commercial or sales inquiries should be directed to Antonia who has set up a page on Facebook called "Hilary Carter Gialerakis".

Printed in Great Britain
by Amazon